Books by Phoebe Nabors

The Soul Power Series
Dragonsoul
Darksoul
Lightsoul

To Shannon,

I hope you enjoy this next installment of the Soul Power Series.

Phoebe Nabors

Darksoul

Copyright © 2019 Phoebe Nabors

All rights reserved. No part of this publication may be reproduced, distributed, or transmitted in any form or by any means, including photocopying, recording, or other electronic or mechanical methods, without the prior written permission of the publisher, except in the case of brief quotations embodied in critical reviews and certain other noncommercial uses permitted by copyright law.

ISBN: 9781721992966

Phoebe Nabors

The Soul Power Series

Darksoul

Phoebe Nabors

Darksoul

Contents

Chapter 1 5
Chapter 2 11
Chapter 3 17
Chapter 4 23
Chapter 5 26
Chapter 6 30
Chapter 7 37
Chapter 8 43
Chapter 9 52
Chapter 10 58
Chapter 11 66
Chapter 12 73
Chapter 13 79
Chapter 14 82
Chapter 15 86
Chapter 16 91
Chapter 17 98
Chapter 18 112
Chapter 19 118
Chapter 20 128
Chapter 21 142
Chapter 22 151
Chapter 23 159
Chapter 24 165
Chapter 25 172

Chapter 26	179
Chapter 27	188
Chapter 28	194
Chapter 29	203
Chapter 30	210
Chapter 31	217
Chapter 32	224
Chapter 33	231
Chapter 34	238
Chapter 35	245
Chapter 36	250
Chapter 37	255
Chapter 38	263
Chapter 39	273
Chapter 40	280
Chapter 41	286
Chapter 42	294
Chapter 43	299
Chapter 44	306
Chapter 45	312
Chapter 46	319
Chapter 47	325
Chapter 1	332

Chapter 1

Dagmar was gone again. He had disappeared three times since they left Fonishia. In the three hundred years that he'd been a part of this family, Conner had never known any of the five dragons he traveled with to leave inexplicably. The longest any of the brothers had been separated, save the middle brother who was still at home, was two days, and that was always either him leaving the group to do business in a town that didn't welcome dragons, or all five of the dragons leaving for a hunt; never had one of them left without explaining themselves, especially for a week at a time.

"He'll be back, Conner," Byron, his oldest friend and the largest dragon he had ever met, spoke directly to his thoughts, *"You know he's been taking this worse than the rest of us; he'd only just begun to trust her."* He knew the truth of his friend's words but didn't understand it. They had been traveling with a young girl, for months. They had all known that she had had magic, even that she had had soul power, the higher form of magic, but she had seemed so innocent that they had all assumed that she had been a Lightsoul.

Lightsouls are known to be kind and gentle, powerful but humble. She had been those things and only Dagmar had suspected the possibility that she could be a Darksoul, but even he had come to trust her eventually, and not two days later, she had used enough power to transform her beautiful form into the dark and smoky image of her true identity. She had lied to all of them and Dagmar had been right not to trust her.

Now, Conner paced by the fire and worried about his adoptive brother. *"Dagmar can take care of himself,"* Snarf, the youngest dragon and formerly the Darksoul's closest friend, spoke now, using the same telepathic speech that was common to all dragons.

"I know that, Snarf," he hadn't meant to yell at the purple dragon. "But where does he go? He refuses to talk about his trips. I don't understand how you all can remain unconcerned."

"Conner," Byron chided him again, *"we all worry about our brother, but most of us understand that he needs his space right now. He barely speaks about anything anymore; why would you expect him to share this with you?"*

Even as he finished speaking, the clouds broke as a huge gust of wind nearly knocked Conner to the ground. Dagmar was colored blue and white, perfectly patterned to hide in the sky as he flew gracefully among the clouds, so it was often difficult to see him approaching until it was too late to brace for the power of his beating wings.

"Welcome back." Conner glared at the dragon as he landed. Dagmar only nodded as he settled between the twin orange dragons, Grezald and Grizwald. He obviously wasn't going to discuss his disappearance. Again.

Conner sat near the fire, stewing over the last several weeks. The amazing family that he'd been a part of since he was a young man just felt broken. Snarf, the joker, was too serious, Grezald and Grizwald weren't playing any pranks, Dagmar was constantly missing, and Conner was in an unceasingly foul mood. Only Byron seemed unfazed by the recent events of their lives, but Conner suspected that that was only because he had always felt the need to be father to all five of his brothers as well as Conner.

The hours seemed to crawl by with no conversation and none of the usual horse playing. Considering how depressing it was, Conner almost couldn't blame Dagmar for wanting to get away occasionally.

"Do you all realize how pathetic you are?" Dagmar suddenly broke the silence, drawing offended glares from all of his companions.

"Excuse me?" Conner looked up from stirring the fire to meet the gaze of the huge blue dragon.

"You're all moping around like you just lost your best friend." That stung, and he knew it would.

"Yes, I suppose we are," Snarf growled at his older brother. *"I wonder why that would be."* The sarcastic tone of the purple dragon drew a soft chuckle from Dagmar.

"And why, may I ask, are you all pouting about it? It's sickening to see such great dragons reduced to a bunch of sniveling children because of a girl."

"She was more than just a girl, Dagmar." Conner leapt up to face him, infuriated by the dismissive nature of his comment. "She was our friend and companion. If you had bothered to get to know her at all, you would understand the significance of that."

"She couldn't have been all that great-"

"You hated her," Conner shouted at the beast, earning shocked gasps from the younger three dragons, "You don't get to chastise us because we didn't."

"No, I didn't hate her," he responded calmly, almost sadly, to Conner's outburst, *"but she really couldn't have been that great if you could so easily flee from her, no questions asked."*

"Dagmar," Byron broke into the argument, *"she was a Darksoul. You had been right, and we left as we should have weeks earlier."*

"What happened to burning the next Darksoul you met on the spot?" he shot a small stream of flame from his nostrils as he spoke. *"Why leave? Why leave one of those vile creatures alive?"*

"One does not simply torch one's friends." The red dragon responded calmly to Dagmar's taunting.

"One does not simply leave one's friend in the middle of the Kotash Sea in a structure made only of water," he countered, huffing. *"One does not simply fly away as one's friend attempts to drown herself with said structure. One does not simply abandon the girl that one claims to care for."*

"She lied to us." Conner balled his fists as his whole body shook with rage. He couldn't believe that Dagmar, the most loyal dragon he had ever known, was turning on them, was accusing them of somehow being the wrongdoers in this situation. "She knew how we felt about Darksouls, and she never-"

"She knew how we felt about Darksouls before she knew that she was one. I probably wouldn't have told you either." He was not backing down. *"How terrified would you have been if you suddenly realized that you were the very creature that the dragons you traveled with swore to destroy? Would you not have been hesitant to share that bit of information with five angry fire-breathing beasts that you hardly knew?"*

"It wouldn't have been a problem. She shouldn't have lied about it."

"Wouldn't it have been?" Her only accuser had somehow become her fiercest defender. *"Wouldn't you have felt just as betrayed? After our last encounter with a Darksoul, can you honestly say that you wouldn't have had the same emotional response?"*

"I am not responding emotionally."

"You all are," he was now roaring at them. Why couldn't he see why this was hard for them? *"Grezald and Grizwald barely speak, you and Byron are continually stewing, Snarf hasn't cracked a joke since leaving Fonishia, and I can't even remember the last time a game of tag made the skies dangerous for smaller creatures. You can't tell me you aren't responding emotionally."* The huge beast stood and walked in a small circle around the group. *"You won't even acknowledge what happened. It's as if you're afraid to mention her."*

"We are not."

"You won't even say her name." Again, he interrupted him. Conner just glared at his friend, afraid of what might come out of his mouth if he opened it again. *"You won't even say her name,"* he barely whispered his repeated accusation, his voice suddenly thick with emotion.

Conner knew he couldn't argue with him anymore. He was right; after all, she had been his only human friend in twenty-five years. Since the death of Byron's mate, none of them had really bothered with humans until she joined them. Sure, they had served and protected whenever they were needed, but they hadn't developed or cultivated any relationships until they rescued the young and innocent slave from her cruel master a few months back. Losing her had hurt worse than any of them cared to acknowledge.

So, maybe he was responding emotionally. That didn't change anything. They had made their decisions: she had lied and they had left. Redemption was not possible.

Chapter 2

"You what?" Briganti shouted angrily at Aleisha as she finished her story. "How foolish, how careless, how stupid can you be?"

"I had to try to save her," she responded calmly to his fury, seemingly incapable of showing any emotion since trying to rescue her mother from Tallen's dungeon a few weeks ago, only to learn that she was already dead, killed by Tallen, the fiercest Darksoul in the region and Aleisha's father. During her wasted rescue attempt, she had revealed to the castle guards that she was not only Tallen's daughter, but a Darksoul as well. It had been her best means of escaping the castle alive, but it meant that her father, who had sold her into slavery, now knew that she had magic. This made her both valuable and dangerous.

"He was never supposed to know until we were ready to strike. I went to great pains to keep your magic a secret from him for two and a half decades and you've ruined it. All my effort was wasted." Briganti continued to pace in front of her, throwing his arms in the air as he ranted. He didn't care that she had lost her mother. He only cared about getting his revenge on Tallen. "He's going to come after you. He'll either claim you as his own or kill you."

"Then teach me how to beat him." She wanted some revenge of her own.

"You can't possibly beat him; he's the strongest Darksoul of our time." Again, he threw his hands in the air flinging his beard into his face in the process.

"I thought that was supposed to be me," she raised an eyebrow at her Dictator, challenging his fickle opinion. "After all, my Dictator is one of the original three. Or does that not mean as much as I was led to believe?"

"I am the strongest Dictator, but that does not make you the strongest Darksoul by default. You need training to reach your full potential."

"I have asked to be trained," as she expected, Briganti didn't even pause to acknowledge her statement. He was still punishing her for leaving Puko with Conner and the dragons a few months back.

"Gabriel was the great Darksoul before your father murdered him and left me with this weak excuse for a replacement." He pointed at her in disgust as he finished.

"He couldn't have been that great if Tallen was able to kill him so easily, and you chose me. Never forget that you chose me." If she had had a choice, she would have been a Dragonsoul like Conner, or even better, she wouldn't have been chosen to have magic at all; it had never caused her anything but trouble. "You should have chosen Locke, like everybody had expected. He would have been honored to be your minion, and would have been free from both you and Tallen."

"Your father," he growled.

"Tallen!" she raised her voice for the first time since returning to Puko. She would not be known as the daughter of that murderer.

"Your father poisoned him. Gabriel never had a chance to fight. If he had, your father would be dead and you would still be a worthless slave in Cedrick's mansion." As soon as he finished speaking, he flew across the room and crashed into his bookshelves, launched by her raging magic.

"Your dark magic had nothing to do with my escape from Cedrick's mansion. I didn't even know I had magic until after Conner and the dragons rescued me." She knew mentioning her former companions would anger her Dictator; he'd been friends with them once, but his bitterness over Gabriel's murder had changed him and he blamed Conner for Aleisha's continual resistance to her "rightful place" as a Darksoul. "You thought to use me as a pawn to exact revenge upon him. I would have been happier if I had never been chosen." She stormed out of his room and marched up the stairs.

She had been staying in the same room she had had the first time she had stayed in Puko. The buildings in this forest city were designed to look like huge trees to blend into the environment. The inside had a long staircase that was carved into the trunk leading to dozens of rooms hollowed out of the larger tree branches. Outside her room, she turned to look across the tree to the room Conner used to occupy, wondering how he was faring and if he would continue to search for the Elixir of Life now that he didn't have her mother's map.

Sighing sadly, she stepped into her room and made her way to the small bookcase she'd had Garret teach her how to make. Selecting her current reading material, she turned to the passage where she'd last stopped and claimed a seat on her bed.

She'd not liked Puko the first time she had stayed here because everyone had been accusing her of being Briganti's chosen babe and had expected her to stay and be trained. They'd treated her with disgust and contempt when she'd made it clear that she wouldn't be their resident magic user. This time, she was welcomed and treated as an honored guest because they all thought she would be their new guard dog, as Gabriel had been before her. She still hated this place and would leave at her first opportunity; she could leave sooner if only she could convince Briganti to start training her, but he seemed quite determined to make her wait until she was prepared to submit to his plans and purposes.

She'd spent most of her time since returning to Puko either reading or convincing the residents to teach her their various trades and crafts. She'd actually found it almost annoying how easy everything became if she applied her magic to it, but she also rather enjoyed the awed expressions from some of the younger residents who hadn't been born when Gabriel was here and using his magic for everything imaginable.

The only thing that concerned her was that, last few times she'd created a vision, where she could see her magic physically manifested as a sort of white mist, it seemed to be getting darker. The first time she'd seen her magic, it appeared a brilliant white, but it seemed that the more she used it, the less brilliant that white became to the point that it was now more of a gray, almost as if it was changing into the black smoke that emanated from her person when in her true form.

She closed the book after staring at the same page for several minutes, standing to return it to the shelf before heading outside to take Soulfire for a run. She had been riding the horse since Conner left him in Fonishia and, somehow, she always felt calmer and safe when with Conner's horse.

Descending the staircase quickly, she nearly ran into Agabeth, the daughter of one of the leaders of Puko. "Good evening, Darksoul," the little girl smiled smugly. Her Uncle had been the most insistent about her need to train with Briganti, and his whole family had counted it a personal victory that she had returned in shame after having been abandoned by her friends.

Aleisha ignored the nasty child and stomped out of the building, turning right upon exiting. She made her way to the small stable, which appeared as no more than a few overgrown bushes. She pushed a few of the branches aside to enter the hollow center and reached for Soulfire. She had made a point of visiting with him every day and had learned quickly how to ride the beast without the saddle that she had been using when she first arrived at Puko.

Pulling herself onto the horse, she grabbed hold of his mane, led him out of the stable and toward the edge of the village.

When she had been here before, she and Conner had practiced her magic next to a stream just outside the village. She led Soulfire to this spot now, letting him take a drink from the cool water before she would take him for a hard run through the thick trees.

Chapter 3

Conner stood in an empty, but oddly familiar room. He had no idea where he was, but he knew he had to get out. He reached out with his mind for any of his brothers. None of them were nearby. Looking around the dimly lit room, he headed toward the only door, opening it to reveal another empty room. He stepped inside and looked at each of the three new doors this room offered.

This seemed eerily familiar as well. He knew he had never been here before, but something about the dark emptiness and soft cobwebs tugged at a memory he couldn't quite reach.

He pulled at one of the doors only to find it locked. Shrugging, he moved to the next, which opened freely. Again, he found a dark, empty room behind the door. He was getting frustrated. Worse, he was getting nervous. He had to get out of this house. Now.

Four empty rooms later, he noticed a light flickering under one of the closed doors. He tugged the doorknob. Locked. He stepped back and pushed toward the door, expecting it to move under the influence of his magic. Nothing happened. He couldn't even feel his magic, couldn't summon it.

What was happening? He had never had trouble summoning his magic. He couldn't imagine what could be wrong. What was he going to do without his magic? He had never been without it in his three-hundred plus years. Taking a deep breath in an attempt to calm himself, he lowered his shoulder toward the door and ran, slamming into the wooden panel and breaking it out of the wall.

He had to shut his eyes against the sudden brightness of the fireplace until his vision adjusted. After a moment, he looked up. This room was fully furnished and beautifully decorated. It was the only room in this strange building that seemed to be in use.

In the center of the room stood the most beautiful woman he'd ever seen, even with swollen eyes and tear-streaked cheeks, just the fact that she was here made her the perfect image. "Conner," she barely whispered his name, reminding him of the last time he'd seen her, the time he discovered her deceit.

He turned and left. "Conner, please. I'm so sorry." He walked away from her agonizing plea as she cried out to him, "Please, I'm sorry." He could hear her screaming through her tears even as he began running from her.

Conner sat up and wiped the sweat from his brow. It used to be that he could go a decade without dreaming; now he had the same nightmare every night. Every night it affected him more, hurt him more to walk away from her.

He tried to shake the image of his precious, weeping girl, but as he lifted his hands to rub his eyes, he found them wet. He also used to never cry.

"Are you ever going to share your dream?" Byron knew that he was having nightmares; it was impossible for him to hide anything from his closest friend, but he also knew that he would not push him for answers.

"Do you think that Dagmar is right? Am I responding too emotionally?" He could almost feel Byron's nod of understanding as he searched for the words to offer.

"Anyone can see that you are responding emotionally, Conner. I don't think that that is the question you are wanting answered." He blew a long, slow breath from his nostrils, as if looking for a way to proceed, *"Why are you responding so passionately? Could it be that you are offended by her lie? How many times has Elam lied to us? You have always forgiven him easily. Are you so offended that she is a Darksoul? Do you truly believe that that changes who she is? Could it be that what offends you most is your own response? Could it be that your difficulty sleeping is a result of your remorse rather than your hurt or anger?*

"You know that you responded wrongly to her deception and revelation. We all did. But what does it change? What value does our remorse have if it does not lead to reparation? This regret, this guilt will lead you down one of two paths if it does not lead you to act. Either you will continue in your self-loathing and distress and will become discouraged and depressed, or you will continue in your self-pity and anger,

believing that your reaction was justified, and you will become embittered and calloused.

"If you were wrong and you do nothing to correct your wrong, it will destroy you, either leading to death, or to corruption. If you were not wrong, that will be revealed as you seek to follow the path of redemption. So, the question becomes: what are you going to do about your regret?"

"What can I do at this point?" the sound of her agonized screams echoed in his ears, "Isn't it too late for redemption?"

"It is never too late for redemption if both parties are willing to forgive," all four of the other dragons voiced their agreement. It seemed they had all grown as tired as he had of the sad state their family had fallen into. Conner nodded and breathed a deep sigh as he let go of the last of his anger, leaving him feeling only sad and a bit lonely.

"Then we can only hope that she will forgive our abandonment."

"Wait, are we actually gonna get to see her again?" Grizwald nearly collided with his twin as his head shot up in excitement. *"We're actually going to go find her?"*

Every head turned toward Conner, waiting for his response. He didn't know why it had to be his decision to make. "How are we going to find her?"

"I know exactly where she is," Dagmar sounded almost offended that he had asked. *"Did you really*

believe that I would let you all simply abandon your friend?"

"I had suspected such an explanation for your disappearances, Dagmar." Byron nodded solemnly, "You were the one who aided her after our untimely exit."

"Did she find her mother?" Snarf stared intently at his older brother, silently begging for a good report.

"She arrived at Tallen's castle but left alone. I was too far away to hear what transpired because she had almost discovered me at least once before then." Snarf lowered his head in defeat and Conner turned his back to the group; he couldn't imagine how discouraging it must have been for her, losing her friends only days before failing to rescue her mother.

"Where is she now?" Byron finally broke the pained silence that had settled over the group.

Dagmar sighed slowly; he seemed reluctant to answer, as if his report was not a pleasant one. *"After leaving Tallen's castle, she returned to Puko. She's been there for a few weeks now, and, though I can't see through the trees well, I believe that Briganti is training her."*

"No!" Conner spun back toward him, his fists clenched painfully by his sides, "He'll ruin her."

"Then I suggest we leave immediately." Byron had barely finished speaking before every dragon was standing and ready for takeoff. It took Conner a moment to douse the smoky remains of last night's fire before throwing the strap of his traveling sack over his shoulder and exploding into his true form.

He didn't usually like to travel in his true form, but they all moved significantly faster if they could fly freely and unencumbered. So, with magic pulsing through his body, he felt his human form melt from his frame in white-hot fire to reveal a creature over seven feet tall with huge wings spread wide, ready to thrust him into the air. In one smooth motion, all six winged creatures lifted themselves off the ground and darted toward the Forest of Karr.

Conner hadn't flown on his own in a long while and had almost forgotten what it felt like. His body hung limp in the air, suspended only by the power of the wind under his wings. He had often held himself board-straight in flight, keeping his body parallel to the ground as he glided over an enemy. The posture struck fear into the hearts of onlookers, as he appeared as a powerful beast, but he found that, even with his great strength, he would soon tire from the strain of holding himself straight. So, while his appearance in flight didn't matter as much as speed, he tucked his legs to his chest and held them with his arms, effectively making himself a large ball suspended by the wings of a dragon.

As the wind rushed through the fur of his wings and the hair of his head, he was tempted to let out a cry of joy, but the urgent reason for his flight silenced the shout before it ever left his lips.

Chapter 4

Aleisha snuck silently into the tree, paying close attention to Briganti's room specifically so as to be sure she would sense him should he choose to wander from his quarters. She had been out with Soulfire a bit longer than she had intended and hoped to make it to her room undetected so as to avoid an unnecessary scolding from her Dictator.

Confident that no one was out in the corridor, she stepped further into the tree and proceeded to make her way to the staircase, silently ascending the trunk. Holding her breath, she passed by Briganti's room, sensing his sleeping form inside. With an inaudible sigh, she made it up the rest of the way to her room, only to pause as she reached for the ivy curtain.

Even knowing the sadness and pain she was asking for if she did, she wanted so very much to turn toward Conner's room, to pretend that he was still there. Dropping her hand, she continued up the stairs to Conner's room, not even pausing before she walked through the curtain.

His room looked just like hers did with a large bed on one wall, a desk and chair on another and a wardrobe on the third. This room had housed the man who had saved her from Cedrick, who had defended her to Briganti, who had taught her how to use her magic. In this room had stood the man whose voice still echoed in her head every time she wanted to lash out in anger, *"Be angry and do not sin."* For this man, she would never follow the examples of her Dictator and father. Even if he hated her now, Conner would always be her dearest human friend.

Taking a deep breath, the tears she'd been trying so long to shed already burning her eyes even as they refused to come, she stepped further into his room, memories from random conversations floating through her mind. She could almost hear Snarf and Conner's laughter in her head as she recalled their water fight next to the Karr River.

She should not have come here. It was better to have never had friends than to have finally known love only to lose it so carelessly, and she could not face the fog of sorrow again for so foolishly seeking out reminders of that which she had lost.

The room seemed to dim as she choked on the tears that never wanted to come. Having predicted what was about to happen, she stumbled over to Conner's bed as quickly as she could, so as to make sure that she was seated before her magic blocked all senses and made it impossible to know where she was.

She managed to reach the bed before her vision went dark. As she scrambled to climb blindly onto the bed, pain shot up her leg as her shin collided with the wooden frame, though it quickly faded as her magic continued to engulf her in the fog of sorrow that blocked every connection to the world around her. Here, in this fog of sorrow, in this empty existence, she could mourn.

If only she had been more careful not to use so much magic in front of her friends, she might have been able to remain with them, though she detested the very idea of the continued lies that would have been necessary as time went on. If only she had told them immediately after finding out what she was, they would never have caught her in a lie, though she knew that they would never have wanted a Darksoul as a companion. If only she had never been chosen by Briganti, she could be with Conner and the dragons even at this very moment. He seemed to be at the center of every pain in her life.

All at once, she could feel again, could see again, could hear the sound of crashing furniture as her magic exploded from her with the force of her pent up rage, thrusting every object in the room towards the walls. *"Be angry and do not sin,"* Conner's voice, ever present in her mind, reminded her of her need to control her magic, rather than simply allowing her emotions to dictate its use.

Sighing, she laid back and stared at the ceiling. She wished he was here. She had so much she wanted to talk to him about. She would do anything to regain his trust. She would do anything if he would give her another chance.

Chapter 5

Conner landed on the soft sand of the Desert of Tyree. They had made good time, only taking three days to fly from the plains of Gennesarat in the west to the western edge of the Forest of Karr. It would have taken a week under normal circumstances, but they had only ever stopped for a few hours at a time to sleep and eat.

They had talked about flying all the way to Puko, but Snarf had suggested that their girl might not be pleased to see them, so a slower, more cautious entrance was decided to be wiser and more courteous to their friend.

Conner closed his eyed and breathed deeply, slowly returning to his human form. Opening his eyes, he stepped onto the first patch of grass at the edge of the desert. He remembered last time he'd come here, hoping that Briganti would help train their new friend, as they had only just discovered that she had magic. He thought it ironic that they were now returning in hopes of preventing that very thing.

"You are no longer welcome here, lizards." Locke, the younger son of the leader of Puko, stood before them. He had not been friendly to either Conner or any of his companions the last time they were here.

"We only need a word with your Darksoul," he hoped that by referring to her with such a term, he could play toward Locke's power-hungry tendencies that he had noticed during their last visit.

Darksoul

"You are no longer welcome here." This was going nowhere, and Conner was in no mood to dally.

"Locke," Ignatius and Fortuna suddenly appeared behind their son, looking quite frustrated, "you are not the leader of Puko." Locke snarled at Conner but submitted to his father and stomped off toward the city.

As soon as he disappeared into the trees, Fortuna ran to Conner and threw her arms around him. "Welcome home, my son." She had always acted as a stand-in mother for Conner, even though he was several centuries older then her.

"Thank you, Mater," he smiled and took her arm before shaking Ignatius' hand, "Is she still living here?"

"She is," he seemed almost sad as he answered.

"She is not well, Conner," Fortuna, too, appeared more distressed than he would have expected, "Something awful has happened to her and it has changed her." She shook her head, "She won't tell me what's wrong and she hardly leaves her room other than to ride the horse." He nodded; he knew that he was largely responsible for her state.

"Can I see her?" The dragons would not enter Puko unwelcomed, but perhaps he could convince her to come see them, if he could get to her. Ignatius nodded solemnly and led him into Puko. It felt strange for him to enter the village without the entire population waiting to greet him as they usually did, but Locke had apparently been correct about his welcome. Not a single person stood in the large open field as they entered. Usually, this area was full of people fellowshipping and doing business. The emptiness suggested an intentional coldness toward their unwelcome guest.

This used to be his favorite place to make his home, save the Dragon's Plateau, as Briganti had given him a room over a century ago, when he had saved Gabriel's life. Gabriel's family had had nothing to offer the Dictator as a bribe to choose their child, and yet he had planned months before his birth to claim the child. Conner had been so impressed with the decision to break from the normal pattern of Darksouls that he had called on the help of Byron and Lorahlie to help him. Gabriel's mother had died in childbirth and Gabriel wouldn't have survived either, if not for their intervention. Briganti had been a loyal friend since. Until, that is, his new chosen babe chose Conner over her Dictator and turned Briganti irreversibly against him.

Conner entered the huge tree where he used to stay, "Good luck, Conner," Fortuna gave him a hug before turning to exit with her husband, "I hope you can get through to her."

"Me too," he turned to the stairs and began climbing, passing by Briganti's room quietly so as to avoid detection and further delay. Upon reaching his destination, he stopped a moment at her ivy curtain and reached out with his magic to sense her presence within. Taking a deep breath to calm his nervousness,

Darksoul

he moved the curtain aside and stepped inside, "Leish."

Chapter 6

Aleisha stood next to her bed staring at the small pool of water as it danced before her eyes. Though she hesitated to use her power for fear that her magic would continue to darken, she desperately wanted to see her mother's face, so she formed her replica in the pool designed to provide fresh water to her room. She had been standing there for almost ten minutes, just staring at her mother, wishing she could have saved her. She wished a lot lately; she wished she had been honest with her friends about her identity, but mostly she wished that she could purge herself of this power that she could feel warring to control her.

"Leish," she was so deep in thought that she almost didn't hear the quiet whisper behind her. She thought of sending the fool back through the entrance and flying down the stairs. Briganti had no right to disturb her in her chambers.

Wait. He called her Leish. Only one person had ever called her Leish. The water sculpture of her mother suddenly splashed all over the floor, soaking the hem of her dress as she spun to face him. She couldn't believe he was here. She couldn't believe he had come to find her. She couldn't believe he had called her Leish. He had once said that he called her that to signify their relationship growing into one of friendship.

"Conner," she almost choked on his name as she felt the tears she needed so long to shed finally form in her eyes. He was here. He just stared at her. He didn't look angry. He almost looked apologetic, though she couldn't imagine why.

"Hey Leish." She ran the dozen feet separating them and threw her arms around him, burying her head in his shoulder as she cried. She was surprised to feel his arms wrap around her as he whispered into her hair, "I'm so sorry, Aleisha, I'm so sorry." Why was he apologizing? He didn't do anything wrong. It didn't matter. He came for her and she was never letting go. "I'm so sorry." He just kept repeating himself. She held tighter.

All the tears she'd been too numb to cry in these last few weeks were suddenly pouring down her cheeks and his shirt. She had never expected to see him again, had never expected the chance to apologize to him if she could stop crying long enough to speak. Yet he not only stood in her room, but he held her in his arms and he offered apology as if he was the one who had been in the wrong. She had never understood him, but she was so very grateful that she knew him, that she had him back.

"The others are waiting just outside of Puko. They would truly appreciate it if you would be willing to see them."

"They're here?" She stepped back and wiped her eyes. She couldn't believe they all came. "Of course I want to see them. Where are they?" He smiled at her, but he didn't look happy like he usually did when he smiled; he looked more relieved than anything. He took her hand in his and led her out of her room and down the long staircase. She held her breath and paused before passing Briganti's room to be sure he wasn't inside. She didn't sense him.

They continued out of the tree and into the large meadow at the entrance of Puko. Crossing the large field of grass, they exited the small village the same way they had entered months before. As soon as she stepped outside of Puko, she could hear her friends.

"She probably refused to see us," Grezald's voice was the first to break into her thoughts, though she almost didn't recognize him without his usual cheerful tone.

"She probably hates us now, and who could blame her?" Grizwald agreed with his twin. Were they talking about her? She didn't hate them. Why would she?

"We were terrible to her." She was horrified to hear Snarf's voice join in with the insanity, *"even if she doesn't hate us, she will probably never trust us again."*

"She doesn't hate any of us." She was somewhat surprised that Dagmar was the only one who had apparently not lost his mind. But then, Dagmar had been the only one to figure out that she was a Darksoul, so perhaps he was the only one who had ever really known her very well. *"You're all idiots."*

"Silence!" All the voices faded as soon as Byron spoke. *"She can hear you."*

Conner stepped out of the woods, bringing her with him. He didn't seem to be aware of the conversation between the dragons, but that made sense; only those whom the dragons allowed to hear them could. That is, only those whom they allowed to hear them and Darksouls. Anyone who allowed a Darksoul to hear their telepathic communications could never hide again, and they had all trusted her with their voices before learning who she was. What she was.

All five of the huge dragons stared at her in silence. For a moment, no one moved or spoke; she was sure she was going to cry again. She couldn't believe they had come back for her. She suddenly laughed and ran to Snarf, burying herself in the soft fur of his chest. The huge purple dragon lowered his long neck to wrap himself around her. *"I am so sorry, Aleisha."* She jerked away from him and folded her arms; she had to know what was bothering everybody.

"Why do you all keep apologizing? I'm the one who was lying to you, I was prepared to beg for forgiveness if I ever saw you again, and yet you are acting like I should be extending forgiveness instead. What did you do?"

"We abandoned you." Grezald sounded like it should be an obvious explanation.

"Of course you did, and I'm grateful," they all looked at each other in confusion. "I expected you to torch me on the spot when you found out what I was. I count it a mercy that you only left."

"Even so," Byron spoke with the same calm voice he always used, *"we did not respond appropriately. As your friends, we should have stayed and given you a*

chance to explain your actions, and as followers of the Creator, we should never have abandoned you when you needed us so desperately."

"But I lied to you. I'm the one who needs your forgiveness."

"And we are all ready and eager to forgive you, Aleisha." Conner placed a hand on her shoulder and turned her toward him. "Now we ask that you forgive us as well. There is not one here who did not do wrong that day."

She stared at him for a moment, bewildered. He seemed so sincere, but why? How could they all be so gracious? She had truly never met anyone like this strange man and his powerful friends.

"Will you accept our apology, Aleisha?" She turned back toward Snarf as he spoke. Were they offering her an opportunity to get her friends back?

"Yes," she felt Conner's hand tighten on her shoulder and he grinned at her when she looked up at him. "Yes, of course I accept your apology. I've hated myself since making you leave. Will you, too, accept mine?" That didn't sound like much of an apology to her, but then again, she had never apologized for anything in her life before; she wasn't sure the proper way to go about such a thing.

"We are all eager to forgive you, Aleisha. May I be the first to welcome you back into our family?" as Dagmar finished speaking, the younger three dragons lifted their heads to let out an excited howling noise. It sounded like a wind dancing through ice crystals in the

winter, shattering the frozen water in a beautiful, yet terrifying roar. She laughed and buried herself in Snarf's fur again, hugging him once more before moving on to each of the others to offer the same gesture.

"Locke told me we had visitors." Conner spun towards Briganti and growled as he entered the circle of friends. "Welcome, all."

"Don't pretend you're suddenly glad to see us again, Briganti. Your welcome party made your thoughts on the matter quite clear."

"You misunderstand," the old man spoke in his most diplomatic voice, "I did not want you to come because I did not want my babe to be upset by your presence. Now that I see that she is glad to be reunited with you, you are as welcome as you have always been." He ended with a grin as he spread his hands to gesture to all present.

"In that case, we thank you for your hospitality. If you give us just a moment alone, we'll join you in our regular rooms." Aleisha glared at Conner for believing him so easily, but he ignored her and nodded at Briganti when he smiled and turned to leave.

"He's lying to you; he wants nothing other than to control me and he-" Conner held his hand up to her and shook his head, silencing her.

"We expected such behavior from our old friend," Byron spoke calmly to her thoughts as she bristled, *"It is best to remain for now and not seek out conflict. We*

will discuss this matter further in the privacy of our rooms later."

Conner raised his eyebrows at her as if asking if she would comply. She wasn't happy about it, but she nodded and turned to lead them all back inside.

Chapter 7

Conner stood in the dragons' large room, pacing as Aleisha told the story of her failed attempt to rescue her mother and her decision to return here. She seemed extremely discontented with her current situation and seemed downright terrified of her own magic. "It just seems like it's changing as I use it, as if it started out thoughtless, emotionless, without motivation or intent of any kind; it was pure. Now, though, it almost feels like, when I use it or when something comes up in which using it would be helpful, it's as if it has a consciousness of its own and it's terrifying. It wants to destroy, it wants to burn, it wants to," she paused, a look of pure fear showing in her eyes, "kill."

He had often wondered why he had never heard of a single decent Darksoul; even Gabriel had ended up calloused, cruel, and corrupt. This development of her magic could explain both that and the fact that Aleisha seemed such a strange exception to the rule. Could it be that, having only just begun to use her magic, she had not used it enough to be transformed into the monster that he knew Darksouls to be? It made sense; after all, by her age, most Darksouls would have spent decades being warped and corrupted by the tainted magic.

"Is it plausible that you could simply refrain from using your magic?" Grezald was the first to speak when she was finished.

"I have tried, but sometimes I don't even realize that I am using it until I feel the pull to use more. I want to be rid of it completely."

"I'm sorry, Aleisha, but I don't think that's possible" - Conner stopped pacing to face her - "I've never heard of anyone losing their magic once they've been chosen."

"Could we ask Elam? If anyone knows, he would." She was practically begging him. He couldn't imagine what pain she must be in, to feel herself being lost and having no power to stop it. "Please."

He highly doubted that Elam would be able to help, but how could he refuse her desperate plea? Even if Elam couldn't help them, they had to try, even if only to get her away from Puko. He looked to Byron for assurance, who nodded only slightly, leaving the final say to him. "When can you be ready to leave?"

"Thank you." She nearly knocked him over when she leapt at him, wrapping him in an unexpectedly powerful hug. "Thank you, thank you." She let go of him and backed up slightly, bouncing in place with excitement like Snarf so often did. "I'm ready to leave right now. Can we go now?"

"It doesn't work like that, Aleisha." He hated deflating her so, but they had to do this right. "It would be rude to leave now; you know how this works here."

"I don't care about being rude to these horrible people," she interrupted him as she crossed her arms with an angry huff, "They are pretentious and cruel, and they don't deserve your unceasing good manners."

"Aleisha," Snarf spoke gently. *"If we treat them as they treat others, we are no better than they. No matter what atrocities they have committed, we must love them as the Creator has commanded."*

She averted her eyes and sighed, "The Creator has so many rules."

"Not really," Byron interjected, *"He just wants us to live in a good relationship with Him and with others. We have all deserved unkindness in the past, even the recent past, yet we are all once again united in love and friendship. Should we not give the same opportunity to everyone?"*

"No! They are horrible people!" She stubbornly locked eyes with the large dragon; the display would have been impressive if she wasn't being so unkind. "I hardly think you can compare us to them."

"Then let me ask you, Aleisha," he patiently continued, *"Who gets to decide when someone is good enough to deserve a second chance? You?"*

She appeared confused by that and looked to Conner as if seeking her answer from him. She opened her mouth to respond, but, as she stared at him, her shoulders slumped; she closed her mouth and looked to the ground in submission.

"We will leave as soon as we can, Aleisha, but we must wait for the appropriate time." He wished he could do something to ease the pained expression she wore, but he had to be a good example for her, even if it hurt him to see her struggle.

They spent most of the evening sitting in the dragons' room, telling stories of the months they were apart and laughing at Snarf and Grizwald as they came up with an endless supply of silly jokes and stupid puns.

"It's getting late." Snarf let out a whining noise when Conner interrupted his favorite joke about a lizard and a frog. "Aleisha and I should be heading back to the main house." He moved to stand but Aleisha put her hand on his arm, stopping him.

"At least let him finish the joke."

"You don't want to hear the end. Trust me," he leaned close so only she could hear him. "He thinks it's the greatest joke in all of comedy, but it's really dumb." He stood and offered her a hand up. He noticed Snarf was glaring at him, but he was alright with that.

"I didn't realize you were capable of being so mean." As they made their way down the flight of stairs, Aleisha poked his ribs and laughed at him.

"If you had heard that joke thousands of times over two and a half centuries, you would have gotten up to run as well." He grinned back at her, then stopped and turned toward her when she stared at him in shock.

"How old are you?"

Oh yeah, he had never actually told her his age. "Three-hundred fifty," he thought for a moment, trying to remember how long it had been since he last asked Grizwald, "fifty-seven. Maybe?" he grinned again, throwing his shoulders back in mock arrogance, "look good for my age, don't I?"

For a second, she said nothing as she continued to stare, wide-eyed, at him. "Nah, I would have guessed at least four-hundred." She broke into a playful grin. "You might look young, but you move like an old man." She jabbed him in the ribs again and ran down the steps away from him.

"Hey!" he laughed and ran after her; she would not get away with that comment.

She jumped down the last few steps and sprinted out of the building, making her way across the meadow and leaving Conner behind. As soon as he reached the open field, he sped up, closing the distance between them until he could reach her.

She yelped when he grabbed her around the waist, "Old man indeed," he said, swinging her around to maintain his balance as he lost momentum. She was laughing so hard that he couldn't help but join her.

Inhaling deeply, he steadied his breathing and gently released her from his grasp. Slinging one arm across her shoulders, he led her, still giggling, toward the main house. "It's good to have you back, Leish." They had only just begun developing their friendship when they had parted. Now he was excited to see how close they would become; he was not used to caring for another human being.

"Thank you. I'm glad you came back." She smiled up at him and wrapped her arm around his waist, walking quietly beside him as they made their way back to their rooms.

Chapter 8

Aleisha woke and rolled in her bed. She'd had a wonderful dream about being reunited with Snarf, Conner, and the other dragons, but that only made waking up to her new life even more unpleasant. Sitting up in bed, she let her sheets fall off of her as a single tear crawled its way down her cheek. If only her dream could be reality.

Sighing heavily, she climbed out of bed and stripped her nightgown off, reaching for her wardrobe to pull out a simple black dress. Briganti had given her the black dresses to symbolize her identity as a Darksoul, but Aleisha only wore them as a symbol of mourning: mourning over her mother's death, her friends' departure, and her own destiny to become pawn to Briganti and slave to her own magic. As soon as she let the hem drop to the floor, she heard the slight rustle of leaves behind her, signaling someone entering her room.

"Morning, Leish." Conner! She spun around and stared at his wonderful smile. It wasn't a dream this time; he really had come back for her. They had all come back for her. "Sleep well?" His smile never faltered as he stepped farther into the room.

She only nodded as she reached up and wiped her last tear away. He was standing right in front of her. She could touch him if she wanted to just to prove that he was real, but she remembered now. The apologies, the promise that they would leave, the reprimand of her attitude toward the people of Puko; it had all been real. "I can't believe you're really here."

"Come on, Aleisha," he laughed quietly as he shook his head, "we don't want to go through that again. We're all here for you now and we're not leaving you this time." He smiled again, "you gonna get ready for breakfast? Snarf will be annoyed if you are late."

She laughed and bounced over to the desk, grabbed her brush, and thrust it into her hair at her scalp, only to get it stuck and wrench a large portion of hair out with her careless ripping. Grimacing, she eased the brush back out and began brushing more gently at the ends of her long hair. She could hear stifled laughter behind her and turned to glare at Conner, who was standing with one hand clamped over his mouth as his shoulders shook with laughter.

"I wouldn't want to be a woman." She could barely understand him through his laughter. "It looks painful."

"I could untangle it with my magic, but I don't like to unless it's necessary." She rubbed the spot on her scalp that was now bare and quite tender; it was going to be sore all day. Conner nodded and stepped closer, lifting his hands to her hair.

"We'll see if this works," he mumbled as he ran his fingers through her hair, eliminating every knot effortlessly and painlessly. "There, you're perfect." He grinned proudly at his work, earning another glare from her. It was not fair that he could use his power without fear of destroying himself.

"Shall we head to breakfast then?" She marched past him and headed down the stairs, leaving him behind her, laughing again.

"You're looking well today, Aleisha." Briganti appeared outside of his room just as Aleisha was about to pass. How could she have forgotten to watch out for him? "Maybe well enough to do some training today?" She wasn't sure what sparked the sudden interest in training her seeing as he had been refusing to these last months, but it made her even more suspicious of him than normal. Perhaps, now that Conner and the dragons were back to challenge his claim over her, he thought that now would be a good time to start acting like a Dictator. "I expect to see you after breakfast, or your friends will not be welcome here."

Conner arrived right behind her and placed one hand on her shoulder. "Snarf has missed his favorite human these last months; it would be a shame not to let him spend the day with her. That might upset him." Conner cocked his head innocently at the old man. "Trust me, you don't want to deal with an offended dragon, especially one with so many brothers to join in his mischiefs." Briganti knew enough not to argue with such a threat. Even in his arrogance, he wouldn't dare start a fight with five dragons and a powerful Dragonsoul. Conner nodded and lightly pushed Aleisha past him and down the rest of the stairs.

"Thank you." She quietly turned to him and offered a weak smile. "I really don't want to train with him. I only even came back here because I didn't know where else to go."

"I know," he leaned closer and whispered, "We're planning on leaving in the next couple of days, so just try to be patient until then." He gently squeezed her shoulder and then dropped his hand to move in front of her, leading her to the dragons' living quarters.

As soon as she stepped on the first step leading up the long stairway to the dragons' room, she heard the powerful sound of Snarf's wings thundering through the air.

She briefly recalled her first experience flying in his grasp. He had been freeing her from Cedrick, her master and owner from the time she was six. She felt that somehow this was no different; he was here to free her from her new, yet equally cruel, master. Even though she was the one foolish enough to seek Briganti out, her loyal friends would not abandon her to suffer the consequences of her folly, and she would be sure not to let them regret their compassion. She would earn the loyalty of her precious friends, even if it took centuries to do so.

Snarf gently placed her on the floor seconds before Byron landed with Conner. As soon as the huge lizard-like fingers unwrapped from around her waist, she turned and ran into her large friend's chest, clutching tightly to his soft fur, and burying her head in his warmth. She heard Conner snicker behind her and mutter something about them being separated for too long. Snarf seemed to be purring in response as he gently wrapped his huge wings around her.

"*Oi, lovebirds,*" Grizwald sounded amused as he called to them. *"Breakfast is getting cold."*

"You dolt!" She heard the low thud of Grezald's paw connecting with his twin's head. *"Breakfast is already cold! It's gonna get hot waiting for Aleisha to finish greeting us if she plans to give us each an equally long embrace."*

"Well, somebody's jealous," Dagmar chuckled lightly. Wait, Dagmar chuckled? Aleisha backed slightly away from Snarf and turned to look at Dagmar. He nodded welcomingly, earning a grin from her. She would have to get used to Dagmar welcoming her; he had been the only one not to leave her when her secret was revealed, but she somehow had still expected him to be cold with her.

"Shall we eat?" Byron broke into her thoughts as he nodded toward a large pot in the center of the room. Conner was already sitting on a pile of leaves next to the food, holding a bowl. On one side of him was a second pile of leaves, presumably meant to be her seat, and on his other side was a basket of bread.

She sat next to him and looked curiously at the pot. It appeared to be filled with gravy of some sort, but Grezald had said that breakfast was cold. Conner broke a piece of bread off of one of the large loaves and handed it to her, keeping the other half for himself. Dipping his bread in the gravy, he shoved it in his mouth, sighing contentedly as he chewed. Breaking another piece of the bread off, he slathered it in gravy and tossed it to Byron, who snatched it out of the air and purred as soon as it touched his tongue. Convinced that she was missing out on something incredible, Aleisha cautiously dipped her bread into the gravy and took a small bite. She had not expected the gravy to be so good cold, but she actually quite enjoyed it.

An hour later, Aleisha tossed the last piece of bread for Snarf to catch, laughing when Grizwald intercepted it in his large jaws. *"Thief,"* Snarf grumbled but looked amused as he watched his brother chomp happily on the last morsel of their breakfast.

"We have discussed the timing of our departure from Puko," Byron spoke, and everyone quieted themselves to listen. *"Considering the difficulty that you're having with the tainted magic, we all agree that we need to seek out Elam's knowledge immediately."* She nodded vigorously, happy to convey the urgency she felt. *"We have decided to depart in the morning. Conner will speak to Briganti tonight to inform him of our decision."* She sighed in relief and felt her shoulders relax as the tension she'd gotten so used to eased. She had really not been looking forward to facing him concerning the matter; she was not as skilled as Conner at handling Briganti's threats and wordplay.

"Elam will be happy to see us again," Grezald hummed quietly and he and Grizwald bobbed their heads in time with the song as he spoke.

Darksoul

"He'll be upset with us for our behavior, more likely." Conner lowered his head and picked at the leaves he was sitting on. "I wonder what he did with my horse."

"It's probably still in the stable," Grizwald sounded confident that he was right.

"Um, actually, Soulfire is here." Grezald and Grizwald stopped humming and everybody stared at her in confusion at her announcement.

"What?" The bewildered look on Conner's face reminded her that the horse hadn't had a name the last time they were together.

"Oh," she felt herself blush and hurried to explain, "Um, I named your horse. Um, he just seemed like he needed a name and you never called him anything but 'horse' so…" he started laughing.

"You named my horse Soulfire?" he asked, "What does that even mean?" At his question, all five dragons joined in his laughter.

"Um, it means…" - she folded her arms and glared at her friends - "Why does it have to mean anything?" This only succeeded in making them laugh harder. "It just seemed like a good name."

"It's a very unique name, surely." Byron chuckled as he responded to her, *"We just assumed that such a unique name would have a unique meaning."*

"It sounds like you've given him his own soul power," Grizwald broke in with his opinion.

"That would be 'Firesoul,'" Grezald sounded completely serious as he corrected his twin. *"Conner could be a Firesoul; he certainly has the personality."*

"Are you saying I'm bright?" Conner offered a huge grin in response to Grezald's comment.

"No," Dagmar shook his head, *"He's saying you remind him of a horse."*

Aleisha chuckled at that, hiding her smile with her hands. Conner winked at her before turning back to glare at Dagmar. *"Um, shouldn't Conner at least go check on his horse?"* Snarf finally joined the conversation, but it seemed odd that he passed up the opportunity to tease Conner for such a serious question. *"After all, Soulfire hasn't seen his master for a few months now; he may think he's been forgotten."*

Conner stood and stretched his back before turning toward Aleisha, "Do you mind showing him to me?" She nodded and accepted his hand up. As they headed down the stairs, she thought of how restless the dragons must be getting being stuck in their room all day, but none of them wanted to join the rest of Puko, either. Maybe that's why Snarf wasn't his usual chipper self today.

"Can we talk later?" She silently reached out to her old friend.

"I would be honored to spend the evening with you, Aleisha." He just didn't sound like himself today.

"Hey, Leish." She hurried after Conner at the sound of his voice. "You okay?"

"Yes, sorry." They made their way slowly down the endless steps. She wondered what could be bothering Snarf; he always seemed so cheerful, but today he didn't even join in with the banter. He was usually the one leading the fun, but even Dagmar was laughing more than him.

She suddenly ran into Conner's chest. "Where are you today? I said your name twice." He wrapped his hands around her arms and gently pushed her far enough away to look at her.

"Does Snarf seem bothered to you?"

"Not as bothered as you do." He smiled gently before frowning worriedly at her. "Is that what's going on in your head? You're worried about Snarf?"

"Of course I'm worried about him! He passed up a perfect opportunity to make a joke about you. He doesn't do that!"

"Snarf hasn't been himself lately." He shook his head and sighed lightly. "None of us have been. He's probably just feeling overwhelmed; a lot has happened in the last few days." He dropped his hands from her arms and turned away from her.

Chapter 9

Conner followed Aleisha through the Common Tree and out the back door. The only stables in Puko were located on the farthest end of the village away from the desert right next to the blacksmith's shop. Conner had only met the blacksmith a few times, but he'd always found him quite pleasant; he hoped that Aleisha had gotten the opportunity to get to know the older man, as he wanted her to have more than just frustration and disdain toward the people of this village. "Good morning, Kellan." Apparently, she had gotten to know him at least slightly because she smiled warmly at him as they neared.

"Aleisha." The gruff man nodded to her before turning to Conner. "Good morning, sir. It's an honor to have you visiting us again."

"Kellan, I hope all is well." He offered him a smile as they passed by his shop to enter the stables, which looked a great deal like a bush to Conner, but he supposed that it still blended in well with the rest of the foliage.

"I hadn't thought of the fact that you would know Kellan."

"Who did you think used to bring my horse to the stables?" he chuckled. "I mean, 'Soulfire.' Who else would have brought Soulfire to the stables?" he grinned and laughed at her attempt to hide her amusement under a glare.

As soon as the horse heard his voice, he lifted his head and started prancing in the stall, eager to be reunited with his master. Conner reached out his hand to the creature and stroked his nose affectionately, stepping closer to wrap his arms around his neck as he whispered soothingly in his ears, quietly sending simple pictures into his mind to show him where they would be going next.

He took a few moments to try to read the horse's thoughts, though it was always rather difficult for beasts to communicate on an intelligible level. He did manage to make out the most important thing he wanted to know, as well as seeing that he and Aleisha had been going on regular rides. "You've taken diligent care of him while I've been gone." He could see that he startled her out of her own mind, as he so often did. "Thank you." She beamed at his praise. "I am a bit disappointed that I didn't get to see your first attempt at riding alone. That would have been fun." He had to suppress his laughter; the horse had seemed rather traumatized by that experience.

"I managed to stay on, but some little girl in Fonishia yelled at me that I was scaring him." Conner laughed at her statement, and this time she joined him.

As their laughter died down, Aleisha got the same distant look he'd seen so many times. Looking around, it didn't take long to spot the sculpture he knew she'd be making with the loose straw; an impressive depiction of the dragons was already forming on the ground in a nearby stall.

"I see you haven't learned to control that yet," She jumped at the sound of his voice, just as he knew she would. "We'll work on that." He thought of the implication of that simple statement 'we'll work on that.' He was voicing a confidence in them having some sort of future together. She was, aside from Briganti and his own Dictator, the first human he really had the capability of having any sort of distant future with. What would that look like, to still be friends with the same human for more than a hundred years? He'd never had a friendship last that long with anyone without wings.

"Why do you do that?" He looked back to Aleisha when she spoke, though he hadn't realized he'd looked away. "You are so focused when we are in a group, so at ease as long as others are around. But whenever we are alone, you are so easily distracted."

"I'm not distracted really." He shrugged, wishing he could fully convey his concern. "I'm just not used to having any human friends." He shifted uncomfortably before taking a seat on a bushel of hay. "The dragons are pretty much the only friends I've been able to trust in the long term; that's why I call them my brothers. Even Elam's loyalty can be bought if someone offers him some new information. Every time I allow myself to care for another human, they've either abandoned or betrayed me." He thought of Alice, the exception. "Or they've died. Everyone from my parents to my Dictator, even Briganti turned away from me after decades of friendship." He nodded to a stool nearby; she didn't need to stand while he ranted.

"When we're alone and I start to open up to you, I remember what it is like to be betrayed by those I care about and I become afraid." He sighed and shook his head, that wasn't exactly how he wanted that to sound. "I don't mean to push you away or anything, Aleisha. I just don't remember how to function in a normal human relationship. It's been so long since I could trust anybody, and quite frankly, I'm afraid. I'm so afraid to trust you not to hurt me."

"Especially since I already have," she didn't look at him as she spoke quietly. He'd not intended for her to come to that conclusion. She was just a young girl who'd barely known life; she'd made a foolish choice based on having almost no life experience and no mentor to teach her how she should have handled that situation.

"You seem to have forgotten who left that day, Aleisha. You were wrong to hide who you are from us, knowing how we felt and how hard we were trying to help you discover your own identity, but I was the one who abandoned you. Not the other way around." He reached out and grasped her hand. She finally lifted her gaze, but only to stare at him in bewilderment. He imagined that she'd not had a lot of experience with people admitting their mistakes with her background, but she would get used to it in their family.

Letting go of her hand, he stood and moved back to the horse. Smiling, he patted his nose one final time before turning back to Aleisha. "Let's get back; you should gather everything you'll need for the journey."

"Do you think it's possible to get rid of my power?" she suddenly seemed extremely intense, as if his answer dictated reality.

"I truly don't know, Aleisha." He sighed and reached up to scratch his neck; that clearly wasn't the answer she had wanted. "I hope so, but my experience tells me that there's probably no way. However, I don't think that the Creator will abandon you to this tainted magic if you truly desire to be free of its evil. If He sees fit, He will provide a way to be free. After all, He frees people from their evil every day; it's just not usually tainted magic that is the origin of that corruption."

"I do want to be free." She looked so desperate.

"You do realize that being free of the tainted magic won't free you from your own corruption?" she looked for a moment like she would object to that, but she eventually nodded.

"I understand that I'll still have a lot of work to do to live like the Creator commands, but it will be a lot easier to resist my violent tendencies without my magic making it so easy to indulge those tendencies and so hard to resist." She huffed in frustration, "I've always battled my anger, but it's almost like every emotion is being amplified to a level I would not normally go when my magic interferes."

Conner nodded as she finished, "I just don't want you to be tempted to use your magic as an excuse. We tend to give our weaknesses more credit than they are due, thereby denying our own responsibility in our failures." He put his arm around her shoulder, hoping to offer some level of support as he could very easily have sounded like he was tearing her down, "We should get back to the main house; we can continue talking about this later if you'd like after you've had time to consider what we've said."

Chapter 10

Aleisha sat on her bed and rolled her dresses as tightly as she could to fit them into her sack. She had decided to leave all of her black dresses behind, as she no longer saw cause to be in mourning; she had even asked Fortuna to make her a white shawl for the journey to add some variety to her otherwise brown wardrobe.

As she shoved the last brown dress into her sack, she stood and walked slowly to her dresser, mentally going through her list of things she would need for her journey. She had never really been attached to things because she had not truly owned anything as a slave and not had opportunity to collect anything of value on her constant travels since leaving her life as a slave, so anything she left behind would not be missed, save Elam's sword and her mother's map. When she left this time, she did not intend to ever come back. Then again, she hadn't intended to return the first time she left either.

She placed her sack on the dresser and began shoving her personal items into the large front pocket. Her brush, her mother's map, and the book that Briganti had given her on magical manipulation of colored textiles filled the front pocket; she would leave everything else.

Kailey stepped timidly into the room, followed by Fortuna. Both women usually held a large smile and rarely ceased talking, but as they eyed the sack on Aleisha's desk, and the sheathed sword next to it, they both frowned with concern, though Fortuna did nod in apparent understanding. "You're leaving again," she didn't ask; this woman and her grandchild were two of Aleisha's only friends in Puko, and they well knew how she hated it here.

"Yes, I am." She smiled weakly at the precious child, opening her arms to welcome her into a hug. Kailey's hugs would be one of the few things she missed when she left. As her little arms wrapped around her waist and squeezed, Aleisha closed her eyes and tried to memorize the feeling of the girl's genuine affection. She had never hated her for her distaste for her magic, had never expected her to be the guardian of Puko, and had never demanded that she act like a normal Darksoul. She had never compared her to Gabriel. She had simply loved as only a child can love. "I'm going to miss you, Kailey."

She heard her sigh deeply as she stepped back and wiped her wet cheeks. "Just don't leave until I finish your new picture, ok. Pater burnt the one I made for you last time you were here and I've been working on one that I know will cheer you up."

"Oh, Kailey." She smiled at the little girl and looked up at Fortuna, who smiled proudly at her grandchild, who was already a more skilled artist than Aleisha ever could hope to be. "We're planning on leaving in the morning; can you finish it by then?"

"Yes!" she nodded with great determination and enthusiasm, "but I need to go work on it if that's all the time I have. It's a picture of Goodman Conner, he's scary, but he's nice, and I know how much you missed him and his dragons." She strode towards the door, stopping before she left to turn back towards Aleisha. "I'm glad you are leaving." Aleisha gasped at the sudden statement. "You've been so sad since you came back, maybe leaving will make you happy."

Her sweet, innocent statement was perhaps the most precious thing Aleisha had ever heard. "Thank you, Kailey. That's very kind of you. I think leaving will make me happy, but I will be a little sad because I'll miss you so much." She smiled at the little girl, who grinned before leaving.

"We will miss you so very much." Fortuna smiled sadly and stepped farther into the room, offering Aleisha a hug before taking a seat at the desk. "But I suppose that I must agree with her sentiment; you don't belong here. You could never be content as Briganti's instrument of rule and you'll never truly be welcome as a leader anyway because you were not born of our women; my sons would forever undermine you and try to manipulate and intimidate you as Briganti does."

"Thank you. You're so very kind to me, Fortuna." She had come to adore this woman, much like Conner had, as a sort of stand-in mother.

"Please, Aleisha, now that Conner has returned to claim you, you may as well call me Mater."

"He didn't," she sighed. Fortuna had never been subtle about her hope that Conner would be wed, but she saw no reason to argue with her about it at this point, "ok, Mater."

"What is this nonsense talk about you leaving again?" Briganti burst into her room shouting, "You came to me for help, and now you think you can just leave on a whim?"

Fortuna, just as terrified of Briganti as most people who knew him well, bolted from her seat and hurried out of the room. Aleisha wished that she could join her in her retreat; she really didn't want to speak with her Dictator, especially about her nearing departure. "This is precisely why those foul beasts are not welcome here; they are determined to destroy all of my work."

"Those 'foul beasts' are the only family I have." How dare he insult them; none of them had done anything to earn his animosity. They had been nothing but kind and respectful, even as he insulted them and treated them more like imposters than guests in his town. "And I don't need your permission to leave. I sought out your help because I thought it best that I learn how to use my power. You have refused to teach me and you neglected to inform me of the true nature of my magic." He folded his arms and raised one eyebrow in mock confusion. "You knew that the magic was tainted, you counted on it corrupting me so that I would become as evil as you." She flinched at a sudden realization, "You have been training me. You've been provoking me, manipulating me into using my magic so that it can mature into the monster that it was meant to become."

"And you still think that you can run away from your troubles. Are you so foolish that you cannot learn from your own past?" He smirked as she remembered the sting of abandonment. He was right; she had tried to run away from her Dictator to hide the fact that she was a Darksoul. That had ended in everyone she loved learning that she was a liar and a coward, but this time was different. She wasn't running from her power and she wasn't lying. This time she was looking for a solution. This time was very different. Wasn't it? "You can never run from who you are, Aleisha. You have been mine since the day you were born and you will be mine until the day you die." She shuttered at that thought, and he sneered at the sight.

"I will be rid of this power," she tried to hold herself confidently, but she heard her voice quiver with doubt, "I will be free of you."

"You think you can be rid of it?" he laughed at her statement; he actually seemed sincere in his amusement for once. "There is no way to be rid of your magic." He stepped closer to her, his usual glare firmly back in place, "Even if there was, how selfish, how ungrateful would you have to be to throw away such an incredible gift? You should be honored that I chose to give you such great power and yet all I hear is complaining."

He leaned close enough to her that she could smell his breath, every bit as stale as Cedrick's had always been. "There is only one way for you to be free of me, and I'm sure Locke would be happy to help you in this matter. His wife is expecting a new child very soon, and I'm sure that that child would be grateful for the power." With that final threat, he turned and slithered out of the room.

Aleisha could feel her pulse speed up as she gasped unsteady breaths. She had known that she was only a pawn to Briganti, had even known that he never cared for her as a person, or even as his chosen babe, but she had never thought that he viewed her as so expendable. He would be just as happy to end her life and restart his path of revenge as he would to win her over to his side to fight Tallen for him. As long as he had his revenge, it didn't matter if she lived or died.

She wondered suddenly if he'd ever planned on letting her live once she had served her purpose, after all, she would only serve as an unpleasant reminder of the man who had murdered his favorite babe.

She fell to her knees and tried to calm her ragged breath as the room began filling with fog; she had never so feared for her life. Even in Cedrick's mansion, she had not felt so disposable, so valueless. She truly was only a pawn, an easily-replaceable, fully-expendable piece in Briganti's sick chess game.

She managed to pull herself up off the floor and stumble her way through the thick smoke to her bed. She had no idea that fear could make her feel so weak; she collapsed onto her bed and closed her eyes, breathing deeply to calm herself.

"Aleisha." Her eyes flew open as she lifted her hand to protect herself. she hadn't expected Briganti to send his minion so quickly, but she would be sure that he would not defeat her easily. Locke may be a great warrior, but she was not so afraid to use her magic that she wouldn't do whatever was necessary to protect herself, even if that meant harming precious Kailey's father.

As his large body crashed against her wardrobe, several of the black dresses fell out and the wooden frame fell forward onto him as he landed on the floor. She raised her hand again; she could barely see through the thick, dark fog in the room, but if she saw the dresser move, she would throw the desk at him. "Whoa, Leish." She gasped and covered her face in embarrassment as Conner struggled to his knees under the weight of the wardrobe.

"I'm sorry, I didn't, I didn't mean…" she just shook her head, not sure how to explain, how to apologize.

He pulled her hands away from her eyes, concern showing even through the ever thickening black cloud. "Are you alright?"

"Why are you asking if I'm alright?" she practically screamed at him, I just threw you into my wall and you're asking if I'm alright? Are you?" She could hear the pitch of her voice steadily climbing higher. She couldn't believe that she had just attacked him. She had thought he was Locke. He didn't even sound like Locke.

"Aleisha, what's going on? You're terrified. Tell me why."

"Briganti threatened me. I thought he had sent Locke to 'free me of my power' as he said he would." She shivered as she spoke; it felt like the strange fog was sucking all heat out of the room. "I was so scared that I didn't even look before I reacted. I was sure you were him. I'm so sorry." Conner's expression hardened into one of pure rage as she told her story. She could see every muscle in his body flex as his grip on her wrist began to tighten.

"You need to stay with Snarf tonight." She didn't recognize the husky, venomous voice that came from Conner's mouth; she shuddered once at the sound of it. "Now, Aleisha." She just nodded and pulled away from him, hurrying toward the door. "Take your things. You won't be returning to this room." She turned and rushed to the desk and grabbed her bag. Flinging it over her shoulder, she picked up Elam's sword and ran out the door.

She had never seen such a fearsome look in Conner's eyes before. As she ran, now blindly save her magical sense, through the ever-thickening fog, she almost pitied Briganti the confrontation he was about to endure.

Chapter 11

Conner stood in Aleisha's room, shaking with rage as he followed her presence until she was outside of the tree. As soon as he could feel her enter the dragons' tree, he was going to be visiting the arrogant Dictator a few floors below.

He closed his eyes and breathed a deep, steady breath. He could sense her presence enter hurriedly into the tree. He was afraid that he had scared her pretty badly with his response to her explanation, as evidenced by her fog's continued thickening as she ran out of the room. He had suspected even before he entered her room that something was amiss, as her magic often reacted to her emotions, but he was shocked to see her in such a state of terror. He would not allow Briganti, or anyone else, to speak to her as he had. He could not be allowed to get away with such disrespect.

Satisfied that Aleisha had reached safety, he turned and exited her room. Stomping down the stairs, he tried to ignore that what he was about to do was wrong. He didn't care if he had to live with the guilt of the old man's blood on his hands for a thousand years; he would happily kill Briganti before he would let anyone threaten Aleisha. He stood outside of Briganti's room, ready to resolve the threat personally.

"Be angry and do not sin," he stood in shock as he heard Aleisha's sweet voice recite the very passage he had spoken to her on so many occasions. How would she react if he went through with this? He was trying

to teach her the way of the Creator, how would this decision affect his efforts? How would it affect her?

She would be safe.

She was so eager to learn, though, to understand. He couldn't show her that his words meant nothing. He couldn't be the reason that she never chose to follow the Creator.

But this killing would be justified. He would be protecting innocence. He shook his head and growled in frustration. He knew that he was lying to himself. What he desired, what he was planning, was murder. It was hate-driven murder and he could not call it anything else.

Taking one final breath, he stepped through the ivy curtain into Briganti's room. "Ah, Conner, good evening." Briganti smiled as usual, but quickly dropped the façade and spoke more cautiously. "You look upset. Is something wrong?" This fool actually looked like he had no idea. He really believed that he could play innocent. Conner only growled again, unsure how to proceed without bloodshed. "Ah," he cleared his throat and nodded, finally having the decency to look concerned. "You spoke to Aleisha." He couldn't speak yet, couldn't move for fear of what he might do to this fool. He should not have come in here yet; he was not ready to let him live for his mistake. "I would like a chance to explain." He was beginning to look properly worried. "You see, she was begging me to take her power away; practically groveling at my feet, really." He tried to smile, but waivered under Conner's intense glare. "I was only playing really; teasing her because the only way to-" Conner lunged forward and wrapped his hand around Briganti's throat. He would not listen to any more of this snake's lies.

"Let me explain something to you concerning Aleisha." He had never before seen such raw fear in Briganti's eyes; then again, he had never grabbed him in anger before. "She does not belong to you. You have no authority over her." He leaned closer to the shaking old man. "She is mine." He paused for a moment to let Briganti nod. "If you or anyone you command touches her, I will rip you to pieces with my bare hands and feed you to Snarf." Shaking with rage, he dropped the worthless old fool and turned to exit the room before he could be tempted to do anything further.

Storming down the stairs, he thought of the implications of what he just said, "She is mine." He wondered what she would have thought of that statement. He didn't mean that he owned her of course; he would never allow anyone to own her again. He simply meant that she was his charge, his friend. He was as much hers as she was his and he would never allow anyone to harm her.

"Goodman Conner," he barely heard Kailey's quiet voice behind him, "Goodman Conner." He turned to ask what she needed, but she jumped away from him, "I'm sorry, sir, I didn't mean to bother you." She looked horrified as she turned to flee. He must still look quite angry. He forced himself to relax before calling after her.

"Kailey, come back, I'm not upset with you." The little girl froze, but did not turn toward him. He sighed; he was no good with kids. He walked up to her and knelt before her; she really looked terrified of him. "I'm sorry, I didn't mean to scare you, Kailey." He gently placed his hand on her shoulder as he watched her large eyes shift uncomfortably as if she was searching for the best escape route. "Did you need something from me?"

"I went to Aleisha's room, but she wasn't there and it looked like something bad had happened. I was going to give her these." She held out a small package.

"Aleisha is in the dragons' room, would you like me to take you to her?" Her expression of fear instantly turned to one of wonder.

"That would be amazing," she almost sounded like she was out of breath. Her awe made him smile as he stood to direct her to the door.

"We'll be leaving earlier than expected, so I'm sure that she'll be happy to see you once more before we go." The little girl's shoulders dropped a little as she nodded. He knew that this child meant quite a bit to Aleisha and it pained him that she would probably not see her again, but he had to get away and he had to get Aleisha away as soon as possible.

As soon as they entered the dragons' tree, Conner called out to Byron to give them a lift. "Ok, Kailey, Byron is going to land and we'll climb onto his back. I need you to trust me to hold you on him while he flies us up." She nodded and stared in wonder at the huge room.

He could hear the familiar rhythm of Byron's wings as he descended quickly and landed mere feet in front of Conner and Kailey. Lowering his head, Byron spread his wings and welcomed his riders onto his back, giving them a few moments to position themselves before taking off.

Holding Kailey in his arms, he could feel her inhale one long breath before holding it in fear. "It's ok, he won't drop us." She let out a tiny breath and held tightly to his arms as Byron ascended the cavern. His huge wings beat loudly on both sides, mimicking the sound of gusting wind.

They were only in the air for a few moments, but he knew that it must have felt like an eternity to Kailey, as she was not used to the sensation of flying. As soon as Byron's feet touched solid ground and his wings returned to his sides, Kailey let out a relieved sigh and loosened her vise grip on Conner's arm.

"Kailey." Aleisha jumped up from her seat next to Snarf and ran towards them with her arms spread wide for a hug. The little girl instantly forgot her fear and jumped down from Byron's back without a thought and ran into Aleisha's arms. "I was afraid that I wouldn't get to see you before we left. I'm so glad you came to see me."

"Goodman Conner said that you are leaving sooner than expected. I expected you to leave in the morning, so does that mean that you are leaving tonight?" Aleisha looked up at him in confusion. He hadn't expected her to tell Aleisha what he said. He had planned on doing that.

"It would not be wise to remain here any longer, considering what has happened." She nodded once at his explanation before returning her attention to Kailey.

"I brought you your shawl." Kailey presented the package that she had shown Conner earlier. Aleisha smiled and took the package, opening it to reveal a shawl too white to have been accomplished without the aid of magic stitched with blue and purple flowers. "Avia Fortuna made it for her wedding, but she said that you can have it because she likes you." He could see Aleisha blinking back tears as she examined the precious gift. He wondered if she realized how great a thing she held; most women in Puko made a tradition of handing down an article from their own wedding for their daughters to wear at their own.

"This is a beautiful picture Kailey." She held a piece of parchment in her hands now and was examining it with great interest, if not a bit of unmasked confusion. He wondered if it was the picture itself or the skill that confused her. He knew that she came from a non-magical town, where typically only master painters and their apprentices had access to supplies and training. In Puko, like in most towns with a resident magic user, usually rare items, such as books and paints, were almost commonplace.

"It's because he loves you. I thought it would make you smile since you haven't much since coming back." Kailey grinned and pointed to the picture with pride. It must be a picture of Aleisha with Snarf; this child was more perceptive than he had realized.

"Thank you, Kailey. It really is a beautiful picture; you've improved so much over the last few months." Kailey beamed at the praise. Aleisha rolled up the picture and gently placed it into her bag. "Come sit with me, Kailey. I'd love to visit before we have to leave."

"Don't feel too bad, Conner," Byron suddenly broke into his thoughts, *"Aleisha will miss this little girl, but she made the choice to leave. You can't take responsibility for the pain it will cause her."* He nodded in understanding; he knew that it was best for everyone that they leave, but it pained him to see Aleisha lose what was so obviously a precious relationship.

Chapter 12

Kailey yawned widely and blinked several times in an obvious attempt to stay awake. "We should get you back to your parents." Aleisha ached at the thought of never seeing her friend again, but she also knew that leaving was the right decision.

Kailey stood and nodded, rubbing her eyes as she did so. Snarf lowered himself for her to climb on as Aleisha held out her arm to help her onto the great beast. Snarf was the smallest of the dragons, so she hoped that he would be a little less scary for Kailey to ride on. Of course, she was so exhausted that she doubted that she would even notice.

Once Kailey and Aleisha were seated securely between Snarf's shoulder blades, Conner climbed up behind them, wrapped his arms around them both, and whispered into her hair, "I'm not letting you leave alone, Aleisha." A moment later, Snarf lifted into the air and dove from the room.

Though it took only a few moments to reach the tree's floor, Kailey was already asleep when they landed. Conner slid from the dragon's back and reached for her. "Just give her to me and finish getting ready to go. I'll leave her with Ignatius and Fortuna; I need to let them know that we're leaving and why. I'll be back as quickly as possible." Aleisha obediently lowered the sleeping girl into his arms and grabbed onto the long fur on the back of Snarf's neck.

"So," Snarf spoke teasingly as he returned to the large room. *"You didn't show me the picture Kailey made for you."*

"You didn't ask to see it," she teased back, smiling at the thought of the sweet girl's innocent assumption, but feeling herself blush at the same thought. *"I'll show you when we get back to the room."* She had been really confused by Kailey's picture. She had expected a portrait of Conner because she had said that that was what it was going to be, but she had not been expecting a picture of him standing protectively beside her, one hand held up at some unseen danger, the other wrapped possessively around her waist. She had been sure she was blushing when she first saw it, but no one seemed to notice, and by Conner's wink at Snarf, she figured he had no idea that he was the 'he' in the picture.

"Aleisha," Dagmar addressed her as soon as her feet hit the ground. *"Do you have everything you need?"* she nodded absentmindedly as she rummaged through her pack to pull out her picture. *"Good, Conner will want to leave as soon as he gets back. We should be ready for him."*

As soon as she unrolled the parchment, Snarf began roaring in laughter. "Hey!" How could he be so rude? Kailey had done a beautiful job. "Stop laughing; she worked really hard on this and she didn't have a lot of time to finish it properly."

"Conner?" He continued laughing as his brothers tried to sneak a look at the curious picture. *"We both*

thought that it was a picture of me. He's gonna get a kick out of this."

"No!" She rolled the parchment quickly and shoved it back in its place. "He doesn't need to know; she's just an innocent kid making an innocent assumption."

"Wait, it's Conner?" Grezald cocked his head at her in confusion. *"I figured by her explanation that it was a portrait of Snarf."*

A huge creature with a human body and black dragon-like wings suddenly landed next to Aleisha, causing her to jump back in shock. What was that thing? Where had it come from? She could hear Snarf continue to snicker as the bizarre creature stared at her with mild curiosity. "You ok, Leish?" it spoke with Conner's voice.

"Conner?" She stared in wonder at her companion as he smiled at her. It did look a little like Conner, she supposed, but the lines of his face were just a little too harsh, his eyes were a little too big and completely gold with no white and a vertical slit where his pupil should have been, and he stood at least a foot taller than Conner.

"Sorry, I guess you've never seen me in my true form" - he shrugged - "I figured that it'd be easier to travel like this." She nodded uncertainly; she had never expected he would look so creepy. His eyes were almost cat-like in their sharpness and his skin had a faint metallic appearance, almost like his skin was made of armor.

"*Shall we depart then?*" Byron's voice suddenly broke into her musings. "*We should go before Briganti works up the courage to try to stop us.*" Aleisha nodded and ran to her things, throwing her pack over her shoulder before she scrambled up Snarf's wing and onto his back.

Each dragon dove out of the room and down to the floor a few hundred feet below. Aleisha watched in amazement as Conner plummeted face first toward the ground, only to right himself mere feet before landing gracefully next to Byron.

As soon as Snarf's feet touched the ground, they all exited the tree together. Fortuna stood in the middle of the field, waiting for them. For a moment no one moved, and Aleisha could see tears welling in the older woman's eyes.

Conner was the first to move. He strode boldly up to her and wrapped both arms and wings around her in a long embrace. Aleisha could tell that they were speaking, but she couldn't hear what was said. As soon as they stepped away from each other, Fortuna turned toward the dragons. "*I pray that one day we will.*" The simple fact that Byron spoke to her was a testament to the close relationship between Fortuna and this small family. The fact that Fortuna had had enough practice speaking with dragons that she'd learned to address him telepathically further evidenced that relationship. "*Perhaps one day we may return to our former estate. Until then, I am honored to call you a friend, to call you Mater.*" After Byron's statement, each dragon addressed her in turn, offering various praise of character and grief over losing her. Aleisha tried not to listen, as she had learned to tell when the dragons intended their thoughts to be private, but she could no more block them out than they could her.

Once the last dragon lowered his head in honor toward her, Aleisha could see her clearly, tears flowing down her ebony cheeks as she smiled at them with an expression that could only be described as motherly. After a moment, she looked towards Aleisha. "Come down, precious one." She wasn't sure quite how to respond; she didn't know Fortuna as well as everyone else, so wasn't necessarily expecting a farewell. As she slid from Snarf's back, Fortuna opened her arms in welcome, offering her the same embrace she had just given Conner. "He's a good man, Aleisha, he's just afraid to love. Be patient with him." Aleisha couldn't help but smile; Fortuna was so very similar to her granddaughter.

She turned away from Fortuna and made her way back onto Snarf's back. She would not miss this village that had been her home for the past several months, but she would miss both Fortuna and Kailey. As each of them lifted into the air, she saw Fortuna waving at them from the ground. She continued waving to the group until they broke through the canopy of leaves that hid Puko from above.

"Probably only a day or two if it's quick," after several minutes of flying in silence, Grizwald's quiet comment captured her attention.

"I can't understand how that dumb horse always finds us." Grezald responded slightly louder, *"How will it even know we left?"*

She covered her ears to block them out; she knew that they hadn't intended for her to hear them and she didn't want to eavesdrop if she could help it.

"Elam will not be able to help this time, Dagmar," now, she heard Byron speaking, apparently a part of an unrelated conversation.

"You don't know that. Even if he's heard a rumor that can lead to someone who can help…"

"You sound like Snarf," Byron sighed, *"I want to help Aleisha as much as any of you do, but I don't think we can this time."*

She couldn't take this much longer; these conversations were none of her business. "Snarf," she leaned forward as she whispered, "can we break from the group for a while? I don't want to overhear them talking." He lifted his head for a moment, telling everyone where they would be before darting away from the group.

"Try to get some sleep, Aleisha. Tomorrow will be another long day of traveling." Nodding absently, she pushed herself off of his neck and in between his shoulders. Wedging herself between his shoulder blades, she curled into a ball and closed her eyes, begging for sleep to claim her.

Chapter 13

Conner landed on Snarf's back and walked carefully up his spine as he flew. As he reached Aleisha, he returned to his normal form before kneeling down to shake her awake. They had been traveling for days, only stopping a couple of hours at a time to let the dragons rest. He was amazed by how much Aleisha slept; he had barely had a chance to speak to her as she spent most of her time either asleep or flying away from the group.

"Hey, we're almost there," she opened her eyes slowly as he spoke to her, yawning widely as she nodded. "I flew ahead and spoke to Elam; he's going to let us stay at the library again."

"This feels so weird." She appeared confused as she looked around her surroundings. "It's like we're reliving our earlier trip; like everything is going to repeat."

"No, Aleisha," he sat down next to her as he spoke, "this time, we're going on the next leg together." She nodded but didn't seem entirely convinced.

"We will never abandon you again, Aleisha," Snarf responded loudly enough to allow everyone to hear, to echo his thoughts in their own reassurances.

When she didn't respond immediately, they let the conversation die. She seemed really troubled as she stared out at the horizon, not that he could blame her for her mood. After all, the last time they'd been here, they had parted without any answers. This time, he could only hope that Elam would have something for them.

"I had forgotten how beautiful it is," she spoke in quiet awe as the circular walls of Fonishia came into view. "I can't wait to get back to the library; Elam forced me to continue the journey after you left and I've wanted to thank him. I thought he was being unreasonable at the time, but I really am grateful."

He couldn't imagine how difficult it must have been for her; she hadn't even known how to ride a horse, yet she had to continue her journey suddenly alone. He'd been horribly ungracious and unloving for leaving her.

"I should tell you something, Conner, so that I'm not hiding anything from you anymore." She looked really nervous; as if she was afraid of how he would react. "Tallen is my father." He could see her searching his face, as if trying to gauge his reaction. He truly damaged their relationship when he left. He could only hope that time would completely heal her trust in him.

"I knew that, Leish." He tried to smile to put her at ease, but he wasn't sure how well he succeeded. "Dagmar followed you after we left. He saw you at Tallen's castle. None of us could hold that against you; you cannot choose your father any more than you can choose to be a Darksoul."

"Oh," she appeared bewildered, "thank you." He leaned closer to her and wrapped one arm around her in a comforting, if not slightly awkward, embrace.

A few minutes later, he walked her through the front gates of Fonishia. "Soulfire won't be here for another day or two, but Byron has promised to keep him safe until we have a chance to collect him." She nodded absently in response as they walked closer to the center of town.

"Aleisha!" Elam's excited voice came thundering out of the crowded streets "Aleisha!" The old man pushed past a few of the civilians to wrap her in a hug. "Conner didn't tell me that you were coming too. I knew that he wouldn't remain upset with you for too long."

"Elam," Conner silenced the librarian mid-rant. "We do have important things to discuss."

"Of course we do," he responded lightheartedly, "you only visit when you have some important question." He shrugged as if in reluctant submission, "Let's go back to the library then. Syris is making lunch."

"Oh, Elam," Aleisha sounded hesitant as she spoke up, "I'd prefer if you didn't discuss our business with Syris this time."

"He's my apprentice," he spoke as if his statement would justify a refusal.

"This is of a much more personal business." At Conner's stern voice, Elam clenched his jaw, but nodded and turned to lead them to the library.

Chapter 14

Aleisha followed Elam into his huge study room and waited impatiently for him to quiet down enough to ask about her magic. For the last ten minutes, he had been explaining some controversy concerning sugar of lead. Apparently men of science from Belmopan were claiming that it was the sweetener, and not the guild master, that was responsible for the increased illnesses.

"So what do you think of it, Conner?" The old man had just finished with his explanation and seemed eager to hear Conner's opinion.

"I studied philosophy, humours, and all kinds of science for almost two-hundred years, Elam," Conner responded in a bored voice. "The only thing that I learned is that scholars don't really know anything." As Elam opened his mouth to protest, Conner shook his head and continued, "One-hundred fifty years ago, they were convinced that everything in the universe moves slowly around Elbot, changing the night sky in a predictable yet infinitely complex pattern. Ten years later, that young star gazer from the north published a paper saying that Elbot circles the sun. The same is true of nearly every aspect of our world: they once said that Elbot was a plane, now they say that it is spherical, but some are moving the conversation to the possibility that it is shaped more like an egg." He shook his head dismissively. "Anyone who can get his writings into the Great Library and claims to have done some vague research can completely change the beliefs of the entire community. Science is too fluid, too fickle for me to care what scholars and philosophers have to say anymore.

"The Creator never changes His mind. He never changes. Neither does His magic. I've had quite enough science; I think I'll stick to my study of His words and His magic, because these scholars don't know what they don't know."

Elam glared at Conner and mumbled some rude words that Aleisha hadn't heard since leaving Cedrick's mansion. While Aleisha didn't have any opinion on the matter, Elam's reaction bothered her. It seemed a petty response to her; he had asked Conner's opinion, so she didn't think he should be so offended by his sharing it.

"Speaking of magic" - Elam clapped his hands and tried to smile at them as he spoke - "I'm sure your question had something to do with magic."

"Yes," Conner smirked as he nodded, "we were wondering if you've ever heard of someone losing their power."

"Can't be done," he shook his head vigorously, dismissing the idea even before Conner finished asking the question, "Once you're chosen, you're stuck for life, sorry."

"Elam, we need any information that you might-"

"You're the one who just said how great it is that magic is so consistent," he huffed in anger, "and now you want to find a loophole when it becomes inconvenient?" He glared at Aleisha as he continued, "Do you know how many people would give their lives to receive the gift you have been given? Are you so ungrateful?" he turned to Conner, "And are you so bigoted that you cannot bear the thought of being companions with a Darksoul? Even a Darksoul who is not vile like the rest? Have you no grace?"

"It's tainted!" he recoiled in surprise at her sudden outburst. "The magic is tainted and it is trying to destroy me. Please, Elam, have you ever heard of someone losing their magic? There has to be some story, some legend that can give us some direction."

Elam closed his eyes and held up a hand to silence them both. When he opened them, his angry expression was replaced with a compassionate one. "There is one legend that I might be able to direct you to." He sighed and shook his head, "I acquired a copy of a journal written by an alleged magic user, who claimed to have lost her power after 'tragic circumstance' robbed her of it." He led them up the spiral staircase past several rows of books. "I can't remember the name of the girl, though." They finally stopped climbing the stairs and stepped onto a wide balcony that stretched the entire length of the room. Elam continued babbling quietly as they passed by hundreds of books, stopping occasionally for Elam to read a few titles only to continue on again. He finally stopped and pulled out a small book entitled "A Powerless Lightsoul." "Here it is," he held it out to Aleisha, "I can't guarantee that this is a true story, but she writes it as if it is, and it's the only example of anyone losing their power that I've ever heard of."

"Thank you, Elam." She stared at the small book in her hands, terrified of what she might find in its pages.

"Now!" He clapped loudly, looking from one of them to the other. "Shall we see what Syris has cooked for us?" he walked past them and headed back to the staircase and began descending without waiting for them."

"Would you like me to read it?" Conner held his hand out to her, offering to take the burden from her.

"Thank you." She smiled and gladly handed the book to him.

"This is why I'm here, Aleisha. I want to help you in any way you need." He smiled at her before dropping one arm around her shoulders and leading her back to the tall staircase. "I have no doubt that we'll find a way for you to be rid of this magic forever."

Chapter 15

Conner sat in Elam's study chair surrounded by maps and notes spread over the table in front of him. He had read the journal while Aleisha was eating with Elam and Syris on the night that they arrived and had spent the last several days trying to piece together her location by the comments in the journal about her home and surroundings.

She had mentioned that most of the buildings in her home were made of stone, and the residents welcomed magic users, which made him suspect that she might reside in Shiloh, though he had never heard of her, despite having trained in Shiloh for decades. She also mentioned vast plains of luscious grass that seemed to go on forever. This made him suspect that she was somewhere in the plains of Tanah Subur.

"Have you learned anything useful?" Aleisha suddenly appeared on the other side of the table. He was surprised to see her, as she had not left her room much the entire time they had been here.

"I'm now convinced that the story was true, but she never revealed how she lost her magic, so we'll have to find her if we want to discover how to duplicate the phenomenon." He pointed to the town of Lambent. "I'm pretty sure that she lives here, so that should be our next destination." He watched her carefully for her reaction; he was worried that she might become discouraged by this constant traveling. It felt like they were going in circles searching for an answer that didn't exist.

Darksoul

She nodded slightly as she stared at the map. "I think Syris is smuggling dragonsilk."

"What?" where did that come from? "Why?"

"Last time I was here, Elam had me train with Syris. He said some things that suggested that he was smuggling for Cedrick." She shifted from one foot to the other, as if she was uncomfortable discussing her former master. "I think it's dragonsilk because of the way he talks about them. He speaks with such utter disrespect, as if they're no better than cattle."

"Aleisha, someone being disrespectful of dragons is not evidence of dealing with dragonsilk." He doubted that she even realized how serious such an accusation was. Dragonsilk had to be harvested from a dragon's wings and was extremely harmful to the dragon. The process was similar in practice to plucking all feathers from a bird's wings would be; the dragon endured severe pain and lost all aerodynamics until the fur grew back. Because of this, the sale of dragonsilk was illegal in all three of the civilized nations.

"He mentioned during lunch today that a dragon is only as good as his magic and his coat." She was not backing down from this.

"Ok." If she was this convinced, maybe he should consider her concerns. "I'll look into it, but we have to be careful; this is a very serious charge." She nodded, looking somehow both relieved and worried.

"So, when do we leave?"

She was certainly changing subjects quickly today. "Tomorrow we'll stock up, then we can leave the next day." She nodded again, opening her mouth to change the subject again no doubt. "Are you alright?"

"I'm fine," she answered quickly, defensively. "Why wouldn't I be?"

"Come on, Leish, what's wrong?"

She frowned and turned slightly away from him. "Elam keeps asking me weird questions, as if he's studying me, and Syris is as rude and provocative as ever, so I'm just really uncomfortable here."

"I'm sorry." He should have known that Elam would bother her. She was probably the first Darksoul to realize that their magic was tainted; her first-hand experience on the much-debated subject would be invaluable to any knowledge-seeker such as Elam. "I'll get them to leave you alone."

She bit her lip and furrowed her brow like she was thinking through a difficult subject, "No, you don't need to." She continued fidgeting as she spoke, "You always want to protect me and I appreciate that, but it shouldn't be your job. You have more important things to worry about."

"No, I don't," he hadn't intended to sound quite so stern. He sighed and reached for her hand, "There is nothing more important to me than you. You are my only human friend and my protégé, and there is nothing that I would not do for you."

She didn't seem completely satisfied by his answer, but she didn't argue.

"Ah, Aleisha" - Syris suddenly came into the study room - "I wondered where you ran off to." He suddenly noticed Conner and glared at their interwoven hands. Conner smirked and moved closer to Aleisha; he couldn't blame the young man for his apparent interest in Aleisha, but he wouldn't allow it either.

"What do you want?" Aleisha didn't seem to notice the silent battle between the two men as she responded in unmasked frustration, a few of the papers on the table falling to the ground under the influence of her magic's response to her emotions.

"I just thought that you'd want to brush up on your fighting technique before you left," he never shifted his glare away from Conner as he spoke.

"Actually," Conner smirked as he interrupted him, "we've found the information we were looking for, so we're heading out now."

"It's the middle of the day, what's your hurry?"

"I'm sure Elam will be anxious to hear about what we learn on our trip, and it is rather time sensitive, so we really shouldn't delay." Aleisha gave him a confused look, but somehow managed to appear relieved at the same time. Conner bent down to retrieve the map they needed and moved to pass Syris, never letting go of Aleisha's hand. "I'm sure we'll have another chance to duel when we return."

As soon as they were out of earshot from Syris, Aleisha spoke up, "What was that about?"

"Territory." He winked at her but didn't elaborate. "We'll be backtracking quite a bit, but the horse will at least enjoy traveling on the plain," he chuckled, remembering her name for his horse, "I mean Soulfire." She smiled in response to his teasing tone. "I think you'll like Lambent; the people are very kind there and it used to be the home of a beloved Lightsoul Dictator named Borealis."

"Used to be?" She cocked her head as she looked toward him in interest.

"No one really knows where he went." He'd only met Borealis once, but he'd liked him. It was too bad that he had disappeared. "One day, he just didn't return home. No one has been able to find him since." He wondered momentarily if this former Lightsoul was Borealis' chosen babe, but it didn't make sense that she would remain in Lambent after he left and no mention of him was made in the entire journal, convincing him that it was written after his departure.

Chapter 16

Aleisha sat in the grass at Snarf's feet. She had gone ahead of Conner to wait with the dragons while he spoke with Elam. She had offered to wait for him, but he had insisted that she go without him. She suspected that he wanted to lecture both Elam and Syris for offending her; otherwise, he never would have allowed her to walk alone without it being necessary.

"You seem deep in thought," Snarf's voice suddenly broke through her thoughts.

"Conner has been acting really protective since you came to Puko. Do you think my reaction made me look weak to him? I know I was a bit of a mess when you showed up."

"Not at all," he shook his large head slowly as he answered. *"He has never indicated that he thinks that of you. More likely, he is being protective because he values you so highly. Being without you for those few months showed each of us just how much we do care for you. We all tend to be more protective of those that we value, even if we know that they do not need us to. I would say, as much as you are able to, you should simply be thankful that he cares enough for you to act on your behalf."*

That made sense; he had just told her basically the same thing not two hours earlier. She hadn't been sure if she believed his explanation, but hearing it from Snarf as well definitely helped.

"So, did Conner say where we are headed?" All five dragons looked her direction when Snarf spoke, indicating that they all heard his question.

"He mentioned a town called Lambent. A former Lightsoul lives there."

"A former Lightsoul? So it is possible." Byron sounded awed; it seemed slightly out of place coming from a dragon who had lived longer than any human could imagine.

Conner suddenly appeared out of the foliage surrounding their meeting place, leading Soulfire by the reins and looking as stern as ever, giving no hint as to how his conversation with Elam went. "All right." He wasted no time reaching Byron's side to mount him. "Shall we head out?" A few of the dragons looked a bit confused by his haste, but none moved to delay him.

Moments later, they were all in the air and Snarf was flying Aleisha away from the group to give her some quiet. *"Are you afraid, Aleisha?"* Snarf's gentle voice entered her consciousness, *"I suspect you are imagining many possible rituals and trials you may be made to endure to be rid of your powers. It only makes sense that you would be nervous."*

"I am more afraid of failing." She sighed as she voiced the concern that had been bothering her since before this journey began, *"It seems that everything that I've set out to do has failed. I can't find the elixir because I can't access the map, I can't save my mother because Tallen killed her, what if we can't find this*

former Lightsoul, or if the circumstances involved in her losing her powers can't be duplicated? Will I be able to fight against my magic? Will I be able to avoid becoming just like every other Darksoul, just like my father?"

Snarf was silent for a long time before answering her, *"I cannot promise that we will have success in this area, Aleisha, so I will not try; false hope is often worse than no hope at all, but I can promise you that you will not face this challenge alone. I realize that it must be very difficult for you to truly trust us again, but we have all decided that, whatever may come, we will not abandon you again."*

"I know that Snarf, it's just..." She wasn't sure how to finish.

"It's just not enough." He didn't sound upset or offended by the idea. He seemed to understand. That was the great thing about Snarf; he liked to joke around a lot, but he could also be very comforting and understanding when he needed to be.

"Snarf?" She'd been meaning to speak to him for a while about something. *"Since you've come back for me, you've seemed unusually somber. What's wrong?"* She could see his head drop a bit.

"Dagmar told us what you did after we left. He told us about having to save you and about keeping an eye on you in your travels afterword. He was the only one who stayed behind to help and he was the only reason we knew where to find you.

"It should have been me who stayed by you, yet I abandoned you. I should have checked on you, yet I didn't bother; didn't want to bother. Yet when we returned, you were willing to pick up where we left off. You welcomed me back as your friend and companion as if I had never wronged you. If anyone deserves that kind of loyalty, it's Dagmar. So, I guess I was just trying to stay out of the way. Allow you and Dagmar the chance to spend more time together."

"No, Snarf." She couldn't believe he actually thought that way. *"I deeply respect Dagmar, and I'll always be grateful to him for saving me, but you are my best friend."* She shook her head, bewildered that she had to reassure him. *"We all messed up in Fonishia. We all responded badly, but we all sought forgiveness and we all received it. Dagmar and I are certainly closer now than we had been, but I see no reason why that should mean that you and I can't be."* Snarf nodded but didn't respond.

"Snarf, I understand how guilty you feel. You think that you are solely responsible for the pain I felt when you left, but Conner believes the same thing of him. I feel that it is me, and not any of you who are to blame for all the pain that I have caused you and myself.

"As I said, we have all sought and received forgiveness; now it is time for us each to accept that forgiveness and move forward. I don't expect any of us will ignore our own or each other's failures in Fonishia, but we cannot allow that one day to become the defining factor in our relationships."

Snarf continued flying silently. For a moment she wondered if he had heard her, but it was impossible that he hadn't. *"Truly, you are wise beyond your years, Aleisha, and kinder than I deserve. Thank you."*

"Thank you, Snarf. Now can you relax a little? I've really missed the light-hearted spin you bring to everything. This family needs that from you." The great dragon nodded again, turning his head toward his brothers just slightly as he did.

"You're right. Hold on." She barely had time to thrust her hands deep into the fur on his neck before he turned sharply toward the group and darted toward Grizwald. The orange dragon let out a surprised yelp as Snarf approached at full speed crashing into him and nearly nocking Aleisha off in the process. The two dragons struggled for a moment to get the upper hand on each other as they wrestled in mid-air, only to break free from each other and dart in opposite directions.

Grezald, seeing the fun that his brothers were having, refused to be left out. While Snarf straightened himself and prepared to strike again, Grezald dove at him from the side, slamming into his side and thrusting Aleisha from her seat. For one, terrifying moment, she fell through the air, only to be caught in Snarf's talons. *"Careful, Grezald! I have a passenger."* She was more than relieved to hear the teasing reprimand, as their travels had been devoid of laughter among the usually jovial youngest dragons.

As Snarf and the twins continued the teasing accusations, Dagmar flew directly underneath Snarf, hovering mere feet away from Aleisha. *"If you fools are going to continue the horseplay, Aleisha needs to ride with me. I won't drop her."* Even as he reprimanded them, he sounded strangely jovial; almost like he was teasing them. Dagmar never teased, though. Did he?

Snarf snickered at his older brother but complied. Placing Aleisha carefully on Dagmar's back, he turned his head to look at her once before flying off to play with his brothers, *"Thank you, Aleisha. Snarf has been too serious of late."*

"You are good for my brothers, Aleisha; they all adore you." Dagmar surprised her by flying further away from the group.

"Thank you, Dagmar. Where are we going?"

"I've noticed that you like to fly separately from the group. I assume that is it out of respect for our privacy?" She was somewhat surprised he had guessed that. *"It is not often that such a young human acts with such consideration for others."* He continued coasting several hundred yards behind Conner and Byron. All three of his younger siblings continued playing as they took turns chasing each other and wrestling in the air. All of the tension that had been making their travels less enjoyable seemed to have completely melted away. *"I was speaking with Conner earlier; he didn't seem to have a solid plan once we reach Lambent."*

"He mentioned a Dictator named Borealis. I assumed the plan was to search out his babe." It seemed pretty obvious to her what needed to be done. *"Is there some reason that we wouldn't?"*

"No one knows where he is, so seeking out his babe could prove difficult." Dagmar sped up to Byron and Conner to include them in the conversation, *"We don't even know if this former Lightsoul was, in fact, Borealis' babe. For all we know, this woman moved to Lambent after Borealis had already left."*

"Dagmar has a good point," Byron interjected, *"Our Lightsoul did not provide a name for her Dictator, so we have no natural starting point for our search. We don't even know for sure if we are heading to the correct town."*

Conner glanced over at her as Byron finished. He looked compassionate as he added his assessment, "We knew before we began that this would be a difficult task. If we don't find anything in Lambent, we will continue searching. We will not abandon you." His firm proclamation was met with immediate grunts of agreement from both Byron and Dagmar.

Chapter 17

Conner gazed at the town before him. It had been many decades since he had last stepped foot in Lambent and he had somewhat missed the pleasant, relaxed feel it had had. In many ways, it was just like any other small town, with only a few dozen houses, a couple of shops, and a temple clustered together in a small area, surrounded by miles of farmland. The unique thing of Lambent was the same as any town which provided home for a powerful magic user; the people of Lambent enjoyed luxuries otherwise impossible even for the wealthiest of men.

The people of Lambent had long since come to expect such luxuries, but the amazing thing of this town, the thing that Conner was convinced was the reason Borealis chose to make his home here, was that those luxuries did not lead to arrogance here. They did not lead to laziness and greed as he had so often seen. Even Puko had long ago abandoned the usually imperative farms that magic could so easily replace.

"Do you suppose Clint still lives?" Byron stood next to him, gazing at the town with the same memories, the same fondness of their most recent visit, near forty years ago now.

"I highly doubt that, though it would be fantastic." He turned slightly, just enough to bring Aleisha into his view. Each day, she seemed to become more nervous. Each day, she tried harder to hide her nervousness. How desperately he hoped that they would find this former Lightsoul here.

"Who is Clint?" Aleisha stepped closer to him as she spoke.

"He was a good friend last time we stayed here." He pointed in the general direction of Clint's farm. "He knew everybody and their business, but still managed to refrain from gossiping about his knowledge. If he is still alive, he would be our best chance of finding this Lightsoul."

"You two should head to his house to seek him out," Dagmar motioned to his brothers before continuing, *"The rest of us would like to head west to see if Burkhart and Genoveva still reside in this region; they may have more knowledge to offer than the townspeople if you cannot find anything out today."*

"It's decided then" - he clapped his hands together and spun toward the group - "Aleisha and I will see what we can learn today, please give the noble pair my respect." Byron nodded solemnly; they had not visited the couple since Lorahlie's death and he was surely not looking forward to having to share the sad news. "We will meet back here at nightfall to discuss our plans for tomorrow." Each of his companions nodded in agreement, so he turned to smile encouragingly at Aleisha before leading her toward Lambent.

"It will be nice when Soulfire catches up, especially if we end up remaining here for several days." She only nodded as she walked silently next to him. "Clint's family has lived on the same farmland for the last two-hundred years, so, if he's still alive, we will find him there." She nodded again. He understood her nervousness, but her silence worried him a little bit, so he tried again, "If we can get some news of Borealis or his chosen babe, then that would give us a good place to start our search for the former Lightsoul."

"And if Clint is dead?" she sounded so lost, so hopeless. She had been disappointed at every turn of her journey; he couldn't imagine how discouraging that must be for her.

"If Clint is dead, we will ask his children for help. I'm sure that they will know who to send us to, even if they don't know themselves where Borealis is." Again, she nodded, falling silent once more. Conner sighed, not at all sure how to revive her spirits.

They walked silently for the last half-mile to the farm. As they neared the house, a young man threw open the door and ran to greet them. "Welcome travelers! Welcome to Lambent." The young man was tall and fit, he had the look of any young man that had grown up working hard with the solid figure and wide shoulders that Conner had come to expect from Clint's family line. "Please, come inside. My wife is making a pot of ginger infusion with honey." He thrust his hand out to shake Conner's enthusiastically before ushering them inside.

"Thank you, sir." Conner gladly followed the young man into the house, careful to keep Aleisha at his side as they entered the small front room.

"Hanna," the man called as he entered the small house. "Hanna, we have guests." He motioned for them to take two seats near the fireplace before taking one himself. "My name is Clint, and this," he gestured proudly as a beautiful young woman with ebony skin and a radiant smile entered the room with two steaming mugs in her hands, "is my wife, Hanna."

"It's lovely to meet you both." Conner smiled at each of them. "My name is Conner, and this is Aleisha." Aleisha finally managed a smile as Hanna gave her one of the steaming mugs. "Thank you for inviting us in."

"We're always pleased to have visitors in our small town." Clint grinned and sipped from his mug, "So, what brings you to Lambent?"

"We're looking for a man who used to live on this farm." Clint looked surprised but leaned forward to continue listening. "His name was Clint; I assume either your father or grandfather."

Clint laughed and placed his mug on the floor next to his seat, "Both my father and grandfather were named Clint. Such a fine name deserves to be passed from generation to generation." He laughed again, like it was a long-standing joke. Conner remembered the endless teasing Clint had endured for his name, as he had been named for a local legend who had been said to fight off a ferocious dragon using only a lasso and a spittoon. He was surprised the name had been passed down at all.

"Your grandfather then; his father's name was Ben." Clint nodded, but his jovial expression disappeared.

"You're too young to have known my grandfather; he died over thirty years ago."

"How did he die?" He had not really been expecting him to still be living, but he had expected a more recent passing, Clint had only been in his mid to late thirties when Conner had seen him last.

"There was a great tragedy in our town. Many men died. My grandfather was one of those men." The stern expression on his face indicated that he would not welcome further questions on the subject. "How did you know him?"

"I knew him when I visited Lambent when I was younger. Clint had always been kind to me, so I was hoping to see him again now that I'm back." Aleisha took a sip from her drink and stared pointedly at the liquid as the men spoke. She looked incredibly uncomfortable.

"Well. I'm sorry you can't see him. I never met him, though I've heard countless tales of the kind man that he was. I've always wanted to be remembered so fondly." He leaned back in his chair, relaxing again as he prepared to change the subject. "I know just about everything there is to know about this town, so if there's someone else you'd like to look up, I can direct you to their families."

Conner nodded and took a gulp of his drink. He had forgotten to drink it while it was hot, but even cool it was the most refreshing thing he'd had in a good while. "This infusion is delicious, ma'am." Hanna smiled and her husband reached to grasp her hand affectionately. "Last time I was here, I stayed with, and studied under, a man named Borealis."

Clint practically leapt from his seat as he thrust his arm toward the door. "Get out!" he shouted at him, all traces of the welcoming young man gone. "I'll not have you come into my house and return my kindness with your lies."

"Clint, please" - Conner stood, but did not move toward the door - "if you'll but give me a moment, I can prove myself to be true."

"I've never met a man seeking out Borealis with just cause. You cannot convince me that your motives are good. You did not know Borealis and you did not know my grandfather. Any fool looking at you can tell you are too young for your story to be true. Now leave my house before I am forced to take action."

Conner breathed deeply but did not move. He should have considered his appearance before entering Lambent; anyone would have been suspicious of his claims. Without another moment's hesitation, he exploded into his true form, sending Clint stumbling back in shock and startling Aleisha onto her feet. He felt her reflexive burst of magic slam into him, but he'd been expecting that, so he managed to stand his ground. "I am the Dragonsoul, Conner. I spent nearly five months in your beautiful town studying under Borealis' mentorship whilst hunting down a band of Banish prophets who had been terrorizing the area. Recently, we have found ourselves in need of a Lightsoul, and I trust Borealis to handle the situation delicately."

Clint still looked terrified, but no longer hostile. Unsteadily reclaiming his seat, he reached out to grasp Hanna's hand again. "Borealis hasn't made his home in this area since the great tragedy that killed my grandfather. I can't tell you where he is now." Conner could almost feel Aleisha slump behind him.

"What about his chosen babe? Surely you know something of her." Clint only shook his head.

"If anyone alive still knows anything, you should speak with the woman who lives outside of town." He rose and pointed out the shutters. "About a mile that way, you'll see a cottage overrun with clover and rabbits. The woman lives there. She lived through the great tragedy and is the only person the old women of the grapevine will leave alone. I don't even know her name."

They made their way to the cottage in silence, each of them too nervous to make any attempt at conversation. Would this old woman be the Lightsoul they sought? Would she be willing to help them? Would she even be able to tell them how she lost her magic?

Finally, they stood on the porch of the cottage, waiting for the woman to answer his knock. From Clint's explanation, he had expected a broken-down shack infested with wild animals, but it was really quite well kept. The porch was clean and the windows were made of clear glass and appeared freshly cleaned. Even the yard, which was, in fact, covered in clover, looked quite intentional, as if the clover had been planted there to attract the rabbits that happily roamed the yard.

The wooden door suddenly opened, revealing an elderly woman with graying hair and deep frown lines. She looked like she hadn't laughed in years. "Can I help you?" she sounded more confused than annoyed that these two strangers had landed on her porch.

"My name is Conner; I'm looking for the chosen babe of Borealis. I need her help."

"Why Borealis' babe, why not the babe of Luscious, Melvin, or Aric?" Just like Clint, she became instantly hostile at the mention of Borealis' name.

"I'm a Dragonsoul. I've studied under Borealis before; I trust him."

"Dragonsoul?" She no longer appeared upset, but awed, "You are Conner, the Great Dragonsoul?" Conner could see Aleisha turn to look at him with obvious confusion at the woman's response. "Please, come inside. I'm preparing lunch; I would be honored if you'd dine with me."

"Thank you," he held the door for Aleisha before stepping inside behind her.

"My name is Eliah" - she held a hand out Aleisha - "What should I call you?"

"Aleisha." She looked exceedingly uncomfortable, "It's lovely to meet you Eliah." Eliah smiled and motioned for them to take a seat on a stuffed couch against the front wall.

"Borealis had sent me on a pilgrimage last time you were here, Conner." Eliah disappeared into the kitchen as she spoke, leaving Conner alone with Aleisha and her bewildered expression. "I was so very disappointed when I returned to hear that I had missed an opportunity to meet the Great Dragonsoul."

"So, you are Borealis' chosen babe, then?" she nodded as she returned to the room. "We have a matter of utmost importance that we must speak to you about."

"If you need anything that I can give, I would be honored to assist the greatest magic user to ever live." She placed a tray of sandwiches on a small table in front of them. "However, I'm afraid you won't find me as capable as most Lightsouls."

"Aleisha is also a magic user, and in need of information that I believe only you possess." He had to be careful. If Eliah still had her power, he did not want to offend her by assuming she had lost it, but if the great tragedy that Clint mentioned was also the tragic circumstances that left Eliah without her power and apparently sent her to this cottage to flee civilization, he did not wish to carelessly open such painful memories.

"As Borealis' babe, I did learn many things, but I would be a fool if I so quickly gave you everything you came for." Her use of past tense was encouraging; if she was still studying under him, she never would have said 'did.' "Not many people have such an opportunity to sit with the babe of Philimina." She leaned forward excitedly and grabbed a sandwich from the plate. Aleisha stared, wide-eyed, at him, looking more upset than he'd ever seen her, direct at him. "Please, share some of your adventures with me and I will give whatever I can."

Conner sighed; he wished he could have a minute alone with Aleisha to find out what she was thinking. "What do you want to know?"

"The dragon." He knew she was going there. "Is it true that you killed it with but a sword?"

"You killed a dragon?" Aleisha looked horrified.

"Not all dragons are as peaceful as my brothers, Aleisha. Just as some human magic users choose to use their powers for evil, some dragons do the same." She still looked horrified, but she stopped glaring at him, "I was following up on dozens of reports of a young Darksoul and his companion dragon who were terrorizing the region west of Shiloh. The legends make it sound as if I faced them alone and simply cut the dragon in two. That is not at all accurate.

"My brothers, Lorahlie, and I went together to face the duo. The Darksoul had amassed quite a large following, and we were met with an army of bandits and magicians led by this dragon and Darksoul. Three days we fought them and three days hundreds of men either died or fled. After the third day, I went to Shiloh to retrieve the sword that Philimina had had made for me when he wanted me to train in war magic." Eliah turned away in disgust; very few magic users other than Darksouls ever studied war magic and those who did, did so in secret to avoid suspicion. "I knew that, in order to end the battle, I would have to end the dragon's life; the Darksoul was an ambitious young lad, but he had neither skill nor power to cause any real damage in a region with so many powerful magic users.

"With sword in hand, I flew over the dragon on Byron's back and dove at him from above. Combining my magic with the sword, I thrust myself into the dragon's back, plunging the sword through scales, muscle, and bone until it reached the heart. The dragon died with the most horrifying roar of pain I'd ever heard, but it died whole."

"Amazing," Eliah sat back and smiled, "an amazing story indeed. Thank you, Conner. Now, what can I do for you?"

"We need to know how to remove someone's magic."

"No!" Eliah shook her head violently, "I cannot aid in such a quest; I will not give you such information."

"Please, Eliah, let us explain," he leaned forward and rested his arms on his thighs.

"There is no explanation that could change my mind. Can you imagine what danger would come if word got out that magic can be forfeited?" she stood and moved to exit the room.

"Excuse me, but if you were so worried about that, why did you write that journal? Why tell the world it is possible if you are so afraid of them knowing that it is?" She stopped just feet from the doorway, tilting her head ever so slightly as she replied in a nervous whisper.

"I sent that journal directly to Griffin, only he and the librarian in charge of the Library of Secret Knowledge should have known of its existence," she turned slightly more toward them, "How did you come into possession of it?"

"Elam, the librarian of Fonishia, has a copy in his collection."

"Elam!" she finally spun around, anger flashing in her eyes at the sound of the librarian's name. "Does anything surpass his lust for knowledge?"

"Does it matter how we know it's possible?" Aleisha pushed herself up from the couch beside him, finally voicing her thoughts. "You have this knowledge and you have not used it for evil. Why can't you trust us to do the same? Our motives are pure. We only want to purge me of magic, no one else."

"You would give up your gift?" Conner wasn't sure who sounded more offended, Aleisha or Eliah. The two women glared at each other from opposite ends of the room, the plate of sandwiches sliding slowly toward the edge of the table as Aleisha visibly fought to control her magic. "What ingratitude, what arrogance would lead you to forsake your own magic, your own Dictator?"

"I am a Darksoul," her voice cracked pitifully as she admitted it. "I wish to follow the Creator, but my magic battles to control me. I have to fight every day not to be overtaken by it; I certainly can't subdue it.

The best I can do is try to ignore it, but even that is failing me. I can feel myself being corrupted by it each day. I must be free." She sounded like she was begging. She sounded so near tears. "Please."

Eliah's shoulders slumped and she sighed, "My poor girl. I've never heard of a Darksoul resisting the tainted magic?"

"You knew?"

"No," she sighed and returned to her chair, pushing the plate of food back to the center of the table as she sat, "I did not know. Many have believed it to be the case, but none has ever proven it."

"But, now that you see that our intentions are pure, will you help us?" Conner pleaded again, hoping, praying that she would relent.

"You say that you wish to follow the Creator?" Aleisha nodded firmly. "Then I shall tell you how I lost my magic; not so that you may be free of yours, but so that you may understand why you never can be."

Eliah covered her mouth and inhaled deeply, "Borealis was more to me than a Dictator, more, even, than a mentor and teacher. He was the only father I ever knew. So, when our town was attacked by a weak Darksoul whom I had offended, Borealis stood by my side; he was as skilled with a sword as any warrior. We sent the Darksoul away pretty easily, but he did not stay gone long." By the clipped sentences and the disjointed flow of her story, it was obvious that she did not enjoy retelling it.

"The Darksoul recruited men from all around, both mortals and magicians. They were taken by promise of riches upon razing our prosperous town. There were so many of them that we were able to see them coming from some distance. We were able to prepare for the attack, but we did not realize just how many magic users we were going to be up against. Burkhart and Genoveva, the dragons that make their home near here, were called upon to aid us, but the battle for our town was still a bloody one with a high cost.

"Dozens of bandits were killed. Dozens of farmers were slaughtered. I cut down nearly every magic user there with the help of the two dragons, but Borealis fought more valiantly than anyone. He fell back to protect the women who had gone to hide with the children. A few of the men, led by a magician, had begun searching for them." She raised her hand again and wiped at the tears that had begun to well in her eyes. "Borealis killed most of the men, but he was struck down by the magician. A woman, Talia, stabbed the magician in the back as he stood over Borealis' dying form. The last I saw of…" she choked back a sob before continuing, "The last I saw of him was his lifeless body lying on the floor of the temple."

She stood and walked to the kitchen doorway again, once more raising a hand to her face, "The end of his life marked the end of my magic. The end of the Borealis Lightsouls, forever."

Chapter 18

Aleisha sat on the couch with her face in her hands. She could not accept that Briganti's death was the only way for her to be free. "So you see, Darksoul, why you can never be free." Eliah sounded truly sympathetic as she spoke, "Any action you take to rid yourself of this tainted magic will only corrupt you further; you cannot kill your Dictator and you cannot have him killed. I wish I could tell you otherwise."

Aleisha heard Eliah's soft footsteps as she retreated to the kitchen. "I knew we were doomed to fail," her shoulders spasmed painfully as she sobbed, "I have failed at every turn in this quest. I knew I shouldn't hope." Conner reached over and gently rubbed her shoulder as she continued crying, "I knew."

"I'm sorry, Leish." Conner continued massaging her shoulder as he spoke, "I wish there was something I could do." She knew that he continued speaking and rubbing her back, but she ceased to hear or feel anything as she continued sobbing and her senses began to fade.

At some point, she lifted her head to wipe her eyes, only to realize that she could not see. She had long since come to realize that sorrow caused her magic to somehow disconnect her from her surroundings. She hadn't even realized it was happening the first time, when she had wandered the streets of Fonishia, not recognizing the people around her or hearing the words they spoke.

She waited a few minutes for her eyes to come into focus, only to realize that she was now alone in the room, but she could hear muffled voices in the next room. She knew that, if she tried to stand before the fog of sorrow left her, she would end up falling before taking her first step. As her vision continued to sharpen and she began to hear individual words in the hushed voices of Conner and Eliah, she stood, wobbling only slightly before moving to join them in the kitchen.

"I would be honored to house you for the night," Eliah's was the first voice she was able to hear clearly.

"Thank you, but my brothers are expecting us to return." If not for seeing his mouth move, she would not have recognized Conner's voice; it sounded forced, almost as if he was having difficulty speaking.

"You still travel with them? I'd love to meet them; I've heard such amazing things."

"I'll speak with them tonight then; perhaps they will wish to visit you as well." He just didn't sound quite right. As she stepped into the kitchen, they both stopped to look up at her.

Eliah smiled sadly at her, but Conner quickly turned his head. He looked like he'd been crying. "I'll ready the horse; he arrived a few minutes ago."

As Conner exited the room, Aleisha turned to Eliah, "What is wrong with him?"

"His dearest friend is hurting," she reached to hand her a cup, to which she only shook her head. "You must realize that your loss is his loss. He cares for you very deeply, Aleisha. More than I've ever seen a magic user care for any human."

"I'm not sure…"

"Soulfire is ready," Conner stopped suddenly as he entered the room. "Sorry, I didn't mean to interrupt."

"I'm ready to go." She was more than ready to go. She was ready to flee as quickly as she could from this place. All she wanted was for something she set out to accomplish to succeed every once in a while. This constant failure, this constant defeat was becoming overwhelming.

She strode past Conner and Eliah, never stopping until she had reached Soulfire and adroitly launched herself onto his back. She had no idea how the horse always knew where to find them, but she was grateful for it; she still didn't feel quite steady on her feet.

"Leish." How dare he call her that after what she'd just been made to hear. "We will find a way for you to be free," Conner approached them cautiously and placed a hand on her arm, which she pulled away from him, earning a wounded look. "I will not abandon you." She did not want to hear his promises; she didn't even want to share the horse with him, but she didn't trust herself to walk and she couldn't deny him his own horse. When he didn't move after a moment, she urged Soulfire forward a step. Conner sighed and pulled himself up behind her, wrapping his arms around her to grab the reins. She should have sat in the back.

"I'm sure either Byron or Dagmar will have an idea of where to go from here," he was obviously trying to comfort her. He had no idea that she was angry at him.

"Why didn't you tell me that Philimina was your Dictator?" Soulfire stopped. "After my deceptive omission about mine almost ruined our relationship, how could you keep that from me?"

"He and I have never had a good relationship."

"And Briganti and I have?" Soulfire started moving again, slowly jostling his riders as he walked. "I have never had a good relationship with my father, either, but I told you about him in order to protect your trust in me," she wouldn't back down from this, wouldn't let him ignore her like this. He had lied to her just as surely as she had lied to him. He had been careless with their newly formed trust, and she had had to learn of his strength from Eliah.

"I didn't see any importance in who my Dictator was. You knew that I was a magic user, you knew that I was a Dragonsoul, you even knew that I had no respect or trust for my Dictator." He sounded offended by her accusation, as if he did not see any wrong in his omission.

"I didn't know about your magic because you told me, Conner. I figured it out." She was getting really frustrated with his flippancy. "I also figured out that you are a Dragonsoul. The only thing that was told me was that you didn't trust your Dictator, and Snarf was the one to tell me that, not you." Could she trust him at all? The horse stumbled as the ground under him shook. "Have you actually told me anything?"

Conner sighed and patted the horse, calming him as he started to panic in the miniature earthquake Aleisha was causing. "You're right. I haven't been open with you," he no longer sounded defensive, at least. "I never talk about Philimina because the memories surrounding the time of my life that I allowed him to be a part of are very painful. I'm sorry; I should have made an exception for you." When she didn't answer him immediately, he continued, "I told you once that I never married because my fiancée was killed. I did not, however, elaborate.

"Philimina takes great pride in the strength of his chosen babe. Consequently, he demands constant training and complete dedication from his babe. For almost a century, I complied; I studied every day, I traveled to the ends of the continent, and even visited Belmopan a few times. I left my family and neglected any friends I might have had. My whole life was centered on mastering my magic, and as long as I continued in that way, Philimina was an amazing mentor and a great friend.

"One day, I befriended a young lady named Alice. I began spending every available moment with her and Philimina began to take offence. Two years after I met Alice, I was prepared to leave my duties as a Dragonsoul and wed her; I had received her father's blessing and we had planned to be married. I do not know how Philimina learned of our plans, as we had long since ceased to communicate because I knew that he did not approve of my change in priorities and he knew that he could not change my mind. But the night before the wedding, I sensed an evil presence in our village and went to investigate. By the time I got to Alice's house, she was dead.

"The next day, the day we should have been married, Philimina arrived in town and told me that it was time to return to my duties. I haven't attempted to have any kind of relationship with him since." Upon finishing his story, Conner urged Soulfire forward on the once again stable ground.

She'd had no idea he'd been hurt so badly, had entirely forgotten that he'd mentioned his slain fiancée. She'd been so harsh. "I'm sorry, Conner," she leaned slightly back to rest against his chest, hoping to convey some small amount of comfort. "I should have trusted you."

"I know, Leish," he sounded like he was choking. "I know that you're hurting. I wish I could fix this," he let go of the reins with one hand to wrap around her torso, hugging her close to him.

Chapter 19

"This is a disturbing development, indeed." Byron paced as Conner relayed the information they received from Eliah. The last rays of sunshine glistened off of his smooth scales as he walked, making him appear almost metallic. *"I can see why she hesitated to offer such information. Can you imagine the wars that would be fought if mortals thought that they could eradicate magic users?"*

"So where do we go from here? We surely can't just give up." Conner was not going to accept defeat this easily. "There has to be something else we can do."

"We can train her to not use her magic," Dagmar spoke up, offering the same suggestion that Grezald had given when they first began this journey. *"Her magic lay dormant until we freed her from Cedrick; surely we can find a way to return it to that state, or at least to weaken it."*

"How would we even begin to accomplish this?" Snarf interjected, *"I've never heard of someone's magic being restrained."* Aleisha sat silently next to him, snuggled tightly in his fur. She hadn't spoken since they returned and Conner suspected that Snarf was speaking for her as much as himself.

"We could always ask-"

"No!" Conner cut Grezald off before he could suggest returning to Fonishia; he did not want to return to the over-inquisitive librarian with the knowledge they now possessed. "We should seek out a different source of information. Elam has shown himself to be predictably importunate with Aleisha, and Syris is no better."

"We could venture to the Great Library, I suppose," Byron stopped pacing and nodded as he thought. *"Even Elam's library does not contain the vast knowledge that Might City has, and we could join you in the Great Library."*

"But Might City is near Tallen's castle," at last, Aleisha joined the conversation.

"Tallen will not bother you while we are near," Dagmar gently reassured her. *"He knows too well the strength of a vengeful dragon to show his face where we are."* She nodded and seemed to relax.

"All right then, Aleisha and I will head out at dawn. You should have no trouble catching up after your visit with Eliah." Conner reached up to scratch his neck, he knew that he should check on Aleisha and see how she was faring, but he didn't want to upset her further by forcing her to talk about the events of the day. He sighed, resigning himself to an unpleasant conversation, and moved to her side.

"Leish," he spoke as quietly as he could as he sat down, "how are you doing with all of this? I know you're overwhelmed and discouraged, but I'm here if you think that talking would help." She only nodded and leaned into him.

She had done the same thing while they were riding; as soon as she ceased to be upset with him, she leaned on him to accept his comfort. So, not knowing how else to help, he wrapped his arms around her trembling form and let her cry into his shoulder. He couldn't imagine how utterly defeated she must feel, how hopelessly lost.

Conner woke before the first light of sunrise, as he always did. He had always enjoyed watching the amazing display of color as the sun emerged over the horizon. As he waited for those first rays to paint streaks across the sky, he shifted his body slightly so that he could see Snarf and Aleisha. She had cried herself to sleep in his arms last night, and was now curled up next to Snarf, burying her head in his fur.

"She seems so fragile of late." Byron must have been watching her too.

"I don't know how to reassure her. I want to tell her that everything will work out, but it very well might not." He laid his head back on Byron's side. *"I would do anything for her if I could; I almost killed Briganti when he threatened her and now I wish I had."*

"Conner," he didn't quite sound like he was reprimanding him, but he would deserve it if he did. *"Aleisha would not be better off for Briganti's death if it came by your vengeful hand. She may be without magic, but she would also be without a godly example. She venerates you and she would see your example as permission to kill whenever she deemed it necessary."*

He looked back over at Aleisha. She appeared troubled even in her sleep. He knew that Byron was right, but he couldn't help feel like it was somehow his fault that she was still hurting. *"What do we do about*

Tallen? I believe that he won't bother her while we are around, but he isn't going to stay completely away either."

"That is a concern." The great dragon surveyed the horizon, as if looking for an answer. *"I would say just don't worry about it too much. We will face that issue when it arises, but we need not concern ourselves with supposition."*

"Might I suggest an early start for those of us who are awake?" Dagmar broke into the conversation, *"The sooner we leave to see this Lightsoul, the sooner we can regroup and head to Might City."*

"I can't head out until Aleisha wakes up; I will not disturb her," Snarf protested the idea, sounding just as somber as Aleisha had been the night before. He wondered if he was as unhappy about the idea of being near Tallen's castle as she was.

"If I may, Snarf," Conner smiled as he spoke; Aleisha was sure to agree with him. *"It might be best if you stay behind to travel with Aleisha and me. I'm sure she would appreciate your company."*

"Brilliant!" Dagmar stood and shot into the air without a moment's hesitation. *"The four of us will go and visit Eliah while you three head to Might City. We'll catch up by nightfall, I'm sure."* All four of the other dragons looked at each other in confusion. What was the urgency? Byron shrugged and moved to stand.

"We will speak with you later then. Take care of her." With that, all four of the older dragons lifted themselves into the air.

"That was odd," he continued watching them for a few minutes. *"What do you suppose the hurry is?"*

"Oh, Dagmar just doesn't like you. That's all," Snarf snickered as he answered, his serious mood apparently forgotten.

Conner laughed gently, *"I don't know why I bother asking you anything."*

"Because I'm brilliant, I suppose." Aleisha mumbled and curled more tightly in Snarf's wing, to which Snarf's amused expression fell to one of disappointment. *"She has no sense of humor in the morning,"* he sighed.

Conner smiled and stood up. Aleisha was always rather difficult in the morning, and having food ready for her would help tremendously. *"I'm going to head to town and get some breakfast."*

Lambent was pretty much the same as he remembered from his last visit. As he walked the streets, he was stopped every hundred feet by a curious resident. Every person offered the same welcome and asked the same questions about news from other towns and cities. By the time he made it to the shop, he had been offered more than a dozen beds and hot meals. "Welcome!" as soon as he entered the shop, a short man with a large belly shouted from behind the counter. "Welcome! What can I do for you?"

"I'm just passing through and I need to pick up some supplies." The man's large grin grew even larger at the news.

"Of course, of course, I'd be delighted to help."

Fifteen minutes later, Conner exited the shop with enough food for the next two days, a new saddlebag to replace the one he'd been using for the last twenty years, and a special treat that was sure to make both Snarf and Aleisha smile.

By the time he made it back to Snarf and Aleisha, Aleisha had woken up and was sitting silently, glaring at a rock. *"Is everything ok?"* By the look on her face, he guessed that asking Snarf would be the better option.

"Quite fine, our beauty just woke up, that's all." Snarf grinned, but Aleisha looked up at Conner, revealing her glare to be just the sleepy expression she wore every morning.

"Mornin'," he smiled at her, trying not to laugh; he'd never met someone so offended by mornings. She only grunted in response and returned to staring at the rock. "I brought breakfast." That got a reaction, sort of. She still made no attempt to move, but her eyes did open slightly wider.

He smiled again, opening his saddlebag to pull out a loaf of bread. Breaking it in half, he handed one piece to her and began eating his half. "The rest of the dragons are going to visit Eliah, so we should head out without them." Again, no response beyond grunting, but her eyes were open all the way now that she was eating.

As soon as she swallowed the last of her bread and drank half of the wineskin, she stretched her arms above her head and stood up. "Ok, I'm ready to go." She made her way to Soulfire to climb onto his back. "How long will it take us to get there?"

"Two days on horseback or one by dragon," he climbed on behind her and reached around her to take hold of the reins. "We could ride Snarf, of course, but the others said that they would like to catch up."

"So, once they catch up, will we be continuing on horseback, or flying the rest of the way?"

"I, for one, am eager to reach Might City," Snarf, who was lumbering along beside them, answered for him. *"I'm pretty sure we are all about ready to land somewhere slightly more permanent; this constant travel is becoming exhausting."*

"I agree." Conner shifted on the horse; the new saddlebag was shifting with each step and it was irritating him. "It will take some time to sift through all the books in the Great Library, so we will be staying there much longer than any of our previous stops."

"I know a woman with an inn in Might City; we might look into staying with her." Aleisha turned her head to speak more easily. "She resides just a few streets into the city."

"The library is at the center of the city, so it might be best to take up residence a bit closer," he paused for a moment, weighing his options. "I own a large home on the same street as the library. If the dragons stay in their rooms at the Great Library, we can meet there without difficulty."

"You own a home?" she sounded surprised, as if it had never occurred to her that he might stay in the same place long enough to need one.

"I own several homes, actually, one in each of the towns and cities that I frequent. Well, almost, I don't own one in Fonishia because I'm usually only there to see Elam, so I just stay at the library or at the inn that we visited our first time there." He chuckled at her obvious confusion. "Over the centuries, a magic user tends to collect quite a bit of wealth. Most powerful magic users invest that wealth and their magic into one residence, like Tallen and his castle or Eliah and her fine glass windows and stuffed furniture, but some, like me, prefer to have a place to put their heads no matter where they might find themselves."

"Oh, that makes sense." With a nod, they descended into silence. Most of the day passed in silence, though Conner suspected that Aleisha and Snarf spoke often. A few times, he'd wanted to try to revive their earlier conversation, but she appeared already occupied, so he let her be.

"How odd," finally, Snarf broke the almost painful silence by letting him in on their conversation. *"I expected that they would have caught up with us by this time."* The sun was nearing the horizon again, prompting them to stop to make camp for the night. The day had been a long, tedious ride without any conversation and Conner was surprised by how exhausted it left him.

"Eliah seemed quite eager to swap stories while we were there" - He slid off of Soulfire's back and reached up to give Aleisha a hand - "If Byron or the twins were in a talkative mood, they could have visited all day."

"Still, I would have expected at least Dagmar to make sure they continued on their journey in a timely manner." He searched the sky all around them, looking for any sign of his brothers, *"Ah well, I suppose we'll have to make camp without them."* Snarf, much like Conner, was not used to being away from his brothers and did not seem to like it in the least.

Conner rummaged through his saddlebag, looking for the treat he had picked up in Lambent. They had been fortunate in the timing of their arrival at Lambent, as it was the peak of harvest and the shopkeeper had just brought in several bushels of freshly-picked apples.

"Leish." He sat down next to her, trying to keep from smiling. It occurred to him that she might have never had the opportunity to enjoy the sweet fruit. She looked up at him but didn't respond; she really was being quite distant today. "I thought you might enjoy an apple." He held it out to her, hoping she would accept it as a peace offering as much as a gift.

"Apple? You got us apples?" Snarf's head shot up so quickly that Conner was surprised he didn't hurt himself.

"Shut up. Aleisha gets first pick."

"Cedrick used to get apples every harvest." She smiled as she accepted the outstretched gift. "I stole a dozen of them once because he never allowed the slaves to enjoy them." She took a bite and sighed with pleasure. "Since it was my responsibility to go to the market that day, I bought extras and told Cedrick that the price was higher than it was. I gave one of the stolen apples to each of the house slaves and two to the man who delivered them in order to keep him silent." She paused and looked at her apple sadly, "It never occurred to me that what I was doing was wrong."

Chapter 20

Aleisha sat next to the dwindling fire; memories of her last visit to Might City playing through her mind as she listened half-heartedly to her companions discuss their next actions. The atmosphere was saturated with excitement as the entire group enthusiastically expressed their joy in returning to the Great Library. Aleisha, who had not particularly enjoyed her last visit, was not nearly as pleased with the prospect of returning to the city.

"We'll be using the platforms, of course," even Dagmar sounded more lively than usual.

"I can't wait to get back to my room," Grizwald was bouncing excitedly in place as he spoke. *"Billy promised that he would move my new shelves in."*

"I'll have to ride Soulfire in, so I'll be skipping out on the platforms today," Conner sounded like he was simply stating a matter of business, no emotion registering either in his voice or on his face, but all five dragons looked his direction with almost sympathetic expressions. "I'll meet you at the library, and I'm sure Aleisha will enjoy the experience of the city from above." He turned and smiled at her. "The Great Library was built partially because of the large population of dragons in the region at the time that Might City was built, before they migrated to the Dragon's Plateau almost a millennium ago. As dragons are known for their love of knowledge and wisdom, the leaders of the city, who had good relations with the dragons, had it designed with them in mind. I think you'll appreciate the resulting architecture."

"We should head out then" - Byron leapt to his feet - *"I think we are all eager to get there and get settled. We have a lot of research to do."* As long as Aleisha had been traveling with this group, she had never seen them ready themselves so quickly. All five dragons were on their feet in a moment and Snarf nearly gave her whiplash yanking her from her position by the fire to place her on his back. Even Conner, who wouldn't be meeting them until later, jumped up and mounted Soulfire so quickly that he startled the poor creature.

"Leish, wait for me to come get you before you go wandering the library; it's really easy to get lost your first time there."

"I can give her a tour; she won't get lost." Snarf reassured him.

"You will not," she could barely hear Conner shouting as they started to put some distance between them. "I'm missing out on her first sight of the library. I won't miss the tour too."

Snarf chuckled as he darted through with incredible grace and speed. Conner had remarked before that one place or another was one of their favorite places to visit, but by the intensity of their excitement and impatience, she suspected that the Great Library was preferred over all else.

It only took a few minutes for the stone walls of Might City to appear on the horizon. Aleisha never tired of seeing cities from above, as they appeared more welcoming when she could see beyond the fortifications. Might City was no exception. When she had been here last, she had not seen much of the city and had, in fact, never ventured more than a few streets in. She had no idea of the vastness of the city, the variety of the buildings, the sheer volume of people swarming the streets of the market and residential districts.

At the very center of the city stood a huge cylindrical tower. The vast building was made of stone and boasted towering marble pillars on each side of the entrance. The huge building was shaped similarly to a rugged stalagmite rising from the floor of a rocky cave, tapering as it grew taller, and flat, irregularly placed platforms jutted out all around the outer wall. Each platform was at least ten feet across and formed a semicircle connected to the building similar to fungus growing on the side of a tree. The platforms each provided an arched entryway framed in beautiful cherry wood. There were so many such platforms that, by the top of the tower, it had been so tapered that it was only probably fifteen feet across. "Is that the Great Library?" she whispered.

"Isn't it beautiful?" Snarf had slowed way down to give her a better view of the library, which had probably a dozen dragons flying around it, moving from platform to platform, visiting each other. She could see each of the other dragons land on their own platforms and disappear into the archways. *"Those of us who have come here regularly are given our own*

rooms to call home when we visit Might City. I'll show you mine." He dove toward a platform near the ones his brothers landed on and settled gracefully on the polished floor.

As soon as Aleisha's feet touched the floor, she could tell it was not regular stone. The surface was smooth but not slick; it was soft and almost felt cushioned. *"It's magic,"* Snarf was watching her with an amused expression. *"Dragons helped build this library, so you will notice quite a few unique features."*

"Wow," she walked closer to the archway, Snarf's eyes never leaving her. As she approached the opening, the inside of the room came into focus, almost as if it had been clouded before and she hadn't noticed until she could see it clearly. The room was large and open, with almost no furnishings cluttering the walking space of the large dragon that lived here.

The entire room was shaped much like an overturned bowl; it had no corners as the smooth walls arched into a softly domed ceiling. One side of the room provided a large pillow, much like the bed of grass Snarf used in Puko. The other side was covered in bookshelves. Several of the shelves boasted statues, artifacts, and other memorabilia, but one of them was packed with old dusty books. Directly across from her was another wooden archway which, upon closer inspection, provided as much privacy as the first had by bringing everything out of focus.

"This is incredible!" she turned toward Snarf and grinned. "This is the most amazing room I've ever seen!" He dropped his head and laughed lightly.

"I'm glad you like it. We dragons tend to use magic quite a bit when we are building, while humans use it more for practical purposes, so our homes tend to evoke an awed response from humans." He suddenly seemed to become aware of the pillow and bounded over to it, *"Ah, how I have missed this bed! No one can make a bed quite as well as the women in the guild."*

"Women in the guild?" As Snarf settled comfortably into his bed, he let out a satisfied sigh. "Women are allowed to join guilds in Might City?"

"Only the magic guild," Snarf tilted his head thoughtfully. *"I keep forgetting that you grew up in Jaboke, one of the only major cities in Ephriat that doesn't allow magic. Magic guilds were set up for those magic users, almost exclusively magicians, whose Dictators never claimed them."*

"I hadn't realized that that was common,"

"Many magician Dictators choose to simply enjoy their immortality and shirk their responsibilities as Dictators. They choose a babe at random when they feel the need to bestow their magic on a new user and move on with their lives, forgetting all about their babes.

"Several decades ago, a magician who had spent his whole life teaching himself how to control magic set up the first magic guild in Might City. The only

criteria for being accepted into the guild is to have unclaimed power and the desire to learn how to wield it. Since then, several Magic Guilds have been built all over Elbot.

"Since the guild is centered in Might City, the guild members often have opportunities to learn directly from dragons, so the women tend to specialize in making enchanted fabrics and clothing."

"I see," she nodded, but she wondered why Conner hadn't suggested she join a guild when he didn't know who her Dictator was. She was sure he had had a good reason, but she couldn't imagine what it might have been.

"May we come in?" Grizwald's voice suddenly broke into her thoughts, causing her to jump in surprise.

"Welcome! Come in, Billy finished with my stone." Both orange dragons came into view as they passed through the enchanted doorway, nodding enthusiastically as they surveyed their surroundings.

"Very nice." Grezald moved closer to the bookshelves and nodded toward a large, deep purple, stone. *"I remember when we found that thing; you were so excited even Grizwald couldn't keep up with you."*

"It's easier to find stones with your hue; of course I would be excited to find one that so closely matches my fur." He didn't sound offended at all by the comment. On the contrary, he seemed quite pleased that the stone had earned comment. *"We were*

traveling to the capitol city of Belmopan a few centuries ago when I found that stone." He turned back to Aleisha, his eyes wide with excitement. *"On the way back to Ephriat, we stopped for a rest on a large port of call. Only one side of the island was settled, as there were vicious rumors concerning a hoarding dragon on the other side.*

"Being the great warriors that we are," Grezald laughed loudly, earning a glare from both Snarf and Grizwald, who was listening intently despite the fact that he'd both been there and had doubtlessly heard this story told several times over the centuries. *"Being the great warriors that we are, we went to investigate and, if needed, free the merchants and residents from the fierce creature, but when we arrived on the other side of the isle, all we discovered was a bored, elderly dragon who was as scared of the people on the other side as they were of him.*

"So, we spent a week staying with the old dragon, keeping him company, listening to his endless, droning stories, and admiring his small hoard. As it turns out, almost his entire hoard came from other parts of the world, as this island didn't seem to have anything interesting to offer, so the people settled wouldn't have had anything to worry about even if he had still been collecting.

"On the last day we were there, Grezald, Grizwald, and I went out to do some more hunting and exploring, not that any of our exploration had produced anything of note to date, and we came to a cliff with a great

waterfall. Upon closer inspection, we realized that there was a large cave behind the waterfall. The inside was simply covered in stalagmites and stalactites; we had to remain in the air for lack of a suitable landing area. Deep inside the cave, we found dozens of carts full of coal and countless antique tools scattered about a huge mass in the middle of the cavern. The place looked like it had been abandoned in a hurry.

"Grezald and I were simply too curious to leave without investigating, so we each stood on one side of the mass and breathed our hottest flame at it. We must have been working on it for a good hour before all the rock fell away and the impurities were burnt off. Grizwald made regular runs to the waterfall outside to bring water to cool the ground and stabilize our small work area. When we finally finished, this beautiful purple stone gleamed before us."

"Snarf just about lost his mind, he was so thrilled," Grezald laughed again, then continued, *"We helped him carry it back to the old dragon's home. We had planned on simply leaving it with him, seeing as it was just too big to carry back to Ephriat, but the old dragon, seeing Snarf's great fascination with the gem, insisted that we break off a large section of it and bring it back for him to add to his collection."* Snarf beamed at the memory. This stone was clearly a very precious possession to him.

"Of course," Snarf's voice sounded slightly less clear than normal, indicating that he had not intended her to hear him. *"We were just telling Aleisha how I*

got my stone." She quickly realized who he had been speaking to when Conner stepped through the archway.

"I'm sure she listened patiently to your nonsensical droning." He smiled and winked at her.

"Not everyone finds my stories as boring as you do. Grizwald certainly appreciates them. Don't you?" Grizwald nodded vigorously; Grezald and Conner only laughed.

"Are you ready to take a tour, Aleisha?" Conner, who was still shaking from his laughter, held an arm out to her.

Giggling at the whole group, she took his arm and followed him out the archway, stopping to wave at Snarf before leaving.

"I'll just show you around the magic section today, as the library is simply too large to explore all in one day, and we'll be spending most of our time in this area anyway." Conner led her out of Snarf's room and down a large hallway; the hallway, much like the platforms and rooms, had no corners. The walls curved upward to make a rounded ceiling and even the corridors that connected to this main hallway seemed to bend off of the main path rather than turning sharply. "It was designed with dragons in mind." Conner noticed her staring at the walls and seemed to know exactly what she was thinking. "Such large creatures sometimes have difficulty making the sharp turns you find in most buildings."

They continued walking the hallway past several of the large rooms like Snarf's room; one of them seemed to glow with an orange light, but she couldn't make out what was producing the glow through the fog of the doorway. At last, Conner turned down one of the curved corridors, which quickly opened up into a vast room much like the main room in Elam's library. The floor had a dozen large tables scattered about, many of which were covered in books and crowded with young people whispering excitedly. The walls stretched upward to a great height, but seemed almost bare, as the many rows of bookshelves looked to have quite a bit of space between them. This design suddenly made sense when a beautiful green dragon landed on one of the wide walkways about halfway up. Even with the space between rows, the balcony appeared crowded as the dragon perused the shelves.

"Welcome to the magic section," Conner whispered and led her deeper into the room, directing her to one of the clear tables. As soon as he sat down, two books appeared in front of him, almost as if they had been there all along, but had been invisible. He frowned and picked one up. "Ah, I forgot to put these away. I like to keep my area clean so that I can find everything." Grabbing the other book, he stood and began walking away, "We just need to return these books and then we can get started."

He stopped by one of the crowded tables and peered at the top book in one of the stacks. "A seamstress!" A young girl looked quite startled and dropped the book she was reading. "From the guild, I assume?" She nodded. "My name is Conner, I knew Warden Peter. Is he still in the area?"

"No sir," she ceased to look startled, and now appeared quite in awe as she stared, unashamed, at Conner, "he died a few months back when some fighting broke out in the Waves of Might. Rumor was that that horrible Darksoul was headed to the battle and Warden Peter went to make sure too much magic wasn't added to the wrong side."

"Oh," Conner looked concerned for a moment, but quickly found himself, "I hope the guild has not suffered too much in his absence."

"We've done quite well, considering," she smiled excitedly. "Warden Peter had been planning on moving east as a sort of ambassador for magic in hopes of building a guild in some city that doesn't currently allow magic. We were pretty well prepared for his departure already when the fighting broke out."

"I'm glad to hear it, thank you." He smiled and moved to leave.

"Dragonsoul?" She nearly leapt out of her seat, all of her books disappearing as she did, "Are you going to be staying in Might City for long?"

"As long as I am needed, miss." The young girl smiled a little too enthusiastically. "We'll be seeing you, then." Again, he moved to leave and, again, she opened her mouth to stop him, but she couldn't seem to think of anything to say.

He led her to a desk at the center of the room, where he placed his two books in front of a studious young man. "I'd like to return these and request a list of books dealing with magical dampening, please."

The young man looked up and smiled. "Of course, sir. Right away." He picked up each book in turn and read the titles before placing them on a large stack of books next to his desk. As Aleisha watched, the stack of books seemed to be slowly diminishing in size as the books on the bottom of the stack disappeared one at a time. "It will take me a few hours to make a comprehensive list, but if you would like to start with a few books that cover the topic broadly, I can point you in the right direction."

"That would be very helpful, thank you." The young man stood and walked them to the nearest staircase.

"Are you doing a report on the topic?" he led them up several more flights before stopping on the same level as the green dragon.

"We would like to learn more about how to dampen magic, specifically." Conner seemed much more willing to speak freely with this young man than he did with Elam, with whom he'd always begun with veiled threats and suspicion. "Are you the head librarian of the magic section?"

"I am," the young man nodded respectfully as they passed by the dragon, who smiled welcomingly at Conner. "My name is Fredrick. I became head librarian of magic two years ago. You've been away for a while?"

"A while, yes. I'm Conner, this is Aleisha," he nodded in her direction. "We'll be spending quite a bit of time here for the planned future."

"It's good to meet you both, let me know any time I can do anything for you." Arriving at a section with some particularly old books, he stopped and pulled out a thick volume. "Now, if you're interested in dampening magic, I would highly recommend reading up on Damion of Mica-Nog. He was one of the first magic users to experiment with such practices, and he is still considered one of the foremost experts on the topic."

"Thank you, Fredrick, we appreciate your help." Fredrick nodded and handed Conner the volume before walking past them and retreating down the staircase. Conner held up the book and eyed it curiously. "Damion of Mica-Nog," he frowned, "that sounds quite familiar." Shrugging, he led her back to the empty table and held a seat out for her.

"What exactly are we looking for, Conner?"

"Anything that will get your magic under control." He took a seat next to her and positioned the book between them. "This isn't a topic I've ever studied before, so I'm not at all sure what that might be." Scanning the first page quickly, he turned to the middle of the book, "Do you know how to read, Aleisha?"

"Yes. Cedrick had me educated so that I could read to him while he enjoyed his brew." He appeared

Darksoul

mildly surprised and relieved at the same time. Her knowledge would greatly speed up the research.

Chapter 21

Damion of Mica-Nog turned out to be a magician who lived in a small town opposed to magic. He, like so many other magicians, had been chosen at birth by a Dictator who was uninterested in training a new chosen babe how to use their magic. As a result of this unfortunate circumstance, he had grown up, much like the rest of the town, despising magic; not realizing that he possessed it.

"As I watched the flowerpot crash into the wall, never having touched it, I knew that my deepest fears and my worst suspicions had been confirmed," Conner read aloud from Damion's journal. "I was a magic user. I had no idea how I was going to deliver this awful news to my parents; they would surely never forgive me for possessing the curse all this time. They would surely disown me."

"I could not bear the thought of it, so I sought a remedy for my condition. I left Mica-Nog and settled in a small hunter's cabin in the forest, hoping to provide myself with some privacy so that I could experiment with my magic. I sought a way to either control it or, much preferably, to be rid of it completely.

"The early days in the cabin were quite rough, as I had no success in preventing my own use of magic, but I refused to give up on my noble quest to be free. I tried every combination of herbs and roots I could think of, as suggested by a woman I met in Cithfrawct, but no plant seemed to hold any real power over me.

Even the brews that left me unconscious for a time seemed only to destabilize my magic and make it all the more unpredictable. On one occasion, when I finally woke up, I found the entire cabin in complete disarray; nearly everything that I had collected and carefully cataloged over the last months was either spilled, burnt, or otherwise destroyed. It appeared as if some great monster had broken into the cabin to devastate all my work. Though I suppose that, in a way, one had, only, I was the monster. I and my magic were every bit as destructive as any beast.

"It was at this point that I decided to seek out a different path for controlling my magic. It occurred to me that my magic could only be controlled with other magic. Fighting fire with fire, as the saying goes, though I would argue that a battle between dragons never ends well for anyone. So, I began searching out a magic that would hinder me from using my power when in its presence.

"Again, it took me many months and hundreds of trials to find a workable solution, but I finally found the answer to my dilemma. I shall have to deliver a copy of my journals to the Great Library, as I am sure my discoveries will be invaluable all over Elbot.

"By my unlikely hand, we may yet even have a cure for the scourge of magic that has cursed our land for so long." Conner scoffed and slammed the book shut.

"Fool!" he said that perhaps louder than he should have, as every eye in the library seemed to be suddenly directed at him. Aleisha, who had been listening intently to him as he read, appeared startled at his sudden outburst. "Magic is not a plague that needs to be eradicated. His fear will be the end of him; it always is." Aleisha dropped her head as if he had just scolded her. He hadn't meant that to be directed at her. She was different from this Damion. He wanted to be rid of his magic for social reasons; so that his family would accept him. She wanted to be free from the corrupting nature of it. Surely she knew that he saw the difference between them.

"I should see if I can find his other journals; it is of no value to know that he succeeded if we do not know how." He stood to leave, taking Damion's journal with him to return to the librarian. As he made his way to the staircase, he looked around to see which of the dragons came today. Snarf and Byron came every day and spent more time in the library than even Conner and Aleisha did, Grezald and Grizwald came nearly every day, but had never enjoyed reading, so spent most of their time speaking with other dragons in the library, trying to find someone with knowledge that hadn't been recorded yet. Dagmar was the one Conner was truly curious to see, as he seemed much less interested in the search then any of the rest of them, despite the fact that it had been his idea to come to the Great Library.

Much to Conner's surprise, today was the first day that he had seen Dagmar in the magic section of the library. He seemed to be speaking with Genevieve, the green female who served as the dragons' librarian in the magic section. Conner knew Genevieve from previous visits to the library, but hadn't yet spoken to her this visit because he knew that she would want to meet Aleisha but would be horrified to learn that she was a Darksoul and even more furious if he didn't tell her and she discovered the fact on her own later on.

Conner stopped at a section that seemed to be solely dedicated to Damion of Maci-nog. In the week since they had arrived at the library, Conner had read four of his journals already, each one dealing with a different angle of his search for magical inhibiters. None of the works, however, seemed to have any real information to offer, only long, complaining monologues about the difficulties of research and short, excited exclamations that he had succeeded. "I don't know why we are wasting our time reading about a man who trusted someone from Cithfrawct." He knew that he was having a dreadfully sour attitude concerning the whole situation; after all, even with all his folly, simply bothering to think of magical inhibition made Damion of Maci-Nog much more qualified to answer Aleisha's problem that Conner wanted to help Aleisha by any means necessary, but he could not imagine that he would need to rely on someone so entirely inept, so completely misinformed, in order to succeed at that task.

Piling the rest of the journals in his arms, he made his way back down the stairway and to Fredrick's desk. "Are there any records of other people using

Damion of Mica-Nog's solutions to ward off magical humans?"

"I do believe that there are," he smiled and reached for a piece of paper, quickly scribbling a few words before continuing, "but you will have better luck finding them in the lore and history section, as the magical item tends to play a rather minor role in the stories." He handed Conner the paper, which simply said, "Lore and History" as if Conner was incapable of remembering simple instructions.

He was ready to go home. "Hey, Leish." As soon as he neared her, he dropped the journals in front of her so that the table would record that they were using them. "Are you ready to head out?" She nodded and stood, placing the book she was reading on the table as she pushed in her chair. *"Byron, Dagmar, Snarf, we're headed home. We'll see you in the morning."* All three dragons bid them goodnight, bringing a smile to Aleisha's exhausted eyes.

As he led Aleisha out of the library, she seemed to be making a point of looking at absolutely anything other than him. She seemed so very distracted by the smallest of things that he didn't think it wise to even attempt making conversation with her until they arrived at the house.

He had been quite pleased when he had first arrived at his house last week to see the good care his hired man, Mathias, had taken. Not a single plank of wood or a single brick seemed in disrepair in the whole of the estate. The garden was well-kept and the single-stall barn smelt as if no horse had entered since the last time he and Soulfire had visited nearly five years ago. Conner had been very careful to make sure that Mathias knew of his pleasure and had gifted him and his family a new set of fine clothes for the coming winter, a gift that did not go unwelcomed.

The door to his home opened for them the moment he and Aleisha stepped foot onto the lowest porch step. "Good evening, sir," Mathias smiled widely as he held the door open for them. "Supper should be ready in just a few minutes, sir."

"Thank you, Mathias." He smiled as the elderly man tried and failed to take Aleisha's cloak for her. She had seemed hesitant to accept the assistance of any of the servants since they had arrived. "You and your family should head home. We can finish everything up here." He looked as if he was going to protest but, upon witnessing Conner easily help Aleisha out of her cloak, he seemed to understand the request.

"Yes, sir," he nodded formally and headed to the kitchen, only to return quickly with his wife and daughter behind him, cloaks in hand. "We'll see you in the morning then, sir, ma'am." Each of them bowed slightly and hurried out the door.

As soon as the door closed behind them, Aleisha seemed to relax ever so slightly. Uncertain what to do for her; he headed to the kitchen to check on their dinner. He found a pot of stew simmering on his wooden stove, the flames nearly out, and a loaf of bread cooling on the table. Quickly finding two bowls, he served the stew and ripped two, good sized sections of bread from the loaf. Where had Aleisha gone? He had expected her to follow him into the kitchen as she had each previous night. Perhaps she was waiting in the dining area; she did seem quite distracted today. Picking up both bowls, he exited the kitchen, only to find that she wasn't in the dining area either.

"Where is she?" Placing their dinner on the table, he went to seek her out. It seemed highly unlikely that she would be in her room, so he made his way past the flight of stairs into the sitting room. Still, he didn't see her, "Aleisha!" he preferred not to raise his voice when not absolutely necessary, but he was at a loss as to where she might be.

"I'm here." He turned around to see that she had not moved from the doorway where he had left her.

"Are you alright, Leish? You seem really distracted today."

"Grizwald told me what day it was earlier," she sighed, looking bewildered, "I guess I've just been a little preoccupied."

"What day is it?" He had no idea to what she could be referring, though he had never been good at keeping track of time, so today could very well be an important holiday and he would have no idea having not been reminded.

He must have looked as puzzled as she did because she chuckled a little, "It's just my birthday. I haven't told anybody."

"Oh." He wasn't sure of the appropriate response to that. Some people he had known wanted well wishes on their birthdays. others would have preferred he not comment. He had no idea which Aleisha would want.

"Most people, at least most people in Jaboke, don't even know when their birthday is because it's really just not important to them." She sighed and walked toward him, "I only know because I was six years old before I was taken from my mother; she had always made a big deal about it. Cedrick knew that I was born in the fall and, being his favorite, I always got a good meal and a new dress out of it, but he never seemed satisfied with my thanks. He used to watch me with an odd, expectant look on his face. I always dreaded my birthday because of him." She wrapped her arms around herself and shivered.

"Leish," he sighed and quickly closed the distance between them, wrapping his arms around her and resting his chin on her head, "You should have told me today was your birthday. I would have planned something slightly more interesting than research."

"Finding the answer today would have been the best birthday present." That's why she seemed so distracted today. She had gotten her hopes up about the search and he had spent the whole day complaining about it.

"I'm so sorry, Leish. Tomorrow, we should take the day off, and the seven of us can go outside the city to just spend some time together." He gently rubbed her back before releasing her. "We will begin to make up for the unpleasant memories of your previous birthdays. We are your family now, Aleisha."

Chapter 22

Aleisha sat at the breakfast table and slowly sipped her hot infusion. Conner had left a few minutes ago to talk to the dragons about where they might go today. He had been so kind yesterday when she had tried, rather clumsily she feared, to tell him how she disliked her birthday. She had been hoping to make it through the day without thinking of it but hadn't been able to keep her mind on anything else.

Conner seemed to take her explanation as evidence that she needed a celebration. She had never even considered that. Swallowing the last of her drink, she stood and wandered around the kitchen, looking for a basket that she could pack for lunch. She eventually found a nice wicker basket tucked in a corner among stacks of canned jellies. In just a few minutes, she had gathered a lovely meal of fresh bread, a jar of jelly, and a wedge of cheese. Wrapping them in a cloth, she placed them in the basket and headed to the front of the house to retrieve her cloak.

The day they had arrived in Might City, Conner had shown up in Snarf's room with a heavy wool cloak on his arm. He had said only that it was meant for Aleisha and had wrapped it around her before she had an opportunity to protest such extravagance. She had since found herself quite grateful for the extra warmth, as fall had arrived and the temperatures were steadily declining.

The front door suddenly opened, letting in a cool blast of air and causing Aleisha to pull her cloak more closely about her body. "Are you ready to head out?" Conner was grinning widely as he stepped inside, closing the door behind him and shivering slightly from being out in the cold.

"Yes, just give me one moment." She darted back to the kitchen to grab the basket before turning back toward the front of the house. Conner had followed her and was eyeing the basket with amusement. "Lunch." She raised it slightly, as if to show off her wares.

Conner simply smiled and offered her his arm. "The dragons have decided that you need a nice relaxing day, so naturally they have planned dozens of things for us to do together." His expression looked like he was trying with everything in him to appear annoyed, but he was failing miserably, suppressed laughter pulling at the corners of his eyes and mouth. "I've talked them out of most of it, as they wanted very much to do some traveling and sight-seeing, but I reminded them, in a very subtle manor I assure you," he winked, "that you have been wanting to cease traveling for a time."

"Thank you," she smiled, "I don't mind traveling if that's what they want to do."

"Today is for you, though, so Snarf came up with a brilliant plan to make everybody happy." He tugged at her gently, pulling her out of the way of a man leading a horse through the street. "Dagmar suggested that I take you to see the family that you stayed with last time you were here and Snarf mentioned that they could use that time to do some of their sight-seeing."

Darksoul

"We're going to see Sophie?" She leaned closer to him to hug his arm as she grinned, "Thank you."

"I was hoping you would like that," he chuckled. At the foot of the Great Library now, she let go of his arm as he opened the door to let her lead the way. He had shown her around the library for the first few days, but now he let her lead in order to better learn her way around.

The shear vastness of the building provided a difficulty for her in learning the layout of the several libraries that lay within, though she was becoming rather confident in finding her way around the western side, as both the Library of Magic and the dragons' rooms were located there. "Whose room are we headed to?"

"Byron's." He watched her constantly as she wandered her way through the halls, as if studying her movement. She suspected he rather enjoyed seeing her become lost, as she always did at least once.

"His is up a few more flights, isn't it?" She looked back to see him nod; now only if she could remember where the stairs were. After a few more wrong turns and a failed attempt to climb the steep ramp that the dragons used to change levels, she finally made her way up several flights of stairs and stopped in front of a large archway with a slight red tinge. "This is Byron's room."

"Yes, very good," Conner nodded approvingly, "Would you like to ask permission to enter, or shall I?"

"I can," she turned toward the doorway and tried to sense Byron on the other side, a much more difficult task than the distance would indicate. *"Can you hear me?"*

"Yes, Aleisha, you are welcome to enter." Conner must have heard the last part as well, for he took her elbow and led her into the room. Byron's was both the largest and plainest of the dragons' rooms. Most of the others' were covered in shelves of valuable stones and artifacts and nearly shone with the intensity of the brightness of the colors. Byron's room, however, held only a single shelf with a few dusty objects. The last time she had visited his room, she had asked about his small collection, only to discover that Byron, or perhaps it had been Lorahlie, was by far the most sentimental of all of the brothers; each object was significant for its role in their family history.

A large smooth stone covered in moss and dirt was displayed at the center of the shelf. She had asked where it had come from, but Byron hadn't wanted to talk about it. Later, Conner had informed her that it had to do with his courtship with Lorahlie, but he would not tell her more. On the edge of the shelf was a large leather saddle, an early attempt to aid Conner in learning to fly. *"It did more harm than good and it was incredibly uncomfortable,"* his laughing voice echoed in her memory, bringing a smile as she surveyed the shelf once more.

"Conner told us that your birthday was yesterday," Grizwald lowered his head to look in her eyes. He

appeared to be trying to intimidate her, *"You should have told me. You know how I enjoy timekeeping. Another significant date to add to my calendar is always much appreciated."*

"I'm sorry, Grizwald, I certainly did not mean to offend you."

"Bah," he jerked his head up, letting out a short laugh, *"No harm was done. We'll celebrate on the proper date next year."* With that, he lowered himself to the floor to allow her to climb on. *"The rest of the fellows are already waiting for us, so we should head out."*

"I wonder who is the most eager for the festivities of the day," Byron chuckled at his younger brother. *"Remember that it is Aleisha whom we are celebrating."*

"Of course, of course." Grizwald bounded out of the room and off the platform, quickly ascending above the library and heading out of the city to the west. *"We are going to take the whole day off to celebrate your birthday. Conner said that you don't have any good birthday memories, so we are going to fix that; you have a family to celebrate with you now."*

"Conner said the same thing. He said that you all are my family now. Does everybody feel that way?" She couldn't help but smile; she never imagined she would have a family.

"Well, I suppose that depends on how you feel." Grizwald landed next to Grezald, who greeted his twin with a merciless head-butt, *"Hey, I have a passenger!*

Be careful!" Snarf and Grezald exploded into fits of laughter at their brother's distress. Dagmar lumbered over and sniffed Aleisha's basket.

"Lunch?"

"I only brought enough for Conner and me. I didn't know whether or not you would be hungry."

"They'll be fine" - Conner reached up to help her down - "They can hunt while we're in the city if they want to."

"So," Snarf settled into the grass. *"We have the whole morning. What shall we talk about first?"* He made a show of formality, as if he was calling an official meeting to order.

"Oh," Grezald nearly leapt into the air in excitement. *"We could tell Aleisha about how Conner came to join our family."*

"Why would she want to know that?" Dagmar looked at his brother in puzzlement, *"We should tell her something interesting."* He paused, presumably trying to think of something that would qualify, *"Perhaps how I joined the family."*

"Weren't you born a part of the family?" She had always assumed that the five dragons were blood relatives; it had never occurred to her that they had adopted each other as Conner had when he called them brothers.

"Why, yes." Dagmar smiled proudly. *"But there are few things as majestic as the birth of a dragon."*

"Dagmar! That's disgusting!" Conner looked horrified as he stared at the large dragon.

"It is her birthday. I would think that such a topic would be quite appropriate." He could tell that his brothers were appalled and he was enjoying their distress thoroughly.

"Is the birth of a dragon something that Aleisha is interested in learning about?" Byron looked to Aleisha, his opinion displayed clearly on his face.

"Um, no thank you." She tried to smile at Dagmar, as she could tell that he was trying to make a joke, but she was just as horrified as the rest of them.

"Perhaps a story of one of our adventures," Grezald was the next to offer a suggestion.

"I think," Byron interjected, *"that Aleisha should have a say."* He turned toward her expectantly.

She had no idea what she was supposed to say. They had never had difficulty making conversation, but suddenly, now that she was being asked for a topic, she couldn't think of a single thing to talk about.

Suddenly, Conner burst into uncontrollable laughter. Snarf, watching the expression on Aleisha's face, followed suit. Before long, everybody was laughing so hard that Grezald and Grizwald were rolling around, holding their bellies and smacking their brothers with their wings, which only succeeded in making them laugh all the harder.

Byron, much to the surprise of everyone present, suddenly pounced on the twins, wrestling with them as they continued to playfully swat at the others. Aleisha had never seen Byron so carefree. "He used to be more like this all the time," Conner moved to her side and whispered as he watched the dragons, "You wouldn't guess to see him now, but, when Lorahlie was alive, he started the horseplay as often as Snarf or the twins did." He continued watching the dragons play, his smile never wavering.

Chapter 23

"This has been the loveliest birthday celebration ever. Thank you all so much." Aleisha smiled like Conner hadn't seen in weeks. As she sat and nibbled on her chunk of cheese, she leaned into Snarf's side affectionately.

"It's been our pleasure to serve you, ma'am." Grezald bowed his head with exaggerated pomp as he spoke in a formal tone.

"We're happy to be able to give you a good day, Leish." Conner chuckled at his brother's antics, "I can only hope the rest of the day goes as well."

"Ah, yes," Dagmar, who had settled in the grass near Aleisha, nodded sleepily, *"you two are going to visit Aleisha's friend. I had almost forgotten about that."*

"Aren't you the one who suggested it?" Aleisha tilted her head at Dagmar, her expression somewhere between confusion and suspicion.

"Why yes, I did suggest it," the blue dragon nodded and grinned mischievously at Conner, *"but Conner vetoed nearly every suggestion any of us gave, so I forgot that mine somehow survived."*

"What would you have expected?" Snarf growled sarcastically, *"It was the only way he was going to get her to himself."* Aleisha giggled at that; she had no concept of how important she was to any of them. She did not realize that any one of them would wish to spend time alone with her.

Conner realized that he was quite fortunate. He and Snarf got to spend more time with her than any of the others, and they both knew that the others envied them for that; this knowledge had even led Snarf to invite Grizwald to pick up Aleisha this morning in his place.

"Whenever you are ready to go, Leish, Snarf and Byron will fly is over to the southern end of the city so that we can enter near Sophie's inn." Again, Aleisha grinned at the thought of visiting her friend. "Then, I'll head back to my house with Byron to get Soulfire so that you can see the rest of the city. It's much too large a city to walk from the gate to the library."

"Thank you, that sounds great." Aleisha smiled and stood. "Can we go now?" Each of the dragons grumbled halfheartedly but stood to bid them goodbye.

"I suppose that means it's time for us to head out" - Dagmar stretched his wings and moved to take off - *"We're overdue for a hunt. You two enjoy yourselves."* With that, he flew off; both orange dragons following close behind him.

Aleisha climbed onto Snarf's back, in such a hurry to see Sophie again that she left her basket behind. Chuckling, Conner picked it up and mounted Byron, placing the basket between his shoulder blades in front of him. Sophie must have been quite important to Aleisha to elicit this level of excitement at seeing her again. Conner wondered what she must be like, though he supposed he was about to find out.

It was a quick flight to the south end of the city, where the gate was guarded by two armed men. "Ho there. What business do you have in Might City?" One of the guards eyed them suspiciously, while the other

Darksoul

stared at Aleisha as if trying to remember something important.

"Tobias," Aleisha smiled at the staring guard, who suddenly broke into a wide grin.

"Aleisha! Did you ever find your mother?"

She shook her head solemnly, "She," she appeared to be fighting off both rage and tears, "she got too close to that Darksoul." The hate evident in her voice both surprised and saddened him. "He murdered her."

"I'm sorry to hear that." Tobias turned to the other guard, "Let them through, Tom, she's a friend." Tom nodded curtly and fell silent. "You make sure you stop to see Sophie while you're here, ok?"

"I will." She smiled one more time as they passed through the gate into a section of the city always filled with children playing in the streets, laughing and lightening the mood of the busy area. Today, they appeared to be playing tag with a small dog which was barking happily as it was being chased. Even as Conner smiled at their antics, he felt the presence of something dark. Worried, he looked around them but saw nothing out of place. Aleisha stopped in front of a building with a sign that read, "Maiden's Song" and turned toward him, "This is Sophie's inn. Beth, her daughter, is usually in the front room to greet guests."

"Great! Then let's head in." He placed a hand on her back and moved slightly in front of her to open the door.

"Aleisha!" a young girl who was wiping tables in the next room looked up and squealed with excitement.

"You came back." She ran toward them and threw herself into Aleisha's arms. "You came back."

Behind the little girl, an older woman entered the room and smiled brightly. "Aleisha!" She, too, smiled widely and ran to embrace Aleisha. After a few moments of excited chatter between the three females, Aleisha turned to Conner.

"This is Conner" - she smiled at him before turning back to them - "This is Sophie and her daughter, Beth." Conner held a hand to greet both women, who watched him with open curiosity.

"It's lovely to meet you both." He smiled; he already liked Aleisha's friends. Anybody who was so glad to see Leish certainly made a good first impression in his mind.

"Come, we were just getting ready to make dinner. Beth is learning how to make bread today." Sophie excitedly chatted away as she led them to the kitchen, which was filled with the mouthwatering aroma of baking bread.

"May I help with the dishes?" Conner couldn't help but smile as he watched the three women together; Aleisha seemed at ease here.

"I guess I'll go get Soulfire, then." At Aleisha's panicked expression, he added, "I saw a stable behind the inn, I'll put Soulfire there until you are ready to go, no matter when that might be." He had to smile at the expression on her face; he wished he had brought her to see Sophie before now.

He headed out the front door, only to stop on the street when he sensed that dark presence again. He frowned at the shadows between the buildings and closed his eyes, hoping to feel where the darkness was coming from. He managed to feel the presence more clearly, convincing him that whatever was causing it was a living creature, but he had no better idea of where it was coming from.

The last time he'd felt something this cold, this oppressive, was the night Alice was murdered. For one, sickening moment, he froze. The sudden dread was enough to paralyze him as he considered what might be lurking in the shadows.

He turned around and reentered the inn. Aleisha, seeing him, came back to the entrance, curiosity evident in her expression. He took a moment to see if he could sense the dark presence in the inn. There was nothing there.

Confident that she would be safe here, he took the few steps separating them and wrapped his arm around her waist, pulling her close enough to whisper in her ear. "Don't leave the building while I'm gone. I'll come back as quickly as I can." He took a moment to rest his head on hers, unsure and terrified at the prospect of leaving her alone, yet unwilling to deny her the opportunity to visit with Sophie.

Eventually, he stepped away, noting her bewildered expression. She didn't appear afraid, as he had somewhat expected. Good, he didn't want to scare her unnecessarily.

Entering the street once again, he walked back to the gate as quickly as he could, *"Byron!"* he called as loudly and as urgently as he could. If Byron wasn't waiting for him when he got to the gate, he would fly himself to the library. *"Byron! I need you at the gate now!"*

"Is something the matter with Aleisha?" Conner looked up to see not only Byron, but all five of the dragons flying directly above him. If not for the library at the center of the city, the sight would have terrified everyone on the ground. As it was, some of the children pointed excitedly, but otherwise they went unnoticed.

"It's most likely nothing, but I would like to retrieve Soulfire as quickly as possible and ask that Dagmar and Snarf remain here watching Sophie's inn."

Chapter 24

Aleisha stood in the middle of the inn, baffled by what had just happened. Aside from the day they left Puko, she had never seen Conner so intense. Shrugging, she turned to rejoin Sophie and Beth in the kitchen, only to see Sophie giving her the same knowing smile that Fortuna so often did when Conner was around.

She shook her head at the older woman's assumptions and scoffed lightly; some women seemed only to care about romance. Aleisha, by contrast, was much more curious about why it had been so urgent to Conner that she remain inside. It surely didn't make any sense to her.

She had barely helped Beth pull the bread from the oven when she heard the front door open once more. Thinking that it was Conner again, she went to greet him. However, the moment she stepped out of the kitchen, Conner's concern suddenly made sense, though she now wondered why he'd been willing to leave her at all.

Before her eyes stood the man whom she hated above all others. Before her stood the man whom she feared even more than Briganti. Before her, stood a tall, thin man veiled in impossibly black smoke. Tallen had found her. He had found her, and she had been foolish enough to walk right into the room in which he waited for her.

"Alencia!" He grinned at the sight of her and opened his arms wide, as if expecting her to come to him for a hug, as if she would want anything to do with him, as if he had any right to expect anything from his daughter whose name he had not even bothered to remember. "Alencia," he repeated the foreign name again, only succeeding in infuriating her more.

"I'm sorry, sir." She forced herself to smile at the vile creature, forced her magic to retreat as she could feel it fighting to lash out at this man who could surely defeat her if she instigated a battle. "I'm afraid I don't know anyone by that name." He had not seen her since she was a small child, so perhaps, if she was careful, she could make him leave without admitting her identity to him. Keeping her wrath and her magic in check would be key to her escape.

"Don't fool with me, Alencia. My captain told me of your visit to my castle several months back." Out of the corner of her eye, she could see Sophie hurrying Beth up the stairs. She truly hoped that she had not heard that last statement. "He told me that my daughter had been looking to reunite with me. Imagine my surprise and pleasure at learning that you are a Darksoul like me, Alencia."

"I am nothing like you." Even as she said it, several tables and chairs suddenly flipped over, crashing on the floor with a loud explosion. This seemed to please Tallen; she had to get her emotions under control.

"My dear Alencia-"

"Aleisha!" so much for not revealing her identity. "My name is Aleisha. If you expected a warm welcome, you should have at least bothered to remember my name." Tallen's eyes darkened. He looked furious, but somehow she didn't think it was directed at her.

"We named you Alencia, after my dear sister. Dorcas promised to afford me that one small favor." As he shook with rage, Aleisha could see the floor around his feet cracking. Taking a deep breath, he cleared his throat, "No matter; Aleisha then."

He stepped closer to her, a small smile playing at his eyes. He looked almost affectionate as he gazed at her; no man had ever looked at her like that, save Conner. She shook her head. She had to remind herself that this man was a skilled liar. Any success she had had tricking Cedrick in the past could not compare to the manipulation Tallen was surely capable of. "As I said, I was quite pleased to hear that you had visited me as well as sorely disappointed that you left before I returned."

"I didn't visit you," she scoffed. "I was only there to rescue my mother from you. I said what I had to in order to get out of there as quickly as possible once I realized that you'd already murdered her." She was surprised by the even tone of her own voice; pleased that nothing in this room went suddenly flying at her outburst.

"I am not proud of the way I handled Dorcas' defiance, but my patience ran out for her after she so vehemently refused to provide the Elixir of Life for you and me." He didn't appear even slightly offended by her words; if anything, he appeared only saddened.

"All I have done since your birth has been for your benefit."

"My benefit?" She could not believe the boldness of this man! Did he really think her that gullible? "Including selling me into slavery?" She could see that that had hurt him, or appeared to have hurt him; he was obviously a skilled actor.

"It was the safest place for you. I had to get you away from your mother. If I'd left you with her, she would have turned you irreversibly against me, but if I'd brought you to live with me after she weaned you, you would have always tried to return to her." His eyes pleaded with her to believe him. She would not. "I never abandoned you to Cedrick. He knew very well the consequences if any harm came to you. Tell me, Alenc-" he cleared his throat, looking pained, "Aleisha, did any man ever lay a hand on you, either to harm or to claim?" How could he have guessed that? Cedrick was known for his cruelty toward his slaves, yet Aleisha had never so much as been threatened by any man under his roof.

"I can see that he took me seriously." He smiled. "You were never intended to remain with Cedrick indefinitely. I was planning on retrieving you once I had the elixir; I knew that it would be easier to convince you of my story if I had the proof to offer to you." He sighed and shook his head. "The last time Dorcas refused me, I lost my temper and she was dead before I could stop my magic from consuming her. As soon as I realized what I had done, I left to take you from Cedrick, hoping that I could find another way to grant you long life.

"When I arrived at Cedrick's mansion, though, he said that you had been taken by a large, purple dragon." He laughed shortly, "If he'd counted the other dragons right, I would have realized who had taken you and tracking you would have been much easier." He had to be telling the truth. How else could he have known that it was Snarf who had been the one to take her from the balcony? Only Cedrick himself would have known that.

"I can imagine the things that Conner and his friends have told you concerning me." At least he had the decency to look ashamed.

"You killed Gabriel, murdered Lorahlie." Surely, he did not think he could convince her of his innocence. Though, he had not tried to deny that he had killed her mother.

"You cannot understand, Aleisha, how I longed for eternal life." He pleaded with her to listen, to understand, "I married your mother foolishly, selfishly trying to gain immortality. When I found her pregnant, my entire focus shifted; all of my motivation became the precious child growing inside your mother's womb. When I found her meeting in secret with another man, I lost my temper; I threw them both in the dungeon.

"I had never worked so furiously to convince her to give me the elixir; I promised her everything I could. I promised to allow her lover to visit her, promised to free her, I even vowed to give up my own use of the elixir. I only begged that she provide it for your benefit. Nothing could convince her to reveal the elixir's location." She couldn't believe that she was still standing here listening to his lies, but she couldn't find the strength to walk away. She had to hear his explanation.

"So, after her repeated refusal, I had to make a new plan; if I could not enjoy eternity with my child, I would find a way to have a few centuries. I knew that no Dragonsoul or Lightsoul Dictators would grant you power and a magician would barely count for a lengthened life, so I sought out a young Darksoul for you to replace. I counted myself quite fortunate to discover Gabriel; he was the most powerful Darksoul and yet he was so young and inexperienced that I easily overtook him, tricking him into sharing a meal. I do not regret killing him, as he was the best way to lengthen your life.

"As for Lorahlie, Briganti's refusal, coupled with your mother's continued defiance, put me in a murderous mood. I felt I had to lash out at someone as my magic would not be contained, and Lorahlie made herself my obvious target when she used her magic to make me leave Puko; I needed to remain until I had succeeded in persuading Briganti." His eyes turned to slits as he cocked his head, "They did tell you that she used her magic on me? I'm sure Conner would not have left that out; he is an honest man if nothing else." After she nodded slightly, he continued, "I am ashamed of my actions toward her; she was a beautiful beast and a gracious dragon. She did not hold my sins against me as most do and would have made a good and honorable elder dragon. I have occasionally wished that I had chosen a more deserving target for my anger, as gentle creatures such as Lorahlie are both precious and rare.

"I know that you think ill of me; I can see it in your eyes, but the simple fact that you are still standing in this room, still listening to my story, gives me great hope, Aleisha." He stepped closer to her, dropping his voice to a whisper, "I dare not hope that you can forgive me for all that I have done, all the pain that I have caused both you and your friends, even so, I must ask. Please, Aleisha, I know that I have done much wrong, and I humbly ask that you forgive me, that you grant me the opportunity to be father to you, rather than monster." She had no idea how she was supposed to respond. She never imagined that he would ask for forgiveness for anything. Was he trying to manipulate her? Was he lying? Everything that he said that she could independently verify was correct. Was there a chance that he was telling her the truth? Could she have been so wrong about her father?

The door of the inn opened once more, revealing Conner's massive form. The moment he saw Tallen standing in front of Aleisha, he exploded into his true form and flew in between them, grabbing Aleisha's arm to pull her more firmly behind him.

Chapter 25

Conner stood in front of Aleisha and glared at Tallen. How dare he show his face! He never should have left Aleisha alone; he should have changed their plans and told Byron that they would be flying back to the library instead of riding Soulfire. As he continued to stare Tallen down, he gently wrapped his wings around Aleisha, shielding her from the monster in front of him.

"Conner," Tallen had chosen to forgo his usual sneer, no doubt in an attempt to make Aleisha more comfortable with him, "I was just introducing myself to my daughter." He only growled at him; he had no right to call Aleisha his daughter, not after everything he had done to her. "I see. I will be going then. I hope to speak with you again, Aleisha." With that, he turned and walked out.

"Conner." He turned so quickly that he almost knocked her over. "I don't know what to think." She moved her mouth silently, as if struggling to find her next words; she looked so fragile, so confused, so troubled, and he had no idea what to do for her. "He knew things: things about growing up in Cedrick's mansion, things about my escape." She looked up at him as if begging for him to explain. "How could he know that it was Snarf who grabbed me from the balcony?"

"I don't know, Leish." She looked like she was ready to start crying, "I'm sorry I left. I had no idea that he was what I was feeling, or I never would have let you out of my sight."

She shuddered and leaned her head on him, "I just wish I knew what to think." Unsure what else he could do for her, he wrapped both arms and wings around her trembling form and held her until she moved to step away. "Sophie and Beth are hiding upstairs. I don't know how much they heard."

He nodded. He had no idea what Tallen might have said to Aleisha, but he had no doubt that Sophie wouldn't have appreciated hearing it. "I'll go check on them."

"You might want to put your wings away." She backed up and wrapped her arms around her middle; he couldn't imagine the turmoil she must be experiencing right now.

Reclaiming his human form, he made his way up the stairs to seek out the lady of the inn. He found her huddled under a desk with her daughter, a knife held out in front of her to ward off any attackers.

"Stay back!" He had to be impressed with her boldness. She was clearly terrified, but she would not sit idly by as some vicious creature attacked her daughter. "I know what you are, and you aren't welcome here."

"Sophie, please." He held up his hands to show her he wasn't hiding anything, "I just want to make sure you're alright."

"We welcomed you into our home, cared for that demon as if she was one of our family." With each word, she seemed to gain courage until she finally made her way out from under the table. "Now I learn that everything she said to us was a lie. You are not welcome here. Leave us before I call the guard."

Conner could only nod; he understood the woman's fears, unjustified though they be. Mostly, he just hurt for Aleisha; she had so looked forward to seeing Sophie and Beth, but now, because of Tallen, they would likely never speak kindly to her again.

Turning to leave her in peace, he slowly descended the stairs to find Aleisha waiting rather impatiently for his return. "Are they ok? What did they hear?"

"They know you're a Darksoul, Leish, I'm sorry." She gasped, closing her eyes and breathing deeply in an obvious attempt to keep herself from crying. He wanted so desperately to comfort her, to tell her that all would be well and that they would forgive her deception, but he could not. He would not raise false hope, and this woman clearly had no mind to overlook Aleisha's origin.

"Let's just go then." She shuddered once more and allowed him to lead her out the door and onto the horse's back. Neither of them spoke the entire ride back to the house, and Conner wished with each step that Soulfire took that he had changed their plans as soon as he had felt that something wasn't right. He wished he had simply stayed with Aleisha and given her a tour of Might City another day.

The massive buildings and countless shops slowly passed by them as they rode quietly to the center of the city, even the most boisterous passers-by failing to catch their attention, until they finally stopped in front of Conner's house. "Welcome home, sir." Mathias came running from the house to grab hold of Soulfire's reins while Conner and Aleisha dismounted. "I had not expected you home so early. Dinner is not yet ready for you, I'm afraid, but I'll get right on that." His usual energetic behavior had never bothered Conner before, but somehow, seeing his smile while Aleisha was hurting, he could not stand to be in his presence. Only the lowest of creatures could smile at this moment.

"Don't worry about it, Mathias; you and your family should head home." The frustrating grin never wavered as he raised a hand to protest. "I will be serving Aleisha today, you and your family need to leave." For a moment, he looked shocked, even hurt, but he quickly found himself and grinned widely.

"Of course, sir." He nearly ran towards the back of the house to retrieve his family, returning to Conner's side before he could so much as make it through the front door. "I wish you both a lovely evening. We shall return in the morning."

As it turned out, Aleisha had no desire to be served. She retreated immediately to her room and refused every request to see her from both Conner and the dragons, even going so far as to scream at him and nearly break the door with the force of whatever she threw at him the last time he tried to check on her. So, unwilling to leave her again, he sat outside her bedroom door all night, watching black fog slowly seep under the door and fill the hallway. Whatever Tallen had said to her, he had terrified her and Conner took that as a personal failure.

He woke painfully as his head quite suddenly slammed onto the floor. Opening his eyes, he saw Aleisha standing above him, confusion and worry pulling her beautiful face into an uncomfortable frown. "Have you been here all night?"

He rolled over to push himself up from the floor, taking a single step back as he stumbled from the ferocity of his sudden headache. "I wanted to be close by in case you needed me." He watched as she tried to understand him; she must have just woken up. "I'm surprised you got up before me; you must be exhausted."

"I didn't sleep" - she nodded to the writing table in her room - "I've been trying to piece together everything Tallen said yesterday. I know that a lot of it was true, so now I'm trying to figure out how much of the rest is." She shook her head in frustration. "I just wish there was some way for me to verify it. He made everything he's done sound so reasonable."

"I would caution you, Aleisha, not to accept that which is suspect simply because the rest of the story is accurate. The best liars will always mingle in the truth in order to gain your trust and make their fiction appear as truth." She nodded but she still looked confused. "You need to sleep, Leish. You won't be able to accomplish anything until you've rested."

"Will you promise not to leave?" She refused to look at him so he couldn't be sure, but she sounded suspiciously close to tears.

"I'll be right here." He claimed the seat at the desk and waited. He refused to leave her side when Mathias came looking for them and nearly called for the doctor at the sight of her sleeping form. He stayed seated when Snarf flew over his house and asked where they were. He continued to wait through his own growling stomach at midday; refusing to leave her room for fear that she would wake up while he searched for food and think that he had left her again.

Finally, after three more visits from Snarf, who had nearly panicked at the news of Tallen's visit, Aleisha rolled over and opened her eyes slightly, staring at him with the same blank expression he'd come to expect from her in the morning. "You stayed." It infuriated him how pleased she sounded. She should have been able to trust that he would be there when she woke. She should never have had reason to doubt his commitment to protecting her. Her simple statement convinced him thoroughly of how completely he had failed her. He would not leave her side again. At any moment that it was possible, he would be near enough to her to step between her and any possible threat to her safety or happiness.

She yawned and crawled out of bed, stumbling when she tried to stand too quickly. "Is there anything to eat?" He chuckled and offered her his arm; at least Tallen hadn't succeeded in ruining her appetite.

"Mathias was here earlier. I'm sure he made breakfast, or at least lunch." She turned toward him, her eyes going wide with horror. "You really needed sleep and I wasn't going to be the one to wake you for something as trivial as food."

She laughed at that, a beautiful, incredible sound after all that had happened yesterday. "Some people consider food a necessity, you know." His stomach chose that unfortunate moment to growl again, apparently in agreement with her statement, making her laugh all the harder.

Chapter 26

Conner was still watching her. Aleisha closed the book that she had had no success concentrating on and turned back towards Conner. "I told you, I'm ok now. You can stop worrying so much." He had been following her around for two days now, refusing to move more than a few feet away from her and, while she was grateful of his attention and care, he was beginning to get on her nerves.

He only smiled and pretended to return to the page he had been supposedly reading for over an hour. They were making absolutely no progress on their search for a solution to her magic, and Byron had mentioned yesterday that they should stay in Might City through the winter. It had surprised Aleisha that he would say that, but everyone seemed confident that Tallen would not approach her again as long as they did not leave her alone. *"He very patiently, very wisely waited for the only time we left you alone,"* Byron had pointed out, *"We will not be repeating that mistake, Aleisha."* He had meant those words very seriously, and now she found herself almost smothered under their constant watchful eyes.

"Conner?" He looked up quickly, nearly slamming the book on the table. "Does it seem to you that all of these stories are the exact same?" He glanced again at the book in front of him before reaching for a closed one at the end of the table. Rereading a few of the pages, his expression darkened.

"They are." He pushed the books away from him in disgust. "We need to head to the history section." He stood and offered her his hand. "I have an idea as to why, but I'll need to check something to be certain."

"An interesting theory," Byron, who was searching a section about halfway up, apparently responded to something Conner said to him, *"What would you have me shift my focus to?"* A moment later, he moved toward Dagmar and the green dragon that he always seemed to be talking to.

Conner confidently led her through a maze of hallways that opened up into a room identical to the Library of Magic that they had just left. Making their way to the librarian's desk, Conner requested a history book that covered a region that Aleisha was unfamiliar with. "Do you know? Is there anything in this book about Damion of Maci-Nog?"

The librarian laughed shortly, "Are you doing a report on Magic Lore?"

"Lore?" Didn't lore usually imply fiction and superstition?

Conner appeared frustrated but unsurprised by the librarian's question. "Fredrick, the magic librarian, is clearly not a magic user and he said that he's been here for two years. How long has he been studying magic?"

"Three years, sir." Conner clenched his jaw and reached up to scratch his neck.

"What happened to Lionel?"

"He died," the librarian eyed Conner suspiciously, "slightly more than two years ago now."

"What happened, may I ask?"

"He traveled to a small village called Lambent to collect a journal written by a Lightsoul there. He was attacked by some robbers on the way back; apparently one of them was a magic user, as I can't imagine how else they could have overwhelmed him." Conner, looking horrified, turned toward Aleisha as the elderly man spoke, "We lost both him and the journal."

"Is there anyone here that we can speak to who might know more about actual, tested magic?" Aleisha had to be impressed with the librarian for remaining so calm; Conner's gritted teeth and harsh growl certainly would have frightened her, had they been directed at her.

"I would suggest trying to see the head librarian. If anyone would know more about a section than the librarian in charge of it, he would."

"Thank you," with that, Conner turned and held out his arm for Aleisha to take again. "The head librarian, Griffin, has been here since the library was built. I don't know why I didn't think to visit him myself. He was a young man when it was built; a Lightsoul with a passion for learning and the capacity to lead the researchers of this city indefinitely. If there is anyone in the whole of Elbot who personally holds more knowledge than Elam, it's Griffin." He led her out of the library and further into the building, through winding tunnels and past several more library sections until they reached a circular room with a large cylindrical tower in the center of it. An immensely tall staircase wound around the cylinder from the floor to the ceiling which, if it was possible, seemed higher even than the ceilings in the library sections.

"This is the center column of the library," Conner nodded toward the stairs, indicating that she should begin the intimidating assent. "Griffin's office is at the top of the tower, though I'm not entirely sure what's inside of it."

"Just how tall is this building," after what felt like hours of climbing, Aleisha stopped for a moment to rest her legs, which felt every bit like they would collapse at any moment.

"I really don't know, exactly. I usually just fly up and it doesn't take long at all." He sounded like he was laughing at her, "For some reason, Griffin enjoys the ridiculous trek; I suspect that it's for no other reason than it affords him a great deal of privacy." They continued walking in silence, saving their breath as they labored on. At last, they reached the end of the stairs, her legs now in such pain that she could have been easily convinced that they were encompassed in flame.

"Come in, my dear scholar, come in." Aleisha nearly fell backwards down the steps at being startled by the booming voice. If not for Conner steadying her, she was sure she would have had to make the awful climb again.

He reached around her and pushed the door open, revealing a large office with one small desk in the center of it. Every bit of wall was covered in bookshelves completely filled with books of all sizes. One small doorway on the other side of the office suggested another room just as filled with volumes as this one.

"Why, Conner, it's good to see you again." An incredibly old man stood from behind the desk, smiling broadly at them both. "And who is this, a young woman or a youthful magic user?"

"This is Aleisha" - Conner smiled every bit as broadly as Griffin - "She is both young and a magic user. You, contrastingly, are looking rather old, Griffin. When was the last time you went out?"

Griffin exploded into uncontrolled laughter and gripped his desk for support as he doubled over. "Rather? Why, I haven't bothered restoring my youth in nearly a century, I'm sure." Still laughing, he clapped Conner on the shoulder and ushered him over to one of the many shelves. "I've been hoping you would visit again. I have a new book I've been wanting to give you." He pulled a dust-covered book from the shelf and handed it to Conner, who stared in awe at the tome, which looked anything but new.

"Is this," he began breathlessly.

"Barkley's journal," Griffin spoke quietly, almost too quietly for Aleisha to hear.

"Leish," Conner spun towards her, excitement evident in both his voice and his expression, "Barkley was the very first Dragonsoul."

"Conner and I have been searching for this journal off and on for," Griffin scrunched his face and thought, "four-hundred years now."

"Considering that I'm only three-hundred fifty-something, that's quite an accomplishment," Conner smirked at the old man's confused expression.

"Oh, must have done my math wrong." He made strange hand motions as he mouthed with great concentration. "Ah, two-hundred years this decade, though I can't be sure which year."

"That sounds more reasonable," Conner continued snickering.

"So, what brings you to my office?" Griffin sat on the edge of his desk and looked expectantly from Conner to Aleisha.

"We have been trying to do some research on magic restraints, but your librarian has proven to be quite useless." Again, Aleisha noted how freely Conner spoke of his intentions compared to his guarded manner in Fonishia.

"Are you trying to restrain someone by using magic on them, or are you trying to restrain someone who has magic from using it?"

"We need to keep someone who has magic from using it." Griffin shook his head. "At least restrain them enough that they really have to try to use it."

The old man gazed at Aleisha with a suspicious look, though she could very well have misread him, as his face was so wrinkled and sagging that he might have been grinning for all she knew. "Are you the magic user who is having trouble controlling their magic?"

She looked to Conner for guidance before nodding slowly. "I see." He turned back to Conner, still looking a bit suspicious. "Is there a reason that she can't join the guild, or even better, have you teach her to control her magic?"

"There is, but I'm afraid I can't share my reason."

"I'm afraid that, aside from the lore about enchantments and talismans from that fool in Maci-Nog, I have never heard of restraining a person's magic." He shrugged and shook his head, "As far as I know, it can't be done."

Aleisha felt like screaming; she was so very tired of failure, but Conner didn't even seem fazed by the old librarian's statement.

"A way to be rid of her magic entirely then?" Why would he ask that? He knew how to be rid of it, and he knew that they could have no part of it.

"Can't be done," Griffin seemed quite displeased that he had even asked.

"Good! You haven't read every book in your library, have you? Where would we look for knowledge you do not possess?"

"Come now, I don't allow a book to enter the library unread." He turned and marched to the closed door on the opposite end of the room. Upon ushering them inside, they saw that the floor dropped away into a bottomless pit lined with bookshelves. "This is my private library; the centermost and largest section in the Great Library: The Library of Unread Volumes. I would not normally allow it, but considering who you are, I happily invite you to browse."

"Is there any way to narrow it down?" Aleisha did not enjoy the idea of having to read every book in this huge room.

"I suppose you could go by the titles, but they aren't sorted or organized in any way yet; that's part of my job." Griffin smiled and shrugged. "We've been busy since expanding our search area to include the other two continents, so I'm a bit behind. I will most certainly aid you in any way that I can.

"Can the dragons come to help?" Griffin broke into an absurd grin the moment the word 'dragons' left Conner's mouth.

"Of course they can!" He nearly danced back to the door of his room. "You should go now and tell them to come right here. They can get in through the roof and may stay as long as they like. And do fly, Conner; it must have taken an age to climb all those stairs."

Conner chuckled as they were impatiently ushered out of the room. "He has always had a special fondness for dragons; they are the only creatures more powerful, more knowledgeable, and longer lived than he could ever be. Would you allow me to fly you down? He makes a good point; it did seem to take a long time to get up here."

"A long time?" That was certainly an understatement. "My legs feel like I got into a fight with a dragon. Absolutely, you may fly me down, and back up when the time comes."

Chuckling, he stepped down a few stairs to give himself some space before exploding into a giant winged creature. Reaching a hand out to her, he guided her down to a more reachable level before wrapping his arms around her and leaping from the spiraling staircase.

Chapter 27

There was just something about learning that had always appealed to Conner. In his younger years, he had been known to lock himself in a room for days, only leaving to collect meals and gather more books. Those days, though, ceased when he met Alice, at first because he enjoyed nothing more than to be in her presence, then because he lost any interest in doing much of anything after she died. By the time he had healed enough from her death and Philimina's betrayal, he had simply gotten out of the habit of his studies and found himself uninterested in picking them up again.

Now, though, sitting in Griffin's office, surrounded by piles of manuscripts and notes, he relished in the knowledge he was gleaning from the many stories and reports. "I had not realized how dull those stories Fredrick directed us to were" - he smiled as he jotted down a note - "I had forgotten how captivating a well-worded report can be." He wasn't talking to anyone in particular, as Aleisha and most of the dragons had long since gone to bed. He supposed the only reason he had spoken at all was his own excitement and great pleasure involved in his task.

"Would you like another cup of tea, Conner, as you share your new discoveries?" Griffin, who had had Byron help him change to a much more youthful form of himself, pulled a steaming pot from his fireplace. Neither Conner nor Griffin wanted to leave their reading to head to bed, so Griffin kept a constant supply of tea brewing, as the hot liquid helped both him and Conner stay awake and alert in the dark, quiet hours of the night.

"Well" - he glanced about at his piles of notes as he accepted the drink - "I haven't found anything on restraining magic yet, but I found an interesting piece on magical barriers. Supposedly, some powerful dragons can learn to enchant a room or building to prevent the use of magic inside. The writer claims that this is used in a prison in Belmopan which houses a rogue magician." He skimmed the page again. "No mention as to whether or not it would work at a smaller size. Maybe a necklace or a cloak could help her."

"Ha!" Griffin grinned mischievously. "That would give a new meaning to a magic user's cloak."

Conner didn't bother laughing. "The only problem is that the only dragon that is known to have accomplished this kind of magic lives in Belmopan, and it's too near winter to attempt a trip so long."

"Well" - Griffin poured himself another cup of tea, taking a moment to inhale the steam before sipping - "I suggest a study of anything written by or about this dragon. It could be that Byron or Dagmar will be able to learn this process without direct tutelage."

"Or," Dagmar interrupted, *"one of us could go alone and seek out the answer. Winter travel is not nearly so dangerous for us as it is for you or Aleisha."*

"Would you really want to leave, though? None of us have ever been without the rest for so long."

"I have managed quite sufficiently in the recent past," he replied quietly, sadly, *"I will not enjoy the journey, or the prolonged separation from my family, but I have no doubt that I will fare better than Aleisha has in recent months and she will be better off for my journey."*

"This sounds more like a declaration than a suggestion." Griffin stood and excitedly hurried about the room, gathering various maps and books. "I will prepare a route for you as quickly as I can, Dagmar. I know how you hate to delay once a decision is made."

"Dagmar, Leish," he paused, unsure how to express his concern.

"Aleisha will not want to see me go, but if I can find the remedy for her torment, it is better for her if I do. It would be better to cause her some temporary disappointment than to leave her in this constant struggle."

"You're leaving?" Aleisha stumbled into the room, her eyes still half closed in sleep.

"We think that we have found a possible solution to your inability to control your magic, but the trip will be too long and arduous for you unless we wait for winter to pass, so I will make the journey alone, thereby speeding the results and keeping you from danger." She didn't appear to comprehend anything he said, but she nodded shortly and flopped into a chair.

"What are you doing up already, Leish?" he had never seen her awake before any of the dragons before, not that her present state could accurately be described as such.

"I couldn't sleep," tears welled in her eyes as she spoke, "I have so many questions, but I'm afraid to ask."

"I'm going to take her for a walk, Dagmar." The large dragon only nodded. "Come on, Leish, let's find you some breakfast." She, too, only nodded, but held her hand out to let him help her up. Chuckling, he pulled her to her feet and led her unsteady form out the door. He considered for a moment flying her down the hundreds of steps, but decided the walking might help her wake up.

They were almost halfway down the long flight before Aleisha finally pulled away from him to walk under her own power. "Conner?" The tears he had noticed earlier still glinted in her eyes, making her appear more vulnerable than she usually did. "I've heard all of the stories about the Creator, about His power, authority, and grace, but I never considered that He knew of me, personally, until I met you." She stopped and squinted at the step in front of her, as if looking to it for her next words. "Snarf said that the Creator is the one who ultimately gave me my power?'

"Yes. He has the ultimate authority and could have easily influenced Briganti to choose someone other than you, had He so desired."

"But you have said that He is good. That anything He does is for the good of those who serve Him, even the rules He gives." He nodded, curious where she was headed with this. "You said earlier that we are to treat everyone with love, even if they have hurt us, but what about Philimina? You said that you have not tried to have a relationship with him because of what he did. So, when does the offence become so great that you are allowed to withhold forgiveness?"

"I'm not withholding forgiveness, Aleisha. He has never given me the opportunity to forgive him." He wasn't sure of the best way to explain to her; forgiveness can be such a difficult concept to put into words. He rubbed the back of his neck and tried again, "In Puko, I told you to treat the residents with love. That stands no matter what the situation. However, I did not say that you were to forgive them, because forgiveness is not a one-person job.

"Just as the Creator cannot forgive us if we do not repent of our wrongs, we cannot forgive if our forgiveness has not been sought. If the people of Puko had admitted that they had treated you poorly and asked for your forgiveness, I would have encouraged you to grant it, as the Creator commands. In this same way, I am prepared to forgive Philimina and I would allow him back into my life if he admitted his wrong and sought my forgiveness, but until that happens, I do not have the opportunity to forgive, and I do not trust that he realizes his wrong and would not repeat it."

"So," she paused again. Suddenly, she looked quite terrified; small tendrils of black fog began forming around her. "So, if someone admits their wrong and seeks forgiveness, we have to forgive them? Even if they killed someone we love? That seems foolish!"

"Leish, do you follow the Creator?"

"I want to." The fog thickened, swirling around them slowly as she struggled with his words.

"He is willing, and even eager, to forgive up to and including the torture and crucifixion of His innocent Son." She choked quietly as a single tear escaped her watery eyes. "If He can forgive us the suffering of the only perfect human ever to live, how could we ever justify withholding forgiveness?"

"We can't," she wiped viciously at her eyes as she was now sobbing, "I can't." He had no idea why she was struggling so fiercely with this, so, since he could think of nothing else to help her, he wrapped his arms around her and let her cry.

Chapter 28

Aleisha pulled back from Conner's comforting embrace and wiped her eyes once more. She was so tired of crying. She felt like she had been crying unceasingly for months. "Thank you, I'm fine now." He didn't look at all convinced, but he would never push her to talk if she indicated that she didn't want to. "So, where is Dagmar going, exactly?"

"There is a dragon in Belmopan who allegedly had been able to enchant a room to prevent a magician from using his power while inside." He offered his arm and they began their descent once more. "We are hoping that Dagmar can learn from him and find a way to miniaturize the enchantment so that it can be applied to an article of clothing for you."

She couldn't believe it. Were they really so close to finding the answer? She was terrified to believe it possible. She was sure that she could not bear another disappointment if they failed. But was there a chance? Conner suddenly grabbed her arm, stopping her from descending any farther. "Be careful, Leish. You need to calm down."

She hadn't realized how dark it had gotten, but the fog was becoming thick enough that she could not see the next step. Frustrated, she tried to take a deep breath, but her irritation hindered her in dispelling the fog that she had not intended to summon. She breathed deeply again, closing her eyes to help her focus on Conner standing beside her, the steps under her feet, the rail leading down to the floor where they wanted to

Darksoul

go. Again she breathed in, this time taking note of each sound, every smell, and the strange feeling of the ice cold fog mixing with the warm air. A few more breaths and she could feel herself relax, the fog slowly dispersing as her fear and excitement waned.

"So, this enchantment," she wasn't sure it was a good idea to continue on this subject, but she had to know what Conner really thought of it, "How likely do you think it is that we'll be able to use this to control my power?"

"Well, the enchantment was strong enough to subdue a magician and keep him in custody, so that makes me optimistic, though, you are significantly stronger than any magician, and I cannot predict how shrinking the magic will affect its usefulness." He, too, clearly would have preferred to switch subjects; he often tried to mingle hope with caution, but always ended up sounding like he had no idea what he expected. "If nothing else, it will give us a starting place from which Byron and Dagmar can branch and experiment until we find something that will work. None of us are going to give up on this."

"Thank you." They turned down a hallway that she did not recognize. "Where are we headed?"

"Snarf's room" - he smiled - "I thought you could do with a few laughs and there's no one better for laughs than Snarf." A few turns later, as they entered the large hallway leading to Snarf's room, she finally understood why she was so lost. She had never tried getting here from Griffin's office before, and everything was mirror image on this side of the library. Seeing her confusion, Conner chuckled, "The library is radially symmetrical. Consequently, it can be a bit difficult to get your bearings if you get turned around."

"Absolutely," Snarf's voice echoed in her mind, signaling their permission to enter his room. *"I never expected to see you up so early, Aleisha."* As usual, Snarf spoke with infectious excitement, quickly bringing a smile to both Aleisha and Conner.

"She couldn't sleep. I thought coming to see you would help," Conner grinned at Snarf's appalled expression.

"I'm not that boring!"

"I didn't say you were, though now that I think of it," Snarf swiped at him with his paw, only to miss when he ducked and nearly hit Aleisha instead.

Glaring at Conner, he turned toward Aleisha. *"I know some pretty good jokes, if you need something to help wake you up."*

"No, please, not your stupid lizard and frog joke." Conner made a face of exaggerated dread.

"That isn't the only joke I know. Besides, I'm here for Aleisha, who, I might add, has a much better taste in humor than you."

"You might say that," Conner nodded thoughtfully, "Though you might also say that she is only trying to be polite."

"You two are crazy," she laughed and turned to Conner. "I will be safe with Snarf if you want to return to Griffin's office." By his expression, that wasn't at all what he wanted, but he nodded accommodatingly and turned to leave.

"Are you all right?" Snarf said as she sat down next to him, burying herself in the safety of his wing.

"I'm so afraid, Snarf. When Tallen found me at Sophie's inn, he asked me to forgive him for all the horrible things he's done to me and the people I love." She took a deep breath, trying to keep the fog from returning. "Conner said that I need to forgive whenever forgiveness is sought, but what if I don't think that he is sincere?"

"I can understand your reluctance, Aleisha, but it isn't our job to judge a person's sincerity, only to forgive."

"I don't want to." She refused to start crying again; she would not give him such power over her. "I hate him."

"I think the proper thing in this situation is to say, 'the Creator has commanded us to love our enemies' but that just sounds like an empty platitude, and I fail to see how it would help you. You know what you need to do, and my repeating it won't change that." He paused, *"I would suggest that you stop looking at this in light of showing favor to Tallen as you will likely never find yourself in a place where you will want to forgive him, but rather approach the issue with the intent that you are showing reverence to the Lord High God. If you remember that you are acting out of*

obedience to the Creator, you may find it a less revolting duty."

"But what if I allow him back into my life and he hurts me again? What if he hurts one of you?"

"Again, it is not for you to worry over such things" - Snarf lowered his head and nuzzled closer to her - *"I cannot imagine the turmoil you are experiencing, Aleisha. The pain at the very idea of facing him, the knowledge that you must love him though you have no admiration for him, the frustration and confusion at your desire to follow the Creator conflicting with your need to protect yourself and your loved ones from some past or future wrong must all be warring inside of you, fighting to control you and dictate your actions. I know that he has hurt you, and I do not pretend to know how badly, but your forgiveness cannot depend on your trust.*

"If you allow him back into your life and he repeats his past behavior, then the relationship is severed again, not to mention his very life if one of my brothers or I can reach him, but it may be that he will not duplicate his mistake. I would advise you against having any expectations either way, should you choose to forgive him, and simply trust that the Creator will honor your choice to honor Him. He will protect you according to His plan, no matter what Tallen would do to you."

"I don't have a choice, do I?" She pushed away from him and stood, pacing slowly in front of him. "If I do forgive him, I open myself up to unimaginable pain.

Yet, if I do not forgive him, then I'm not following the Creator and that would be much worse than anything Tallen can do to me." She sighed; she knew what she had to do, she was just afraid, "Will you come with me?"

"Of course, Aleisha, I would be glad to be there to support you." He motioned for her to reclaim her spot next to him. *"I have missed you these last weeks since Conner decreed that you were not to leave his side. Tell me how you've been. How has the research gone? Has Conner given you any room to breathe?"*

They spent the next hour reliving some of the most boring days of her life. She told him how she had had to sleep on Griffin's floor most nights because Conner did not want to leave his studies, yet would not let her go home without him. She told him of the strange experience of watching the weathered old man she had met not long ago transform into the young adult who stayed up all hours of the night to study with Conner. "Does their magic give them some strange ability to never sleep?"

"I wouldn't think so, but I have noticed that human magic users seem to get bored with the idea of sleeping as they get older. I don't think I've ever met a human more than a couple of hundred years old that actually sleeps as much as you or I do."

Finally, after several more minutes of stories of Griffin's tea and Conner's near silent behavior, she reached the events of the morning, explaining the plan for Dagmar to travel to Belmopan and learn to enchant fabric from which they would make her a new set of clothes.

"That seems an odd choice," he remarked, *"you would be required to wear the same thing every day. I would expect they would make something slightly less limiting."*

"Maybe we can talk them into making me a cloak instead. I could wear a cloak every day without having to worry about washing it nearly as often and it would not be nearly so restrictive." She smiled. "It would be a bit ironic that I refused the cloak that Briganti offered me to represent my magic, only to replace it with one that suppresses it."

"That would be quite fun," he chuckled, *"and if you found yourself in an emergency where you needed to use your magic, you could simply shed your cloak without any worry of immodesty."*

She could just imagine herself in Tallen's castle again, the captain approaching her threateningly only for her to calmly undo her cloak's fastening, dropping it to the ground a moment before he was thrown at the wall behind him. She would wait until she was satisfied he would stay down and then silently bend down to retrieve her cloak, refastening it without so much as a stray glance at the prone captain. "That could make for some interesting situations."

"It does surprise me, though, that Dagmar volunteered to leave the group. He really must care for you even more than I realized."

"I should talk to him about Tallen; he knows all about loving someone he's suspicious of." He had certainly shown her more grace in her continual deception than she felt she was capable of offering to Tallen. "I wonder what made him welcome me even when he knew I was lying to you all."

"Dagmar has always been the brother that I have the least in common with; I've always been too trusting and he's always been too suspicious, I've been energetic and rambunctious while he's quiet and reserved, I've struggled with forgiveness while he's struggled with trust." He lifted his head suddenly and stared at his doorway. *"I think you could gain quite a lot from talking to Dagmar."*

"Byron wants to see everybody in his room," Grezald's voice interrupted their conversation. Snarf simply nodded and stood, pausing long enough for Aleisha to exit before him. *"Hey, Aleisha, I thought Conner was still in the office."*

"He is as far as I know. I convinced him to leave me with Snarf this morning."

"He must be pretty confident that Tallen has backed off then. Last I saw him, he was still saying that he wouldn't trust anyone but himself with your safety." Grezald led them down the hallway, bouncing cheerfully as he walked and swinging his tail at Snarf as they rounded each corner. Snarf managed to dodge most of the time, only getting hit once as they rounded the last corner and Grezald nearly whipped him in the

side of the head, turning afterwards to offer a mischievous smile.

Snarf responded to his older brother's play with an exaggerated sigh, *"Remember, Aleisha, maturity does not always come with age. One must strive to leave the folly of their childhood behind them, lest it follow them into their old age."* He must not have realized how close they were to Byron's room, as Grezald, snickering at Snarf's feigned dignity, called for Grizwald's assistance moments before both orange dragons pounced on Snarf even as he finished speaking.

Chapter 29

Grizwald suddenly launched himself from a sitting position and flew out of Byron's room. For a moment, Byron, Dagmar, and Conner looked at each other in confusion, but at Snarf's sudden yelp of surprise, they each returned to their previous activities. Conner was looking at a map of Elbot, helping Byron find the most direct route from Might City, Ephriat to Sprino, Belmopan.

Aleisha appeared through the doorway, laughing as she found her way to his side. "Snarf and the twins are wrestling. I don't think Grizwald even knows why; he's just there because Grezald called him." She sat down next to him and glanced at the map in front of him.

"Those guys are crazy." He was glad to see her smiling again; even Dagmar had commented on her mood the other day and they were all becoming more concerned each day.

"If you three will get in here, we have some news to share with you," Byron's usually patient voice betrayed just the slightest irritation. All three of the youngest dragons immediately entered the room silently with heads bowed and tails dragging behind them. *"Thank you. Conner and Griffin found an account of an enchantment being used to restrain a magician's power and would very much like to learn more about this enchantment, perhaps even toward the possibility of adapting it for the purpose of helping Aleisha better control her magic.*

"The largest obstacle is that the dragon who developed this enchantment lives in Belmopan, and, with the quickly approaching winter, we simply cannot risk the trip with Conner and Aleisha accompanying us. So, since Dagmar and I are the most experienced in enchantments, we have decided that it would be best for one of us to make the trip to Belmopan, learn all that we can from this dragon, and return to design a cloak for Aleisha that will, hopefully, restrain her power." Grezald and Grizwald looked panicked at the news, but Snarf hardly responded at all. Aleisha must have already told him of their plans. *"Dagmar has volunteered to be the one to go, but I would be much more comfortable with this arrangement if one of you would go with him. I cannot, as I am the strongest among us and need to remain here on the possibility that Tallen returns."*

"I will go with him," Grizwald did not hesitate. *"When will we be leaving?"*

"Let me go too, then," Grezald piped up before Dagmar had a chance to reply, *"If Grizwald is going, I am too."*

"No Grezald, we need you here." At the sight of the younger dragon's panic, Byron shook his head slowly. *"Aleisha is our first priority; we can spare two of us to chase down this information, but it would be unwise to dwindle our numbers too far, lest Tallen should grow bold."*

Grezald looked to his twin with the tears welling at the corners of his wide eyes. Grizwald must have said something quite touching right then, because Aleisha gasped as her hands flew to her face to wipe her own tears before dashing to hug him. Grezald finally lowered his head and nodded, apparently resigning himself to the idea of being away from his twin for the first time, as far as Conner knew, since birth.

Grizwald, his own brave expression wavering, nodded to Dagmar to continue. *"We should leave as soon as possible, so that we can return quickly,"* Dagmar spoke gently to his little brother, *"We are working on plotting the most efficient course. After we are done, I think we should head straight out."*

"Before you go" - Aleisha shot a worried look at Snarf, who nodded - "Before you go, I was wondering if we could take a flight around the city."

After a moment's pause, Dagmar stood and walked to the landing platform, Aleisha only a few steps behind him. "Is she alright?" Snarf only nodded again but he looked rather troubled.

"As we mentioned earlier, Dagmar will be trying to learn how to enchant a cloak for Aleisha to wear to aid her in controlling her magic. We do not know, however, whether he will need the fabric or the materials with which to make the fabric, so while they are gone, we can busy ourselves with collecting the materials needed for each likely scenario." Byron spoke with no emotion, giving direction in a detached monotone.

"What kind of materials are we looking for?" He hadn't considered the need to enchant the very fabric they used to make the cloak. "Are some materials better suited to enchantment than others?"

"Dragonsilk would give the greatest chance of success." Byron, Grezald, and Grizwald all stared at Snarf in horror, *"Considering that she is the most powerful Darksoul on all of Elbot; it only makes sense that we should begin with our best option. I would gladly offer my own fur for the sake of Aleisha's cloak."*

Conner had never heard of a dragon making such an offer. If not for the firm set of his enormous jaw, he wouldn't have been sure he had heard him right.

"Snarf," it was a strange thing, indeed, to hear Byron in awe, *"What you are offering, you will not be able to fly for months."*

"Then we should harvest the materials as soon as possible so that we will be able to leave as soon as winter is up. I'm quite certain that Aleisha will not wish to remain here long after that."

At that moment, Dagmar and Aleisha reentered through the outside doorway, Aleisha looking quite shaken and Dagmar appearing deeply saddened. *"I think,"* he sounded as if he had aged centuries in the brief minutes he'd been gone. *"Grizwald and I should leave immediately. If we stop to rest when we reach the ocean, we should be able to fly straight across without much trouble. That way, we can get to Belmopan as quickly as possible, and, hopefully, return before the winter is up."* All eyes fell on Aleisha. What had they talked about? Why did she

Darksoul

look so sad? Was that black fog forming around her hem?

Three days had passed since Dagmar and Grizwald had left, and Conner had barely seen Aleisha. He knew where she was, of course, and could hear her crying in her bedroom upstairs, but she would not open the door for him.

As far as he knew, Snarf had not yet told her that they would be making her cloak from his fur, so he did not think that that was the cause of her distress, in fact, he was pretty sure that whatever she was crying over was what she and Dagmar had spoken about before he left. Oh, how he wished she would just talk to him. How he longed to comfort her concerning whatever turmoil was causing such grief.

"Conner?" He nearly leapt from his chair at the sound of her voice. "I need to ask your help." She still looked like she was ready to dissolve into tears at any moment, but at least she was out of her room.

"Anything, what do you need?"

"I need to go to Tallen's castle." That was, perhaps, the last thing he would ever have expected her to say. "He has asked for my forgiveness, and I need-" she took a deep breath before continuing. "I need your help to face him. I'm so afraid, Conner."

He couldn't believe what he was hearing. Tallen had apologized? He had humbled himself enough to seek forgiveness? If it hadn't been Aleisha making such claims, he would think that he was being lied to.

"Leish." He had watched her struggle with anger since he had met her. He was amazed that the same girl he had chastened less than a year ago for burning down Briganti's room while he was still inside was the same woman who was now ready to offer forgiveness to the man who she had so often said that she hated. "Leish, I'm so proud of you."

That did it. A powerful gust of wind blasted from where she stood as she choked out a hard sob. The fire in the hearth vanished and the book he'd been trying to read flew off the table, which toppled over moments later. Even as the room darkened, he could see Aleisha finally lose her battle against her tears as another sob broke through the otherwise silent room. He hurried over to her, grasping her shoulders to keep her focus on him. "I'm so proud of you," he repeated.

"I am so scared."

"I know." She squeezed her eyes shut, gasping uncontrollably as she tried to slow her breathing. "I'll be right beside you. I'm not leaving you, Leish."

Opening her eyes, she stepped away from him. "We should leave now, then. I've put this off long enough." She marched to the front door, stopping only long enough for him to catch up and help her with her cloak. He wasn't sure if he'd ever walked so quickly in his life as he did while trying to keep up with Aleisha on her way to the library; she seemed determined to get this whole thing over with before she lost her nerve.

Darksoul

She didn't enter the library, as he had expected, but rather walked around the edge of the building until they came to a patch of grass about the same size as the landing platforms all up the outside of the building. Moments after they entered the grassy area, Snarf landed in front of them. Aleisha wordlessly climbed onto Snarf's back, sitting just far enough forward to leave room for Conner to join her. This must have been why Snarf said he wasn't ready for him to shave his wings yet; he'd already known Aleisha's plans.

Chapter 30

Aleisha was done feeling. She couldn't afford to feel anything if she was going to see Tallen. Anything other than stoicism would likely result in someone being badly hurt, and she couldn't let that happen, not now that Conner had said that he was proud of her. Not now that Dagmar and Grizwald were risking their safety and comfort by flying hundreds of miles to seek out an answer that none of them knew for sure would work.

Conner being beside her would help. She knew that if she began to lose control, he would grab her hand, whisper instructions, or place himself between her and Tallen, whatever he felt was necessary to help her stay focused.

The castle was so very much closer to Might City than she had realized. Though, she had gone by horse last time she made this trip and she had been only just learning how to stay on Soulfire's back. Memories of her nightly sparring matches with her magical foe flashed through her mind; how she suddenly wished she'd stopped to grab the sword Elam had given her. *"I'm afraid that I can't come in with you, Aleisha, but I will be just a cry away. If you need me, I will either find or make a way to get to you."* Snarf landed just outside of the castle walls, drawing terrified looks from the guards.

"Thank you." Conner helped her down from Snarf's back and grabbed her hand, taking a protective stance beside her as they approached the castle.

Darksoul

On the drawbridge stood a lone guard glaring purposefully at Snarf, "What business do you have here?"

"We seek an audience with Tallen." He appeared to be ready to deny them entrance; she supposed arriving on a dragon raised understandable suspicion. "I am his daughter; he'll want to see me." She hoped being honest with him was a wise decision, but, if not for Conner standing by her, she would have found another way in.

The guard raised one hand over his head, motioning to someone on the wall. "Tallen doesn't have any children." Several more guards appeared in the gatehouse behind him, weapons drawn. Perhaps the truth wasn't the best idea.

"Is Captain Darek Moore available? He can verify my claim." Conner had taken an aggressive stance; she had to get the situation under control before one of them attacked.

"Do you need me, Aleisha?" Even Snarf was preparing to strike now. Perhaps they should not have come.

"Ah, Alencia, I was beginning to worry that you had forgotten to return." The captain pushed through the crowd of armed men, stopping directly in front of her. "You said that you would return in weeks. It's been months."

"I'm here now, so take me to my father." He made no move to obey. "Before things get ugly again, Captain."

That worked. Captain Moore had witnessed her choke one of his men with nearly to death with her magic last time she'd been here, so he would not dare defy her. Moving aside, he instructed his men to let her through. "I'll inform your father of your return, Alencia." With that, he scurried away.

"Alencia?" Conner, following close behind her, whispered in confusion.

"Apparently, Tallen wanted to name me Alencia, after his sister, but my mother always called me Aleisha." The bailey was busy with activity as men and women, carrying packages and rolling barrels, hurried from building to building.

When they reached the front steps of the keep, Aleisha stopped. From the two large wooden doors, the stairway fanned out as it descended until it ran the entire width of the building at the base. This was where she was forced into Cedrick's wagon so long ago. She stood in this very same spot the last time she had seen her mother. "Leish" - Conner grabbed hold of her hand again - "It's ok. I'm here."

The men at the top of the stairs holding the doors open for them looked at each other in confusion, wondering, no doubt, why they just stood at the bottom of the steps. Sighing, she lifted her chin defiantly and marched up the steps. Tallen would not intimidate her any more.

The great hall was exactly as she remembered it; exactly as it had been in the replica she had made in the Kotash Sea. As she stepped through the doorway, she heard one of the guards gasp and crash into the door. Taking another step into the keep, she saw a young girl turn and run upon seeing them. "Leish, I know you're terrified, but you're scaring these people." She hadn't even noticed the black fog filling the space around her. "You need to try to calm down."

"I can't." She could see her father watching her with an unreadable expression from the other side of the hall. "I don't think I can do this." The air seemed to grow colder as it became nearly impossible to see through her ever-growing cloud of fog. People all around her were screaming in terror, and she could hear doors slamming and the heavy footfalls of armored men running away from her. She couldn't breathe through the fog.

"Aleisha!" Conner had somehow made his way in front of her and was grabbing hold of both of her shoulders. She was going to pass out. "You need to calm down. He cannot do anything to you as long as I am here."

"I'm here. Does she need me?" Snarf's voice reverberated through her consciousness. *"Of course,"* he must have been talking to Conner, *"Aleisha, we're still here; Conner and I will be with you the whole time, but you have to decide that you are going to be ok."*

She squeezed her eyes shut and tried to remember why she was here. She was following the Creator now, and if He said to forgive, surely He would help her do that. Conner and Snarf continued offering calming, reassuring words. Finally, she gasped, pulling precious air into her starving lungs. "Good, Leish, you're ok. You're ok." Opening her eyes, she continued taking in short, refreshing breaths.

Slowly, she took the black fog under her control until she could once again see Conner before her. Smiling, he reclaimed his place at her side. Once she could clearly see the room around her, she noted that she, Conner, and Tallen were the only people who remained in the great hall; everybody else had fled from her. Tallen looked decidedly worried as he watched her walk slowly forward, no longer holding her head quite so high.

"There are easier ways to be granted a private audience with me, Alen-" He shook his head in frustration, "I mean Aleisha."

"I've come to accept your apology." Tallen's mouth fell open at her declaration. "I've come to tell you that I" - she clenched her jaw, tears welling once more in her eyes - "that I forgive you." She hadn't thought that it would physically hurt to say those words to him.

"You-" he looked to Conner. "What? You would not let her lie to me." He turned back to her. "I never thought-" he stepped closer to them, his eyes wide with wonder and confusion, "I mean, I had hoped, but- Why?"

"I am following the Creator now; He says that I have to forgive you, so I will."

Again, he looked to Conner before turning back to her. "The Creator?" He smiled and shook his head, some of the confusion gone to be replaced with the colder expression she'd expected. "I should have known you were following Him when I learned with whom you were traveling." He continued walking toward them, any sign of doubt gone completely. "I suppose I should thank you, Conner, for teaching her the ways of your God; I'll never follow Him myself, but I always appreciate dealing with those who do."

"I wondered when she said that you'd sought forgiveness," Conner sounded perfectly polite, as if speaking to a businessman rather than an enemy, "what could have led you to do such a thing. I had almost dared to hope that you had changed your mind about the One True God."

"Even Darksouls are capable of benevolence occasionally," Tallen sneered at Conner. "There is nothing on this planet that I would not do for my daughter." He turned to look back at Aleisha. "I did not realize how badly I'd hurt you until I saw the look in your eyes when I said the wrong name; that is when I chose to apologize." Directing his gaze back at Conner, he added, "Only Aleisha could elicit such a response, though, so do not expect such behavior directed at you, dragon boy."

"As long as we understand each other." How was he so calm? Though Tallen had done horrible things to his family and even remained unrepentant, Conner's voice held no hint of anger or offence. In fact, he sounded almost amused.

"I must invite you both to stay for dinner." He backed up a step and clapped loudly. "After Dorcas died, I thought I'd lost any chance of my daughter living a long life, and now I learn not only that she has magic, but that I might have a relationship with her; it's more than I dared hope for." Suddenly, he seemed quite frustrated as he looked about the room. He clapped again and waited. "Cowering fools." lifting one hand toward a side door, he ripped it from its hinges, revealing a terrified guard cowering behind it. "You, go to the kitchen and have them prepare a feast. My daughter has come back to me!"

Chapter 31

Aleisha looked like she was ready to panic again. Tallen had called a half-dozen people into the great hall to give instructions on the grand feast he was preparing for them, despite the fact that they had never agreed to stay. "Bring in more coal; it's getting near winter and we don't want our guests to grow cold."

After the last servant ran from the hall, Tallen, smiling broadly, strode over to them. "You're both welcome to stay as long as you like; I would love to get to know you, my daughter, and I know that you would be more comfortable if the dragon boy was part of that process."

"We can't stay here." Conner had to give her credit, at least she looked like she was trying to be civil, even if she did look ready to bolt at a moment's notice. "The others will be worried if we don't return soon."

"Nonsense." Tallen didn't seem the slightest bit worried, "Conner would never leave the dragons without them having some sort of arrangement if he doesn't return. When they come to check on you two, we'll simply explain the situation. They can even land in my courtyard, if they like, to get a better sight of everything; make sure all is well and you're here of your own will, that sort of thing."

"I think that Aleisha and I should go speak to Snarf." Conner was of the opinion that they should accept the dinner invitation, but he refused to bring that up in front of Tallen, for fear of Aleisha feeling pressured.

"Of course, dinner won't be ready for a few hours, so you can head back to the library and talk to all of them if you like. Invite them to come too, if that would make Aleisha more comfortable."

"We'll do that then." Aleisha turned to glare at him, so he added, "If we don't return, we've refused your invitation."

"Oh, yes, of course." He looked devastated as he stared at Aleisha, as if he hadn't considered that they might refuse him. He didn't appear even the slightest bit angry, though, as he would have expected were he not sincere in his attitude toward Aleisha. That certainly helped Conner relax a bit.

The way back to the library was relatively quiet. Aleisha was too uncomfortable to carry on any sort of conversation, Snarf was so shocked by Tallen's response and offer that he was, for once, completely speechless, and Conner was replaying the entire scene over and over, looking for any hint of deception or manipulation on Tallen's part. The only small excitement came when Snarf, apparently still lost in thought, flew into the midst of a large flock of birds.

As soon as they landed on Byron's platform, both he and Grezald came out to greet them, *"How did it go?"* Byron had been just as impressed as Conner when Aleisha told him of her plan to visit Tallen, and was no doubt eager to hear that Tallen's repentance had been the result of his turning his life over to the Creator.

"He invited us to a feast that he's preparing in my honor," Aleisha looked extremely uncomfortable discussing the situation. "He said that Conner and I are welcome to stay in his castle so that he and I can get to know each other better. I'm not sure that I want to."

"I'm sure you know how impressed we all are that you even went to him, Aleisha," Snarf and Grezald both nodded vigorously at Byron's statement, *"but I would not be comfortable having you stay there, so far from our protection."*

"He did say that we could invite any or all of you to stay as well," Conner offered, climbing down from Snarf's back as he did. "He says that all he cares about is Aleisha's comfort."

"And do you believe him, Conner?" All eyes turned to him. Aleisha looked at him pleadingly, though he wasn't sure if she wanted a positive answer or a negative one. He suspected that she didn't know, either.

"Honestly, Byron, I don't know," he rubbed at his neck as he struggled to find the words to accurately relay his thoughts. "He certainly seemed sincere, and I detected no anger at all when I suggested that we may not return, but I know that he is a master deceiver and I realize that he may make me a fool." He sighed, frustrated and confused about the whole situation. "I personally think that you, Aleisha, and I should return. You are the most biased against him, so if you believe him, he is most likely genuine. I do not think, however, that Snarf or Grezald should come because Snarf has things to tend to and if Grezald were to arrive without Grizwald, Tallen would know that he was gone and, in the event that he is trying to manipulate us, I don't want him to know that our numbers are depleted."

"I would be ok with that if that's what Aleisha wants."

"I don't know what I want" - she slid from Snarf's back and began pacing - "I guess I want to know the truth. He said that he's been protecting me my entire life, and he knows things that suggest that he has been, but that's so contrary to my understanding of him. I just don't know what to believe."

"Then we should return." Byron turned his head toward the doorway, as if listening for something. *"Griffin is here, so I'll let him know that we will be gone. Are you ready Snarf?"*

"Yes!" Aleisha clearly had no idea what was going on; she looked from Byron to Snarf and back again, confusion playing across her face. Snarf had mentioned that he wanted her dragonsilk cloak to be a surprise, so it made sense how vague they were being.

"Good day to you all." Griffin burst through the doorway, grinning broadly. "Are we ready to-"

"Yes, quite ready. Lead the way," Snarf cut him off before he had an opportunity to blurt out their plans in front of Aleisha. *"I wish you good luck, Aleisha, and I truly hope that Tallen is all that he seems."* With that, Snarf, Grezald, and Griffin left to shave Snarf's wings.

"I suppose we should head out then." Byron knelt to allow them to climb onto his back. As soon as Aleisha was situated, Conner climbed on behind her, wrapping

his arms around her middle to keep her secure. *"We don't want to keep him waiting when he's prepared a feast for you."*

"Conner," Aleisha finally spoke when they neared Tallen's castle once again, "how long are we planning on staying?"

"Until either we have outstayed our welcome or you say you want to leave, whichever comes first." Byron nodded at Conner's answer. "You are why we are here, so you have the most say."

Byron began his descent into the courtyard, sending dozens of people scurrying away into various buildings, screaming in terror. At the sound of the commotion, the keep doors opened to reveal Tallen's tall form. He smiled in greeting, not the cruel, arrogant smile that he usually wore, but the welcoming, pleasant smile one would expect from a father greeting his daughter. "Just in time; the table is being set even now for your feast, Aleisha, and I have several servants making accommodations for all five of your dragon friends." He looked to Byron and frowned.

Conner, thinking that it may be dangerous to remain on Byron's back if Tallen said something foolish, climbed to the ground and reached to aid Aleisha in her own dismounting. The moment her feet touched the ground, Tallen moved forward only to stop at Byron's threatening growl.

To everyone's great surprise, Tallen knelt before the red dragon. Even hidden behind closed doors, the confused whispers of the castle residents filled the courtyard. "I accept that I deserve whatever revenge you seek, Byron," he stared at the ground as he spoke, "but I ask that you grant me pardon as I finally have more to live for than power and greed."

"I'll take that as an apology, or as close as he is capable of. Tell him that I will pardon him," Byron growled again, *"that I forgive him."* He, much like Aleisha had, sounded like he was gagging on the words.

"He accepts your apology." Tallen lifted his head, searching Byron's stone expression.

"Very well, I suppose I can sleep without worry now. Thank you, Byron." Standing, he turned to lead them into the keep. "Open them all the way, fool, you'll never have enough room for our dragon guest if you keep them half closed." A terrified guard hurried to the doors to push them open further in order to let Byron walk through.

The great hall had been transformed in the hours that they were gone from the cold, stern bareness that they had walked into earlier to a bustling banquet, servants rushing about to finish setting the table, lighting tall candles, and arranging pillows in five large makeshift seats for the five dragons. "I'm surprised, Byron, that none of your brothers came," Tallen, taking a seat at the head of the table, addressed Byron boldly.

"Tell him that I will not answer him, no matter how tiresome his attempts at conversation become."

"Our brothers don't have the patience Byron does; they would not so kindly ignore your rude attempts to get them to talk." Tallen glared, but did not respond.

"Very well, then I shall leave him in peace, since my conversation is so very offensive to him." His eyes darted to Aleisha. "I do hope that they don't keep you out; such an existence sounds dreadfully lonely."

"I have Conner to talk to, and I know that the dragons will do whatever they deem best in every situation, so I'm not offended by them," the skill with which she responded, deceiving but never lying, bothered Conner. She sounded like she had had a bit of practice manipulating the truth. Perhaps a skill she had picked up as a slave?

Grunting, Tallen lifted a goblet, "No matter, shall we begin?"

Chapter 32

Aleisha had never had to endure a more awkward meal in her life; neither Conner nor Tallen had taken their eyes off of her the entire time they were at the table. She wasn't sure which was worse; Conner watching her with a worried expression, as if he thought she might collapse if he took his gaze from her, or Tallen staring at her as if she were some rare artifact to be put on display.

She had simply sat there, trying to ignore both men as they spoke threats barely veiled by their forced politeness. Only Byron had had anything interesting to say, and spent most of the meal trying to distract her from the two men trying to lay claim to her. *"Conner is simply protective of you,"* he had said at least a dozen times over the course of the meal. *"I've never seen him so possessive,"* he added the last time he said it, *"at least not since Alice died."* After that statement, he'd grown silent, refusing to discuss the matter further.

Now, she sat with her back to the wall of the room Tallen had had prepared for her, listening to Conner, who sat on the other side of the wall, telling a story about an old magician who had started to build a castle very similar to this one, only to run out of money halfway through. "He wasn't a very talented magician, so he couldn't build it himself, and the workers he had hired kept raising their prices because they thought that magic users had unlimited resources," he stopped to chuckle at that. "He ended up chasing them all away and shutting himself up in his half-finished castle for the rest of his life, refusing to see anyone ever again because he had so thoroughly lost respect for his fellow humans."

"Why would you tell me that? That's such a sad story," he laughed at her distress.

"I was trying to make a point."

"I can't imagine what it was supposed to be" - she heard him sigh through the thick wall - "You shouldn't trust builders?"

"No," he laughed again, "you can't depend on your magic to fix all of your problems." She wondered what she'd done to make him think that he needed to tell her that. "Too many magic users forget how to use their hands or their minds. They become less than they could be for their laziness and complacency. I want to see you succeed in every possible way, Leish, and I want you to know that I'll be right here with you, cheering you on, encouraging you, and never, ever letting you cheat yourself by taking careless shortcuts."

"Thank you, Conner." There was a knock on her door. She heard Conner jump up and hurry to his own.

"Conner," she heard Tallen's voice just outside the room, "I suppose I should have realized that you would not let me see my own daughter." His voice carried the usual frustrated tone that it did when speaking to Conner.

"You can certainly ask her if she wants to speak with you, but I assure you, I will not allow you to trouble her." Again, he knocked.

She supposed she could not ignore him forever. She opened the door but stood squarely in the middle of the doorway to keep him from pushing past her into the room. "May I speak with you privately, Aleisha?" He spoke formally, intimidated by Conner's unwavering glare, most likely.

She nodded and pulled the door slightly more open, letting him in. With a nervous glance at Conner, she followed him into her room and closed the door behind her. "What do you want?" He had made his way to her fireplace and was playing with the flames, making them shoot out at odd angles as he smirked at them.

"I have worried about you since the day your mother told me she was pregnant with you, Aleisha; it is the natural way of a parent." He turned to face her squarely, returning the flames to their former state. "I wonder, why does Conner, the chosen babe of Philimina, trust you, a Darksoul?" He stepped closer to her, watching her with a strange expression. "You look troubled; did he not tell you who his Dictator was?"

"I knew." She did, however, wonder how Tallen knew. Didn't Conner say that he didn't like to advertise his heritage? Perhaps he had met Tallen before Philimina betrayed him.

"I'm surprised. Usually Conner is rather tight-lipped about the subject. Quite truthfully, I was shocked to see him claim his true form in front of you; I had been of the understanding that he didn't like telling anyone even that he has soul power, much less who his Dictator is." She wasn't sure where he intended to go with this line of conversation, but she wished he would get on with it. "Or did you figure it out on your own? You do seem an intelligent girl, you must have deduced his background; surely he would never have told you willingly."

"Why do you care how I know his past? It's really not any of your business what he has and hasn't told me."

"I see I've touched a sore spot in your relationship," he shook his head, sighing, "I had hoped that I was wrong, of course, but I suspected that Conner had been no more forthcoming with you than he had been with Alice."

"What do you mean?" Why was he bringing her up? Why did he even know about her?

"Has Conner ever actually told you anything about himself, or have you had to figure everything out on your own?" Her face must have shown her hurt, because Tallen frowned sympathetically. "Oh, Aleisha, I know that you've not had many friends in your short life, but you really should hold higher standards for those you surround yourself with; you deserve better than a man whom you cannot trust."

"I do trust him." His predictable manipulation was making it difficult for her to keep an even tone. The fact that it was working, that her every question concerning Conner seemed to be rushing to the front of her mind, infuriated her further.

"Even through the lies and omissions?" Tallen shook his head, wide eyed. "I appreciate your kindness, Aleisha; I have benefited from it myself in your returning to me, and I know that I do not hold any authority over you, but I cannot stand by silently and watch his abuse of your trust. I must, at minimum, voice my concern and ask that you examine your relationship with this man. Ask yourself if you truly do benefit from knowing him. Ask yourself if that benefit outweighs the secrets and manipulation."

"You are right." His mouth twitched into the slightest of smiles. "You do not have any authority over me. How dare you call into question Conner's motivation while you stand here manipulating me as you accuse him of doing? I know very well that Conner does not share his past, and I have been frustrated on more than one occasion upon realizing some important detail that he neglected to share with me. I have seen him play the emotions of those who might hold information which he seeks, and I have no doubt he has, to some extent, done the same thing to me." As she continued to speak, the flames behind Tallen flickered violently, responding to her memory of the day she learned of Conner's Dictator.

"My trust in him does not depend on his sharing of every detail with me. Could it really be called trust if I demanded to know everything before I believed him?" Tallen opened his mouth, eager to answer. "No! My trust in Conner is not based on his honesty or his openness; otherwise, I would not trust him at all. I trust Conner because I know that he loves me. I know that there is nothing on the whole of Elbot that he values over me, so I know that, whatever secrets he may keep, everything that he does concerning me is for my good, and so I trust that he will never hurt or harm me because he values me too highly to deal carelessly with me."

"How can you say such foolish things?" Tallen threw his arms up in frustration and claimed the chair near the fire, leveling a glare at her as he did. "With all his lies, with all his manipulation, how do you know that he's not just using you for his own gain? Believe me, Aleisha, when your interests conflict with his own, he will abandon you."

"Do you think that it is in his interest to be here? He would like nothing more than to never have to be in your presence again; it is for my sake that he endures your taunting." He did not look convinced, so she tried again. "He defended me to Dagmar when he tried to have me sent away from the group, he came after me after I lied to him and offered both forgiveness for my actions and repentance for his own wrong response, he even defended me to Briganti, my own Dictator, when he threatened my life for not conforming to his will." The fire exploded from the hearth, catching the edge of Tallen's cape on fire as he leapt from his chair.

"He what?" the floor around Tallen's feet cracked in a splintering pattern as Tallen roared. At the murderous look in his eyes, Aleisha fell silent, suddenly too afraid of his rage-fed magic to respond.

The door suddenly flew open a moment before Conner was between them. "It's time for you to leave, Tallen." Much to her surprise, he nodded and left without another word, his cape still smoldering, leaving a black trail behind him as he left.

"I mentioned Briganti's threat. I shouldn't have done that." Conner turned and reached for her hands, offering the comfort of his touch as he so often did.

"That was, perhaps, unwise," he nodded.

"His magic manifests itself like mine," she nodded to the floor, where it looked as if a large boulder had been dropped where Tallen had been standing.

"Yes," he frowned, "that is odd." He looked away from her for a moment.

"Yes," Byron replied to whatever Conner just said, *"he appears to be heading to the dungeon. Would you like me to stop him?"* He paused, *"Alright then, even if you're asleep?"*

Conner sighed and rubbed his eyes. "You should try to get some rest, Leish. I'll be right through that wall if you need me." He pointed toward his room. Once she nodded, he turned to exit, leaving her alone with her confusion.

Tallen was every bit as manipulative as she'd expected him to be, but somehow, through his accusations and assumptions, he seemed perfectly sincere in his concern for her. Was that, too, manipulation?

Chapter 33

Conner paced slowly in his room, waiting for Aleisha to wake up. Byron had woken him up nearly two hours ago to tell him that Tallen had exited the dungeon and was headed back up the stairs. Conner had tried to speak to him when he arrived at their level, but Tallen had simply said that he was going to bed and staggered past him, leaving the scent of smoke behind him.

Hearing the explosion last night in Aleisha's room convinced Conner that, even if he was perfectly sincere and meant no harm to Aleisha, she would not be safe being alone with him. It did, however, also convince him that Tallen must be at least partially sincere in his affection for Aleisha since news of her safety being threatened sent him into such an emotional state.

Finally, he heard her stirring in the next room, stumbling about as she slowly awoke. He chuckled and wondered, as he had many times in the past, how she had survived as a slave in the house of a cruel master if she could not wake up early, clear of mind and ready to serve.

"Tallen has returned to the great hall," the noises from Aleisha's room ceased as Byron spoke.

"Thank you, Byron. Aleisha just woke up, so we should be down there soon."

"Conner?" she was apparently standing immediately on the opposite side of the wall, as her voice came though clearly, or as clearly as it ever did upon waking. "What if he's still angry about last night?" She sounded more concerned than scared, surprising him with her care for the man whom she'd hated for so long.

"We'll deal with that when the time comes. For now, we should just head down to get some breakfast; I know you must be hungry."

"Ugh, why don't you have to deal with normal bodily functions?" He heard her hit the wall with something as she moaned, "You don't eat, you don't sleep, do you even have to go to the bathroom?"

"That is a very personal question, Aleisha," he chuckled at her obvious annoyance. "And I do eat and sleep, just not as much as some people."

She mumbled something in response as he pushed away from the wall, making his way to the door. He only had to wait a few moments before Aleisha opened her door and, carefully unbraiding her messy hair, claimed her place next to him. Tallen was already seated by the time they arrived in the great hall and was surveying the food with distaste. "Ah, Aleisha." He nearly jumped out of his seat when he finally noticed them. "So good to see you up. Did you sleep well, my dear?" Aleisha barely grunted and moved closer to Conner, clearly too sleepy to attempt anything more yet. "And Conner, welcome. I do hope you'll pardon my behavior last night; I was in a rather foul mood I'm afraid." He nodded. He understood, of course, how angry Tallen had been at the news of Briganti's threat, but he did not trust him to respond properly, especially considering how poorly he had responded himself. "Well, since no one is feeling chatty, let's eat. It's not what I requested, but it should still be eatable, at least." With a disgusted glance at the plate of steaming scones, he reclaimed his seat.

"Thank you, Tallen. It looks delicious." Conner had always enjoyed a good scone. Pulling a chair out for Aleisha, he helped her into her seat before claiming the one next to her.

"So, what are you doing in Might City?" Tallen selected one of the scones at the base of the pile, inspecting it closely before grunting and biting into it. "You've hardly left the library. Please don't tell me you're training her with books, Conner, the best way to learn is by doing."

"Perhaps, but we've had limited success with her training, as I've never taught a magic user before and we obviously don't want her Dictator involved." He took a sip from the cup before him, carefully choosing his next words, "So, while we are limited in the hands-on lessons, she is learning a great deal from the resources in the Great Library."

"Have you considered the guild? Or perhaps finding another Dictator to teach her? I'm sure Flanen, my Dictator, would be happy to be involved with my daughter's training." Aleisha shook her head vigorously at Tallen's suggestion, holding a hand up to her full mouth and urgently mumbling something unintelligible through the food.

"I don't think she would trust anyone else to train her at this point." he smirked at Tallen's raised eyebrow. "One can only endure so much betrayal before they lose the ability to trust."

"Well then, I won't bother offering my own assistance," somehow, he managed to keep any offence out of his voice or expression. One could almost believe that he was entirely sincere in his interest in Aleisha's wellbeing, almost, if not for centuries of deceit and manipulation.

"Do you have a library?" Aleisha, who had finally emptied her mouth, seemed entirely oblivious to the current direction of the conversation.

"Library?" Tallen laughed, "Why ever would I need a library? I live but a short distance from the most complete library in all of Elbot."

"I was just hoping," she paused, "Well, I've always enjoyed reading, so I was hoping that you had some books available."

"Perhaps I can interest you instead in a tour of my castle; we have so very much to talk about before I leave in a week." Tallen grinned and took a long drink.

"You're leaving?" Conner hoped that he didn't sound as suspicious as he was.

"Yes, well I didn't expect any visitors, so I'll have to ask that you excuse me while I tend to some important matters," he appeared all business as he spoke, but something very dark played in his eyes. "I realize that you will be eternally suspicious of me, Conner, but I must ask that you allow me some level of privacy, as I have been accustomed to sharing nothing with anyone until yesterday."

The rest of the meal passed uneventfully, as everyone seemed rather uncomfortable in each other's presence. At one point, Tallen tried to speak with Byron and was met with an angry growl and another warning that he would receive no response; that ended any attempts at conversation for the remainder of the meal.

Aleisha was the last of them still working on her breakfast. She seemed to be taking a huge amount of time chewing each bite as her mind apparently wandered. As soon as her empty cup touched the table, Tallen sprang from his seat, clapping his hands excitedly. "Come, let me show you my home." He ushered them out of their seats and toward the stairs. "There is so much that you haven't seen yet."

Aleisha climbed the stairs confidently, more familiar with her surroundings than Tallen could have anticipated. As Conner moved to follow her, Tallen grasped his arm, stopping him. "Aleisha told me that you defended her from her Dictator," he spoke quietly, so as not to allow Aleisha to hear, "I want you to know that I appreciate that. She is the only thing that matters to me and I can respect anyone who sees her true value as I do." With that, he released him and hurried up the stairs to Aleisha, motioning grandly at various art pieces displayed in the hall.

All three of them walked the entirety of the keep together, Aleisha staring in wonder at each grand room, Tallen boasting splendidly about every expensive and rare artifact, and Conner following closely, unimpressed by the overindulgence and lack of originality. Conner had been in dozens of castles over the three and a half centuries he had traveled the three continents of Elbot and nearly all of them had the same basic layout as this one: the ground floor housed a great hall and some storage rooms, the second floor had guestrooms and a chapel, though Tallen's chapel didn't look to get much use, and the third floor made up Tallen's personal chambers.

"I designed this entire floor personally," he gestured proudly at their surroundings. "The sitting area, especially, is quite grand, don't you think?" Indeed it was; the polished stone walls were covered in paintings and tapestries of the most intricate design. Several pillars were set up around the room, displaying books and vases from around Ephriat and Belmopan. In one corner stood an elegant shrine with the image of a young girl carved into the stone face, a silk cloth draped over the sides of it, and several letters piled on top.

"Is that me?" Aleisha walked toward the shrine and reached out to touch the girl's face. Now that he looked closer, the girl did hold a striking resemblance to Aleisha.

"It is," Tallen's voice sounded wistful and reminiscent as he watched his daughter finger the stack of letters, "I told you that I never abandoned you. I made sure to keep close attention so that I could protect you from any danger Cedrick might put you in." Aleisha sat in front of the shrine, her back to them, and stared, unmoving, at the evidence of Tallen's story.

"I thought that you didn't care," when she finally spoke, she sounded like she was choking. "I thought that you saw me as no more than cattle to be bred and sold at a profit."

"No, Aleisha, you are my daughter." He moved to join her, but Conner put a hand on his shoulder, stopping him, and shook his head; Aleisha did not need his comforting touch yet, she would not welcome him yet. "I was cruel, I was manipulative, but I have always adored you. You are the only thing I have ever held at higher value than myself."

She stood and turned toward them, tears still wet on her cheeks. "Thank you for showing me this. I didn't believe you before," and with that, the tears stopped. Conner could see a change in her expression, invisible to anyone who did not know her well, surely unnoticed by Tallen. The terrified, exhausted, angry expression that she had worn constantly since he'd found her at Puko just a few months ago was gone. She didn't look happy, but she finally looked calm.

Chapter 34

Aleisha woke as she always did, with her braid wrapped around her neck, the sound of Conner pacing in the next room waiting for her to wake up, and dozens of feet scurrying about downstairs as Tallen's ever-present rarely-seen servants worked tirelessly to prepare a delicious meal that he would find disgusting.

She'd grown used to this new normal over the past few days, though she remained irreversibly uncomfortable being waited on. Untangling herself from her hair, she rolled out of bed and stumbled over to the wall separating her from Conner. "Morning," even trying as hard as she had to sound normal, her greeting still came out sounding very much as if she'd been being strangled as she attempted to speak.

"Good morning, Leish. Did you sleep well?" Conner, on the other hand, always sounded like he was laughing at her in the morning, probably because he was.

"I'm hungry." She heard him chuckle, confirming her suspicion.

"Of course you are. I'll come get you and we can go find some food." She tried to hurry to her bed to retrieve her dress, which she'd dropped on the floor while preparing for bed last night, but she wasn't quite as coordinated in the morning as she normally was and somehow managed to trip on a crack in the floor and landed with a loud thud several feet from her bed.

"Are you ok, Leish?" Conner knocked urgently on her door at the sound of her clumsiness; she only managed to moan, but he seemed to understand and waited patiently for her to get dressed and comb out her braid before opening the door for him. "In the future, you may want to refrain from any sort of dexterous activity this early in the morning." He grinned at her as she attempted to push past him to get to the hallway and the scent of food.

"You were waiting for me; I was trying to get ready quickly."

"You were the one who was hungry," he chuckled again, apparently in a good mood this morning. "I don't care how long it takes you to get ready for breakfast." He offered his arm and helped her down the stairs, bringing her into the great hall and to the table spread with steaming bread and several jars of various jams.

"Good morning," Tallen, too, seemed in an unusually good mood as he greeted them with a smile, not even pausing to glare at Conner as he normally did. "The incompetent cook finally managed to prepare exactly what I demanded this morning; this is sure to be a good day." He motioned enthusiastically at their seats, impatient for them to sit down so that he could enjoy his breakfast. "Tell me, Aleisha, what is your favorite jam?"

She shrugged, moaning slightly more loudly than intended; she'd never had jam before, Cedrick didn't allow the slaves into the fruit.

"No matter, I'm sure you will find them all delicious." He reached for a large roll and a jar of strawberry jam. "I was thinking that today we could all visit in the sitting room upstairs. The last few days have been so busy and full of distractions and we can have some privacy on my floor."

"Thank you, that's a very kind offer," Conner replied for her, as he had taken to doing for the first hours after they got up; Tallen had seemed offended by him at first, but quickly realized that she was not good at communicating this early.

Tallen shrugged and went about enjoying his morning meal, sighing contentedly as he bit into various slabs of bread covered in several kinds of jams. Aleisha ate more slowly, taking the same time on her one slice of bread as Tallen did on three of his.

"How is the Darksoul this morning?" Byron's voice was not clear enough for her to be confident that he had meant his question for her, but she could not tell from Conner's face whether or not he had answered him. *"I see. Well, I suppose we cannot complain about that."* Apparently he had.

"Come, I'll have the cook prepare some mulled wine for us; I know how certain members of our party do not handle the cold." Tallen smirked at Conner, who rolled his eyes and pushed the chair out to stand.

"Actually, Byron and I have some things we need to discuss, so I will have to join you in about an hour or so," with that, he nodded to Aleisha and marched out of the room, heading to the rear courtyard to meet Byron.

Aleisha supposed that she had no way of avoiding spending the morning with Tallen. Swallowing the last bit of her breakfast, she, too, pushed out her chair to stand, following Tallen as he led the way to the third-floor sitting area.

"It was good of him to give us a few moments alone," he appeared almost confused as he pulled his eyebrows together as he spoke. "I suppose he has finally come to realize that he cannot keep you from me forever. After all, I am your father; I have rights." He ended with his usual haughty expression, destroying any favor he might have earned.

"Rights?" How dare he attempt to make such a claim, after everything he had done. "Rights?" He honestly appeared bewildered by her offence. "If you had ever had any rights you would have forfeited them when you sold me to Cedrick. You have no right to me."

"Now, Aleisha, I know that you cannot truly believe that," he spoke to her as if she were a small child he was reprimanding. "We both know that you would not have remained here so long in your obvious distaste for all things affiliated with me unless you realized that I had some right to you. Now, I would like to take that right and grow it into more of a privilege. I want you to be here because you desire to know your father rather than because you feel you have no choice."

"I am here because the Creator says that I have to forgive you, not because I think you somehow deserve anything other than my scorn and Byron's revenge."

She could feel her magic already trying to take action based on her emotions, an even more difficult reflex to smother this early in the morning. "And if you ever truly wanted me to desire a relationship of any kind with you, you would stop attempting to prove your devotion to me with blood. I hate that you justify murder by saying that it somehow benefited me. I am not a monster like you."

"Every creature that I have killed since learning of your conception has been for your benefit; your refusal to believe that does not nullify its validity." He snarled, but seemed to catch himself and took a deep breath, responding more calmly when he spoke again, "I have explained my actions to you once already, Aleisha. I do not feel that I should have to do so again. Gabriel had to die in order for you to have long life while I urged your mother to give me the elixir, Lorahlie was an unfortunate casualty when her magic seemed to make Gabriel's death a vain effort, and your mother had to die for refusing to grant immortality to her own child." He threw his arms up and paced in front of the fireplace, grumbling, "I am only trying to be a good father to you and you will not allow me even the courtesy of telling me why my actions offend you; most people would be honored that I went to such great lengths for them."

"No, they would not," she scoffed. Could he truly believe that? Was this his honest view of the world? Was he so warped by his magic, or had he been taught to think this way? "Most people serve the people they love, not sell them into slavery, kill their mother, and threaten their friends."

"Stop telling me what I'm doing wrong," he had never shouted at her before, but now he stood panting in front of the flames, the black smoke of his true form beginning to form about his body as he apparently struggled to control his magic. "Tell me what I should be doing. Tell me how you want to be loved, not how you don't."

What could she say to that? He looked almost desperate; he looked like a man who always knew what to do but found himself at a loss. But what could she say? She could describe for him all day what love was not, she could explain all the ways he had failed and describe a thousand ways he had hurt her, but how could she say what she wanted? She didn't really know what she wanted. She wanted a father. She had no idea what that meant. "Ask Conner; he knows how to love."

"Conner," he nearly spat his name, "of course you would direct me to him." He sighed and turned away from her, his smoky cloak swirling gently as he did. "He would know how to love you, wouldn't he?" She almost didn't hear him for his whispering.

"He's the one who first treated me like a human rather than a commodity, he's the one who first protected me rather than threatening me, he was the first person who ever took the time to teach me anything that would benefit me more than him. He can tell you anything you need to know about sacrificial love," he didn't look like he was still listening, but she suspected that he was. After all, for all of his shortcomings, even Conner believed that Tallen's affection for her was sincere. "Perhaps, if you ask him, he can even teach you how to be a father."

Chapter 35

Conner had no idea what he had missed while he was outside, but both Aleisha and Tallen seemed to be in strange moods today. When he'd finally made it up to the sitting room, Tallen looked to him with an almost pleading expression before scurrying out of the room, leaving him alone with Aleisha for a few minutes before eventually returning.

Whatever had transpired had apparently brought them to some sort of mutual understanding, for, upon his return, today was finally the first time Tallen had entered the sitting room without Aleisha glaring at him. She'd looked up, of course, had acknowledged his presence, but she'd been down-right civil, almost pleasant as he took a seat across the room from them.

Now, Conner sat next to Aleisha on a large bench while he and Tallen attempted, as they had been doing for the better part of a week now, to entertain Aleisha with stories from their pasts, and prove to each other how seriously each of them took their roles in her life as protector.

"Aleisha," Tallen smiled as he addressed her, though it looked more forced than Conner had previously noted in any of their previous dealings, "would you mind terribly if I asked for a moment in private with Conner?"

She looked to him for his answer, so he nodded. "Of course." She stood to leave, pausing at the door to look back at them with concerned suspicion.

As soon as the door closed behind her, Conner leaned forward, resting his forearms on his knees for what was sure to be an interesting conversation. "What do you want to talk about?"

"Aleisha," he said shortly before standing, stretching himself to his full height. This was going to be another battle in which both of them would vow their undying affection for her and accuse the other of not caring for her properly.

"I figured that; there really isn't anything else that we could possibly discuss." He, too, stood, smirking as he rose a good four inches higher than Tallen. Tallen was a large man, but Conner had rarely met anyone taller than himself, especially when one of the dragons decided that he needed to gain a few inches when they renewed his youthful physique.

"Well," he cleared his throat and took a few steps away, "I'm concerned. You seem to have an unnatural attachment to my daughter."

"Unnatural?" In all of the verbal sparring matches they'd had over the past week, he'd not used that particular word before. "I'm afraid I have no idea to what you are referring."

"I'll have you know that I am not yet twenty-eight decades." He sneered, jutting his chin out in defiance.

"Ok?" he could not imagine where he was going with this line of bizarre and unrelated statements, "and the relevance is…"

"I know you to be nearly forty!" Why he was shouting as if Conner had intentionally been older than him, he had no idea. Why, further, that seemed to matter, baffled him beyond imagination.

"First of all, I am only three and a half centuries, not nearly four," Tallen did not look ready to back down from his argument. Conner just wanted to know what they were arguing about. "Secondly, why are you so offended by that?"

"I will not have my daughter going with a man older even than me, and by nearly a century." That was, perhaps, the last thing he would have expected.

"Wait a second" - he threw his hands up in front of him, as if he could stop this irrational man's words from reaching him - "'going with?'"

"I will not have you preying on her."

"Preying on her?" He dropped his hands and growled, "I do not wait for her to be alone so that I can corner her and force her to see me when she clearly does not want to, I do not verbally attack the other people in her life in an attempt to make her question her trust of them, I do not claim to care for her whilst having done nothing for her save sell her into slavery, make her prey for a vindictive Dictator, and murder her mother. If anyone in this messed up relationship is preying on your daughter, it is you, sir, not me."

"She is but a child, and you have taken advantage of that, making her trust you with your false appearance and bending her to your will until she cannot have her own." Thick smoke began swirling around Tallen's feet, momentarily confusing Conner as he wondered what he had to fear before realizing that the Darksoul was claiming his true form. He did not intend this argument to end prematurely.

"She is not a child and I never could have taken advantage of her naivety, because she does not trust easily and will not follow blindly after those she knows to be lying to her. If you knew her at all, you would realize that she is incapable of being a victim even if I had planned to make her one." As Tallen finished changing into his true form, his dark cloak surrounding him in smoke and shielding his eyes from view, Conner felt the floor beneath him tremble slightly. Tallen was evidently attempting to restrain his magic and his rage, not the course he ever would have expected him to take but an interesting choice.

"Know that if you ever do pursue my daughter that I will not take kindly to your advances." The floor shook again and the fire burst from the hearth momentarily before Tallen took it under control. Conner refused to react; he would remain the calm and controlled of the magic users no matter how tempted he was to level the dangerously unstable man before him. "I've only just now received her back into my life and I will not allow anyone that I perceive to be a threat to either her safety or happiness to sabotage our newfound relationship. I do not fear you, your dragon wings, or your so-called brothers, and I will do whatever is necessary for my daughter up to and including killing a few dragons, if ever the need arises. You will treat her with the utmost respect and dignity, as if your very life depended on it."

Conner had to admit that Tallen, in this case as so many others since they arrived, was only trying, even if clumsily, to be a good father to his daughter. He could not fault him wanting to ensure that his own daughter's future lived up the standard that he had set out of his best attempt at love. "If I were to pursue Aleisha, I would hold myself to the highest standards of propriety," his calm tone seemed to catch Tallen off guard, as he was likely expecting more hostility, as had been the norm, "and you can be certain that no other man on the whole of Elbot would treat her better than me, but I have not been pursuing her, partially because of the impropriety of it. I will not seek to further my relationship with a woman while we live under the same roof; I will not be a source of temptation for your daughter, I will assure you. I adore her every bit as much as I now see that you do."

Chapter 36

Aleisha sat in the courtyard behind the keep, buried in Byron's fur to keep her warm in the ever-lowering temperatures. She had thought of going to her room and starting a fire while waiting for Conner and Tallen to finish whatever argument Tallen wanted to have today, but she saw Byron so rarely, as he was not comfortable being inside when not absolutely necessary, and she quite missed the feeling of the warm, comforting embrace that the dragon offered.

"Do you think that we could visit Snarf today?" More than anything else, she missed Snarf, and had dreamt of flying with him three times in this last week.

"I'll speak with Conner, but I do believe that Snarf was hoping that we would keep you away from the library until he has had a chance to finish your," he stopped abruptly, *"gift. Yes, he's making you a gift and he wants it to be a surprise."*

Snarf was making her a gift? She couldn't imagine what she'd done to merit such favor. *"Why don't you suggest that he simply hide the gift? Then I would be able to visit him without him worrying about it."*

"No, that won't work," Byron shook his large head, *"There would simply be no way to hide it; we'll just have to be patient. Of course, if you want to leave Tallen's castle, I will aid you with that, but I doubt greatly if Snarf will grant you passage into his room until the surprise is finished."*

"Will you tell me what the surprise is?" she suspected she already knew the answer, but it couldn't hurt to ask.

"Of course not! It's a surprise." He failed to sound offended, his stern voice betraying a small amount of laughter, *"I usually leave it to the twins to ruin surprises and share secrets."*

They fell back into silence, Byron watching a flock of birds which had landed in the courtyard and Aleisha puzzling over the mysterious surprise. What could he possibly be preparing for her that he couldn't hide?

"What has he done now?" For a moment, she thought that Byron was talking to her, but when she looked around his large chest, she saw Conner exiting the keep and heading toward them, looking rather annoyed. *"Oh, I had forgotten that you are older than him. Why does that matter?"* She really was trying not to listen to Byron's side of the conversation, as Conner clearly either didn't want her included or didn't realize she was sitting there, *"Not that I can think of; you've always been a perfect gentleman."*

She picked a couple of long pieces of grass, focusing closer than necessary on the strips as she carefully braided them together, trying to keep her attention from the voice in her head, *"It is a perfectly logical conclusion, you must admit. After all, you are a human male, she is a human female, and any fool can see that you care for her."* She dropped the grass. What had Tallen said? Sighing in exasperation, she gathered a few more strips of grass, overlapping the old strands with the new to continue her plait. *"Well, you certainly wouldn't hear any complaint from us; we all rather enjoy her recent addition."*

She held up her braided rope, testing the length against the circumference of her head. *"Why don't you ask her that?"* It wasn't long enough yet, so she continued plucking lengths of grass. *"Have Snarf ask her, then, or Dagmar."* Finally, the rope reached around her head. She picked one last long strip of grass, weaving it through the top and bottom of her braid to secure it into a circle. *"You, of all people, should realize the significance of the centuries; why you would ever bother with such trivial impatience is simply incomprehensible. It's an excuse!"*

She pulled a few more blades of grass, preparing to weave them into some kind of decoration for her grass crown. *"Well, she's right here, so you could ask her yourself."*

Conner rounded the huge dragon, stopping next to Aleisha to sit down. "Move over, Leish, I need some warmth too." He gently pushed her over, wedging himself between her and Byron's wing and sending her further into the soft warmth of his furry body. "So, why are we outside in this uncomfortable weather?"

"I wanted Byron to bring me to Snarf, but he refused. He said that there was some surprise that he didn't want me privy to." She watched his face carefully, hoping for some clue about the mystery.

He looked like he was trying not to smile as he reached up to rub his eyes. "We usually let the twins share all of our secrets." She should have known he would say that.

"So, what did Tallen want to talk about?"

"Oh, the usual," he shrugged, "threats of violence mostly and the reminder that he would do anything for his daughter 'up to and including killing a few dragons, if ever the need arises.' I mostly just ignored him at that point."

"You just let him threaten you like that?" Again, he shrugged, as if it was not important.

"You are his highest priority, Leish; his threats are the only way he knows how to show love." He pulled his legs up to his chest and shivered, "Why, again, are we out in this horrid climate?"

"I didn't want to be alone, and it's really not that bad out yet." If not for the breeze, it would have felt more like spring than winter.

"He's always been a bit of a wimp when it comes to the cold," Byron's comment drew an offended glare from Conner. *"One winter, he refused to go outside without being in his true form so that he could wrap himself in his wings to keep the cold air out."*

"We weren't all born with fur coats," he grumbled as he shivered again.

"Quite right, but Aleisha isn't complaining."

"We can go inside if you're that cold." She couldn't help but smile at the sight of him; he looked so harmless, so very opposite to his usually powerful presence.

"I'm fine, I just prefer the heat; I am a Dragonsoul," he was obviously trying to sound tough, but only succeeded in making himself appear even more pitiful.

"You cannot blame everything on being a Dragonsoul."

"Watch me." Aleisha had to turn away; she did not want Conner to see that she was laughing at him. "Ok, fine then, if you're both just going to laugh at my pain, then I think I will go inside." He stood and marched away from them, evoking raucous laughter from Byron.

"Maybe I should go in too," Aleisha stood, shivering as she left the comfort of Byron's wing to be hit by the frigid wind.

"You do realize that he's not actually offended?"

"I thought not, but I'd be more comfortable if he wasn't alone with Tallen any more than necessary; they're likely to kill each other one day."

"I doubt that very much, Aleisha. Both men care more for you than I believe you will ever know; that fact alone will keep them from ever harming each other for fear of hurting you."

Chapter 37

"Too cold?" Tallen barely looked up from the parchment he was standing over when Conner walked back into the room.

"Byron is keeping her warm." He took a seat next to the hearth, holding his hands out to warm them in the heat of the flame. "Are you leaving Ephriat?"

"Of course not, why would you think that?" This time, he turned his full attention to Conner.

"You are studying a map; I would think that you would be familiar enough with most of Ephriat that you wouldn't need one." Tallen had dodged every attempt on Conner's part to discover what 'important business' would be taking him from the castle so close to winter, so it was slightly surprising that he answered him at all.

"I neither do as much traveling as you, nor do I have the advantage of an aerial view in my travels." He returned to his map. "My business is my own, Conner, and I would appreciate it if you would cease your incessant prodding."

"I just want to be sure that you will not be doing anything that could cause Aleisha harm, either directly or indirectly." At his angry glare, he added, "I realize, of course, that you would never do her intentional harm, but you may very well push her away if you are not careful, and that would hurt her indirectly.

"You need not worry; I will not harm my relationship with my daughter." Looking bored again, he returned once more to his map.

"Tallen." Both men looked to the doorway as Aleisha walked in. She looked from Conner to Tallen and back, "Is everything ok?"

"Of course," - he smiled and held a hand out to invite her to join him - "Tallen and I were just talking." That didn't seem to reassure her. She draped her cloak over a chair before moving to stand next to him.

"When are you leaving?" She pulled a grass crown from her hair and tossed it in the flames.

"Tomorrow morning," Tallen smiled as he spoke, a stark contrast to the glare he always offered Conner, "I should return by the end of winter." Aleisha nodded, looking thoughtful.

"We should winter in Might City then; Byron and I have never been away from the others this long and, by your request earlier, I assume you want to return to them as much as we do." He was pleased to see her smile at his suggestion. "We'll leave as soon as we see Tallen off, then."

"When I return," Tallen spoke again, recapturing their attention, "may I assume that I will be welcome to see my daughter at the library, or should I just wait for you to decide to seek me out again?" Aleisha looked to Conner to answer.

"Of course; we have no authority to deny you access to the Great Library. I cannot, however, promise that any of the dragons will grant you welcome into their rooms." He reached up to rub his neck. "In fact, I can guarantee that none of them will let you in, so you should look for us in one of the library sections, though I cannot say which one you might find us in at that point."

"They allow you in?" Tallen directed an odd look at Aleisha.

"Of course." She seemed shocked that he would ask such a thing. "Why wouldn't they?"

"You are a Darksoul" - his eyes narrowed - "are you not?"

"None of us knew what Aleisha was until several weeks after she joined us," Conner saw no need to try to deny Aleisha's abilities, "As you well know, my brothers don't bother trying to hide themselves if they know that they cannot."

"You can hear all of them?" Tallen stared at Aleisha in awe. "What is it like?"

"Chaos." She stretched to her full height and jutted out her chin, mirroring her father's angry stance from earlier. "It's not as pleasant or as helpful as you would assume; I hear overlapping voices and half-conversations. It's little more than a headache."

"Fascinating!" He stood and rolled his map. "I've rarely had the privilege of hearing a dragon speak; I simply can't imagine having their voices constantly in my mind."

"I will never pursue the voice of any dragon not already in my mind and neither should you."

"Aleisha" - he shook his head, smiling - "you are still so young. In time you will come to realize how important power is." He turned to Conner, "I have some last-minute preparations to tend to. I'm sure I will see you both at dinner." With one final glare, he left the room.

"He is never going to accept the fact that I don't want to be like him." Aleisha relaxed her stance and sighed, "Power seems like an exhausting ambition."

"Exhausting and consuming" - he stood to face her at eye level - "lust for power has led many great men to do terrible things."

"Like Philimina?" He nodded. "What about knowledge?"

"Lust for knowledge led Elam to apparently have a librarian robbed and killed so that he could have knowledge that was not contained even in the Great Library." She sighed again and reached up to rub her eyes. "Anything that we value above the Creator will eventually lead us to corruption, Aleisha. He is the only source of good."

"Is He more important to you than Byron?" She frowned.

"Yes, and Byron would be concerned if he heard otherwise." She looked confused and it occurred to him that they'd never actually talked in depth about what it means to follow the Creator; he'd always taken for granted the idea that she already knew. He would be sure to remedy that in future conversations.

"Is He more important than me?" Pure innocence. Neither her voice nor her expression betrayed any amount of sarcasm or offence. He hadn't realized that she knew how important she was to him.

"Yes, Leish, He's even more important than you." She looked bewildered, as if she had not considered that he held anything or anyone above her. "If I did not serve the Creator first, then I could never serve you so well. He is the source of both my goodness and my love, and without Him, I would be no better than Elam, Philimina, Tallen, or even Briganti." She opened her mouth, obviously prepared to argue. "What would I serve if I did not serve the Lord?"

"Well, I don't know for sure." She was back to looking confused.

"Most likely, I would have served Alice first." She had an odd response to that, folding her arms and taking a defensive stance. "I would have killed Philimina for killing her; I would have lost my magic, robbed the world of the strongest line of Dragonsouls, and died centuries ago." He lowered his head to look more directly in her eyes. "If, for some reason, I had decided not to kill Philimina, I might have become consumed by my mourning, being corrupted by bitterness and guilt, or maybe I would have become as obsessed as Elam with knowledge, Philimina with magic, Tallen with power, or Briganti with revenge.

"See, Aleisha, the Creator is my anchor, my compass, and my map. Without Him, I would be a slave to my own understanding, desires, and ambition."

"But you would still be good." He wasn't sure why she was so insistent, "You would have to be."

"Why?"

"Because you're Conner," she began pacing, throwing her arms up in confusion as she frantically tried to explain. "You're kind, you're selfless, you're," she stopped and stared at him, shrugging, "you're you."

"But what makes me kind and selfless? It doesn't come from me." She continued to stare blankly at him. "I was not kind and selfless before I came to follow the Creator; I was arrogant and self-centered. I am the most powerful Dragonsoul alive, perhaps the most powerful ever to live, and that aspect of who I was, was the most important thing in my life. I used to seek out foes who might provide me with a challenge in order to prove that I could not be defeated."

"That doesn't sound like you."

"It's not me, Leish. Hasn't been me for hundreds of years, but it was me for a long time." He reclaimed his seat, nodding at a chair near him to invite her to join him. "Do you remember that I told you that my life was centered on my magic while I was still being mentored by Philimina?"

She nodded slowly, "Before you met Alice."

"Yes, Alice was the most unique person I had ever met; she seemed always to be in a pleasant mood, she was more patient than anyone deserved, and she was the only non-magic user that didn't treat me like some kind of god." He chuckled at Aleisha's darkened expression, "Her boldness with me, tempered but the most interesting contrast of her humility, is what drew me to her.

"As I said, I began to spend every available moment with her; I was fascinated and intrigued by her, it was several months after I met her that I came to realize that the great difference between her and everybody else was her love of the Creator. She explained that her kindness and patience with everyone around her was her way of showing her devotion to the Creator. She told me that, since she could not do anything for or give anything to the Creator, she took to serving those around her and giving of herself to His creation, other people.

"It was her testimony and her honest virtue that led me to give myself and my life to the Creator. I had only ever given Him my words before meeting Alice, such a beautiful example of His love, and coming to desire the same joy and devotion that she possessed."

"So, she is why you are who you are?"

"Not exactly." He reached to scratch at his neck. How could he better explain? "She led me to Him, but He made me who I am."

"I always assumed that Byron…" - she dropped her head into her hands - "I'm so confused."

"Byron has taught me a great deal about the Creator and had aided me in my understanding of His word, but Alice was the one who not only led me to follow the Creator, but introduced me to the dragons." She jerked her head up to stare, wide eyed, at him. He chuckled again, "I am not their natural brother, you know."

"Obviously!" - she glared at him - "I just assumed that you'd always known them, I guess."

"Nope," he grinned, "just a couple of centuries is all."

"I need to think." She dropped her head again, moaning, "It's just so much."

"I understand" - he stood to give her some space - "I'll see you at dinner, Leish."

As he left the sitting room, he replayed everything he's said through his mind; he desperately hoped that he's explained well. He felt a little foolish that he hadn't made sure that Alesha properly understood what following the Creator meant; he'd just been following Him for so long himself, that he tended to forget what it was like not to know the truth, not to know how incredibly personal and life-changing such a decision had to be.

Chapter 38

"Will you at least be following the regular trade routes? With winter setting in, even you ought to take precautions." Aleisha was vaguely aware of Conner and Tallen arguing again; they seemed to enjoy nothing more than to probe each other for some unimportant piece of information, only to be offended and suspicious when the other did the same thing. Aleisha had more important things to think about.

Conner had said a lot before dinner about what it meant to serve the Creator, and she had been thinking of nothing else since. She couldn't imagine placing the Creator as her highest priority. What did that even mean? Conner was not a priest, but he claimed that he served the Creator first, so it obviously did not mean that he was extravagantly religious, and she certainly didn't see the pretentious piety that she'd often glimpsed at the chapel in Jaboke.

He mentioned that Alice served the people around her in order to serve the Creator, but what did that mean? Conner treated the people of Puko with kindness even when they were cruel to him, but he did not give in to Briganti's demands. Did that mean that, even in serving, he had a choice when to serve? Or did it mean that he only served when he was giving of himself, rather than others?

"I hear that the Nejave Mountains are swarming with outlaws, so I would avoid that area even if I were going to Jaboke again," Tallen ripped into a loaf of bread and passed a large piece to Aleisha as he spoke.

How does one prioritize a being that they can neither see nor hear? How does one know if their actions further the cause of such a being? Conner had told her that the Creator wants His creation to live loving Him and loving others, but if she were to take that as the Creator's cause, would she be prioritizing the Creator, or Conner? She was sure she could trust anything that Conner said, but doesn't even that place him as her highest authority? Would she be able to deny something that Conner told her if she were to hear from someone else that the Creator did not agree with him? How would she even know which of the two to believe? She would obviously believe Conner, but does that not make Conner her god rather than the Lord?

She groaned and pushed her plate away, drawing the attention of both men. "I'm going to bed." With that, she stood and hurried to her room before either of them had a chance to respond. *"Byron, are you available?"*

"I'm here Aleisha," his deep voice echoed in her mind, *"Is everything alright?"*

"Conner said that anything we value above the Creator will lead to corruption, is that true?" She stoked the dying fire in the hearth, adding more wood to revive the flame.

"Quite true, I'm afraid. I've seen it hundreds of times over the course of my years." His voice suddenly lost some of its clarity, *"Yes, I'm speaking with her now."*

"Conner?" he must have been asking Byron to check on her.

"He is concerned about you." She nodded before realizing that he couldn't see her silent reply.

"But how do we value a being we cannot know?"

"Can't we know Him?" Byron paused, she wasn't sure how to respond. *"The Creator is not so mysterious, Aleisha, He has given us the scripture, His word, so that we may know Him and His commands."*

"I've heard of this scripture." She did not have fond memories of her trips to the chapel; the priest spoke of loving your neighbor, but esteemed Cedrick, the cruelest man in Jaboke as some kind of saint. *"I've not been impressed with those who have presented it."*

"Where do you think Conner gets his values and guidelines? Everything that he has told you concerning anger, being kind to those who are cruel to us, and forgiveness has come from his study of the scriptures."

"But, if I choose to follow the Creator because Conner wants me to, am I not serving Conner over the Creator?" She sat on the foot of her bed, staring at the fireplace.

"Is he why you have chosen to follow Him?"

"He is, and all of you," she sighed. *"You are all so good and I want to be like you, but now Conner is telling me that I can't be good unless I place the Creator even above you, but now if I do, won't I be doing so out of my love for all of you? So now has it not become impossible to truly serve the Creator*

before you? Won't my service of Him always be tainted by my service of you?"

"You are correct that, if you chose to serve the Creator because it is what we would want for you, your conversion would be a false one." He paused again, *"Your decision to follow him cannot and should not be based on emotion. Your affection toward Conner, Snarf, or Dagmar cannot be your basis for your service of the Lord. Has Conner told you of his testimony?"*

"Yes, he told me that Alice led him to follow the Creator."

"And if his devotion to the Creator had been based on his devotion to Alice, then he would have easily either returned to his former way of life because the object of his devotion was taken from him, or he might have turned completely away from the Creator because He had allowed her to be taken from him.

"However, because his decision to serve the Creator was based, not on emotion, but on a realization that the religious piety that he had formerly practiced had not gained him anything, and that only choosing to serve the Creator above all else would grant him a right relationship with the Lord, his loss of Alice, while it hurt him deeply and he mourned bitterly for her, did not mark the end of his relationship with the Creator."

She heaved a deep sigh and laid down, staring at the ceiling as she tried to sort through everything she has

Darksoul

just heard. *"Does that help, Aleisha?"* Byron's voice broke through her thoughts once more.

"I don't know. I'm just so confused and overwhelmed. I think I just need to think for a while."

"Let me know if you have any more questions."

"Thank you." Perhaps she should see if the Great Library had a copy of the scriptures. Perhaps reading for herself what the Creator had to say would help her to separate Conner and the dragons from her thoughts of the Creator. Perhaps then she could make an intelligent decision concerning her future service of the Creator.

She must have replayed the conversations of the day a dozen times as she lay on her bed, her legs hanging limply off the side of her bed. Though she puzzled for hours over her endless questions; by the time the sun shone through the narrow crack between the heavy curtains and the warm fire had dwindled once more to a small flickering flame, she was no closer to a resolution, though she was now quite thoroughly exhausted.

She heard a loud pounding on her door, confirming her suspicion that morning had, in fact, come. Moaning, she moved to roll out of bed, only to realize that both feet were asleep, a side effect of her unfortunate position, no doubt. Groaning as she tried to stomp the blood back into her lower legs, she held tightly to the bed post to keep herself upright. The pounding continued. "I'm trying," she groaned again at the sound of her own unrecognizable voice. No wonder Conner always teased her in the mornings; she was a mess.

As soon as she could feel her feet again, she grabbed her cloak to hide the fact that she'd never changed for the night and staggered painfully to the door, stumbling into it and smacking her head into the wood. "Stupid door." She yanked on the door, flinging it open and sending herself stumbling back several feet before landing on her backside with a great thud. "Stupid door."

Conner came rushing into her room, kneeling before her with a shocked and worried expression. "Are you alright, Leish?" - he reached for her hand to help her up - "I know you don't handle mornings well, but you look even more exhausted than normal."

"Forgot to sleep." She accepted his hand and let him pull her up. "Door knocked me over."

He chuckled, "The door knocked you over?" She nodded, yawning. "Let me help you get downstairs. Tallen will be leaving soon and he would regret not getting to see you before he departed." He chuckled again, "If this half-asleep version of you counts, that is." As usual, Conner seemed to feel the need to speak endlessly first thing in the morning. "Byron wants to leave immediately after Tallen does, as we are not welcome by the servants and we have no need to stay any longer. I'm sure that you will be able to get some sleep on the way back to Might City, though I would suggest that you remember to sleep at night from now

Darksoul

on, as you don't seem to be able to handle skipping sleep as well as some."

"Shut up," she moaned, much to Conner's amusement, "tired." He continued half-dragging her down the steps in silence, chuckling occasionally as she stumbled over her own feet and grumbled about the stairs.

The moment they entered the great hall, Aleisha was overwhelmed by the noise. Dozens of servants rushed about the room, carrying crates and sacks from a large disorganized pile in the center of the room, through several doors either to the waiting cart outside or to one of the many storage rooms on this floor. From somewhere in the chaos, she heard Tallen's cheerful cry, "Aleisha, my daughter." She didn't bother trying to sort out the confusing images before her; she knew that, if she waited long enough, Tallen would make his way over to them, and she didn't have the energy to try to figure out from which direction he would be coming. "What's wrong my dear?" Upon reaching them, Tallen's eyes widened in alarm.

"Aleisha is not a morning person," Conner replied with great importance, "she is simply having a bit more difficulty even than normal waking up this morning."

"Ah, I see," his cheery tone had returned and he clapped as he grinned at her. "I'm so glad that you made it down before I set out; you have no idea how much it means to me that you made the effort, especially since you are not feeling quite well yet." He turned and briskly marched toward the pile the servants were working on, motioning behind him to urge them to follow. "Since I will be gone for many weeks, I would like to leave you with a couple of gifts."

She knew that she should respond with some customary formality, but she couldn't remember the appropriate words. Tallen, digging through the pile until he apparently found what he was looking for, shouted angrily at a nearby servant for not having finished sorting the random mass of packages. Turning back to them, he held out a leather-bound book to Aleisha, "My gift to my daughter. I have held this for you since the day you were born, though I began my work on it decades earlier."

"Thank you," Conner whispered into her hair as she took it, reminding her of the pleasantry she'd forgotten earlier.

"Thank," she mumbled, accepting the item and examining it. The binding was made of one long piece of leather that wrapped around the whole of the book twice and tied shut. Untying the thong, she carefully unwrapped it to reveal the highest quality paper she'd ever seen adorned with thick hand-written script, *Concerning Alencia, my Beloved Daughter.* She had to read it several times, stumbling over her misspelled name before remembering that Tallen had said that her mother had promised to name her after his sister.

Turning the page to read the first entry, she gasped, *You, my daughter, were not born to die. Your witch of a mother has refused to save your life, but I will never betray you as she has; I will find the Elixir of Life. You and I will live forever together in this castle in which you were born. Together, we will grow in knowledge and power; we will increase our wealth and influence; and one day, many centuries from today, this precious day of your birth, when we have learned all that we can, when we have conquered all that we please, and when we control all that we see, we will rule the whole of Elbot, and every creature will worship you as I do.*

If not for her most recent conversations with Conner and Byron, she might have been flattered, if not a bit uncomfortable, but reading this now, she found herself disgusted, though slightly more trusting of Tallen's many claims of his devotion to her. She reached to turn the page again, but was stopped by Conner's hand reaching to close the volume for her. Horrified at the thought that he'd read what Tallen had written, she turned to look at him, only to see him nodding toward Tallen, reminding her that he was holding another gift for her.

Tallen held out a neatly folded pile of cloth, "You wear a fine cloak, Aleisha." She eyed the material suspiciously as she took it from him. "But I think that this one will fit you rather better. It was my first cloak, and I would be honored if you would accept it." As she feared, the black cloth unfolded into a Darksoul cloak, the enchanted hem smoking as she shook it out. If not for her exhaustion, she would have been furious. She dropped it on the floor before her, sickened by the very sight of it. Why did the men in her life so want her to wear one of these wretched things?

Tallen flinched as his cloak crumpled to the ground. She found that she did not care if she offended him; he had offended her with his 'gifts.'

"Aleisha," Conner reprimanded her quietly before bending down to retrieve the cloak, folding it over his own arm before addressing Tallen, "As I said, she is not a morning person, and the cloak she wears now was also a gift, so I do hope you do not take offence at her exhausted manners." Why was he trying to comfort him? He knew how she felt about being a Darksoul.

"I see." Tallen still looked disappointed, but he now eyed Conner with an almost possessive glare. "I should have realized that it came from you." It was probably because she was so tired, but she thought she heard a growl in Tallen's voice. "Well then" - he turned back to Aleisha, forcing a smile - "It's time I head off. I will see you at the start of spring."

"Yeah," she mumbled. Tallen grabbed one last package and, throwing his head back splendidly, he strode past them and exited without another word. A few minutes passed in silence before Conner took hold of her arm and led her out the front door.

Chapter 39

Conner helped Aleisha onto Byron's back and helped her get comfortable. As he expected, she fell asleep moments after curling up in his arms. He could not be more relieved that they were finally returning to Might City; he had done his best to endure their stay at Tallen's castle with a right attitude but he had not been able to truly relax since they'd arrived.

Byron, too, seemed focused solely on returning to their brothers, so neither of them made any attempt at conversation. Conner had to fight the urge to pull Aleisha's new book from her arms to get a glimpse of the text. She'd seemed rather distressed as she read it and he wanted to know why, but it wasn't his place to snoop in her belongings. He could not imagine what Tallen might have written to his daughter twenty-five years ago that he would still consider relevant enough to give to her now, but he suspected that the book was not as old as he claimed. It should not be too difficult to detect if Tallen had attempted to deceive her, after all, he had thought that Aleisha had been given a different name at birth, so if her name was anywhere in the book, depending on which name he used, they might be able to detect a lie, even if they could not verify the truth.

In his musings, Conner did not realize how far they had traveled until Byron landed gently on his platform. Almost immediately, Grezald landed next to them, bouncing excitedly as he urged Conner off of Byron's back. *"Quietly, Grezald, Aleisha is trying to sleep."*

He eased her from his lap as he slid from Byron's back.

"What? No! Snarf has been driving me crazy; I need to get her to his room as quickly as possible."

"I suppose that means he doesn't care to keep his secret anymore," Byron chuckled as he turned to take off again, *"I'll bring her right there, but it's up to Snarf to wake her up."* He leapt from his platform and glided down to Snarf's which glowed slightly purple.

Did he want to head down immediately, or should he give Aleisha and Snarf a moment to enjoy their reunion? He didn't want to miss her reaction when she saw his shaved wings. Smiling at the thought of Snarf's selfless offer, he burst into his true form and dove from the balcony, followed closely by Grezald, and landed on Snarf's platform a moment after Byron disappeared into the room. *"Come in, please. You have been gone so long."*

Smiling, he stepped through the barrier to see Snarf for the first time in a week. *"Hey baldy,"* he grinned at Snarf's squirming. *"How are you doing?"*

"I will be glad to have it back; I had not realized how frigid winter can be." He had never seen a dragon shiver before, but Snarf's whole body vibrated and his wings twitched violently as he complained about the weather. *"Byron said that Aleisha has been sleeping since you left Tallen's castle."*

"Yes, she apparently forgot to sleep last night, so I would suggest trying not to wake her until absolutely necessary." He looked over at her sleeping form,

which they had somehow managed to get down from Byron's back and onto Snarf's bed without disturbing her. *"We had an interesting discussion yesterday about priorities, so I suspect that that has quite a bit to do with her restlessness."*

"So, tell me about your visit with Tallen. Did everything go smoothly?" Both Grezald and Byron perked up at his question, apparently hearing what Snarf had said.

"Well. I think that Tallen is sincere in his affection for Aleisha, but he has no concept of real love, so he resorts to everything from manipulation to worship to convince her of his devotion. He left this morning and said that he won't be back until spring, so that's the reason for the timing of our return, though I think that Aleisha was just about ready to come back anyway had Tallen not left." He turned to Byron, *"Would you add anything?"*

"Aleisha seems unwaveringly suspicious of her father; that may be a good thing to be aware of, should you choose to bring him up in front of her. Also, Tallen has it in his head that Conner has been or soon will be in pursuit of Aleisha." Both younger dragons looked to Conner with wildly excited expressions, earning a chuckle and a shake of his head; he had not intended that to be a part of Byron's addition. *"What of you then? Do either of you have anything to report?"*

"Snarf hasn't ceased to complain about the cold since we had his wings shaved." As expected, Grezald

did not pass up the opportunity to torment his younger brother who growled teasingly in response.

"And Grezald hasn't ceased to complain of his loneliness since Grizwald left," Grezald offered an exaggerated pout and a nod at Snarf's reply.

"Snarf," Aleisha, who sounded like she might still be sleeping, mumbled from Snarf's bed. Her head appeared over the cushion as she stretched to see her beloved friend, a sleepy smile spreading across her face as she spotted him. "Snarf," she repeated his name as she turned and, nearly falling from her place in the large bed, clumsily made her way to the floor. Stopping but a moment to regain her balance, she dropped the book that Tallen had given her and dashed at Snarf, burying herself in the fur of his neck and front. "I missed you, Snarf. I missed you so much." Snarf grinned as he wrapped one arm around her, completely hiding her from view.

"Note how she didn't even notice me standing here," Grezald did his best to sound offended, but he was too excited to be convincing.

"I'm sorry, Grezald, I wasn't sure if you were really here; after all, I've never heard of one half of an entity living without the other half." She turned away from Snarf as she spoke, giggling at the shocked expression on Grezald's face; rarely did anyone tease him, save Grizwald and Snarf, and he clearly wasn't prepared with an appropriate response.

"It's good to have you back, Leish" - she turned to him, confused - "you've been so tense lately, you haven't seemed like yourself." She smiled before suddenly turning back to Snarf.

"Byron said that you have a surprise for me and that you wouldn't want to see me because of it."

All three dragons looked at her with the most comical expressions of confusion mixed with amusement; they sometimes forgot how enormous they were and how easy it would be for someone as small as a human to miss large details that were glaringly obvious from their greater perspective.

"You may not be able to rely on Snarf's protection from the cold this winter; he's a bit bald, you see," he chuckled as her eyes widened and she shook her head, looking horrified as she turned to her large purple friend, staring intently at his wings.

"Who did this to you?" Of all the possible responses, Conner had not expected such passionate anger at her realization; if not for the magical glow the room gave off, he was sure that whatever fire they used would now be leaping from its source with great fervor. As it was, a shockwave pulsed from her body, knocking Conner back a step and throwing the bed against the far wall. "Who hurt you?"

"I am not hurt, Aleisha. It was my choice to have my wings shaved." Though Snarf tried to soothe her, Conner could see her shaking with rage even as he spoke, *"Your new cloak, the cloak that we will use to help suppress your magic, will be made of dragonsilk. It was my decision and it is my honor to give of myself to help heal you and to help keep you warm."* The

room fell into silence as Aleisha stared at Snarf. Conner wished that he could see her expression as she realized what he was saying; she had to know what a great sacrifice he had made for her. *"You still do not know how we love you, Aleisha? There is not one in this group who would not give their very life for you, yet you are shocked that I would give my fur?"*

"You love me?" She stepped back and looked about the room, her confused eyes resting on Conner before she continued, "Of course, I knew. I just didn't realize…" she stopped again, clearly searching for the words.

"A hug from me." At Snarf's request, Conner stepped forward to wrap his arms around Aleisha, offering the embrace Snarf wished to be able to give her.

"And me." At Grezald's agreement, Aleisha snorted into his shoulder, the first of her tears dampening his shirt as she sobbed.

"From me as well," as Byron's voice joined the others, the room seemed to fill with a warm light, brighter than he'd ever seen, yet somehow not blinding. If he wasn't mistaken, they had just learned how her magic manifested itself in joy.

They stood there a few minutes, Aleisha sobbing softly into his shoulder while all three dragons stood by, lowering their heads in silent accord. "I'm sorry," she sniffed as she finally pulled away from him. "I have no idea why I'm crying; I'm not sad at all." She looked about the group, grinning so wide that she

Darksoul

looked like she was going to start again. "Thank you all. Thank you."

Chapter 40

Aleisha looked around the room at these beautiful creatures she was so fortunate to know. Where would she be right now if not for them? A few weeks ago, she had thought that, without Conner, she would still be in Cedrick's mansion, but recent revelations left her wondering at the accuracy of that assumption.

Tallen had said that he went to retrieve her shortly after she was rescued. Would he have been able to convince her of his sincerity? Would she still have discovered her magic? Would she now be serving Tallen's will? Would she have used her newfound magic to try to kill the man who imprisoned her mother and sold her into slavery? Would he have, in his warped dedication to her, let her kill him? Would he have, in his anger and lust for power, killed her?

She shivered. All she could know for certain is that she was indeed lucky to have met Conner that day in the market. But had it been luck? Conner had said that he was there quite intentionally. He had been looking for a girl whom he had been sent by the Lord to help. Was this journey, this relationship, this family, a gift from the Creator? Why would He choose to bless her so? Did He love her as Conner and the dragons did?

"Byron?" The large dragon lowered his head even further than it had been, nearly touching his nose to her head.

"Yes?"

"We are supposed to value the Creator above everything including each other?" He nodded. "Does the Creator value us more than we value each other?"

"That is an interesting question" - he smiled at her - *"May I ask how you came to wonder such a thing?"*

"The priest always said that the Creator is consistent, and it just seems like a consistent God would have to value us so much if He demands such devotion from us."

He nodded, *"The Creator is the source of love, so without Him, we are not capable of loving as He commands us to. That is why, even though Tallen adores you and places you above everything else in this life, he still tries to bend you to his will. He does not know how, even though he values you greatly, to do that which is best for you, regardless of his own desires.*

"Because of this, that the Creator is the source of all love, He is the only One who can truly love completely and perfectly. Not even Conner, in his selfless choice to accompany you to Tallen's castle despite his own hatred for him, or Snarf's generous gift of his fur and his flight, nor even Dagmar's loyalty to you when even Conner, Snarf, the twins, and I abandoned you can ever begin to show you the depth of love the Creator shows towards you and the care He gives you. Even your very breath is a precious gift that He delights to give you, even as you reject Him."

"He sent you to find me in Jaboke."

"Yes."

"I want to follow Him," she nodded, determined. "I want to put Him first like you and Conner do." If the Creator could love her so much that He sent Conner to rescue her, if this same Creator was the Creator from the fables who let His own son be tortured as punishment in place of the evil men who deserved it, if He could teach her to love as she was loved, then she could serve Him gladly. She could even place a God like that above her beloved friends.

"All that is required to have a right relationship with Him is your repentance. Do you believe that you are a sinner in need of His forgiveness?" She nodded, feeling the tears welling in her eyes again. How terrible a sinner was she? She had hurt so many people in her anger, she had used her beauty and position in Cedrick's house for years to manipulate people into giving her whatever she desired, she had hated her own father, and had wished ill on more people than she would bother to count. *"Then all you need is to admit your wrong to Him and ask His forgiveness. You can know that He will forgive you, because He let His own Son die so that He might; He would not waste such a sacrifice."*

"Ok, I want to do this now. Where do I find a priest?" Conner frowned at that.

"Aleisha, the scriptures say that the Son is our priest. You can go to Him directly through prayer. You do not need any man to assist you." She had never heard of this before; the priest in Jaboke had always made it clear that he was the only path to the Creator.

Darksoul

"How do I do that?"

"Just talk to Him like you do to me" - he smiled - "You could even talk to Him like you do to the dragons; He is the creator of the universe, so He won't have a problem hearing you." She nodded, but she wasn't sure she understood.

"I'll try." She closed her eyes and tried to picture this God with whom she was trying to speak. *"Creator, I've never spoken to You, but Snarf told me that You knew me before I was conceived, so I know that you know why I'm trying to talk to you now. I have not served You and my wrong priorities have led me to all kinds of evils. I beg Your forgiveness for my wrongs, and I thank You for sacrificing Your Son to make that forgiveness possible. I ask that You teach me to correct my mistakes, to place You above all else in this world, yes even above Conner, Snarf, and their brothers."* She opened her eyes and looked to Conner, "and that's all?"

"That's where your journey begins." He smiled and clapped her shoulder, "You will quickly learn that you will never reach 'all' while still on Elbot. Even I do not follow the Creator perfectly and I have been serving Him for two and a half centuries now."

"Well, this is awesome," Snarf bounced in place as he spoke, though she wasn't sure if it was his boundless energy or the cold that made him do so. *"It's always a wonderful thing to witness someone make such a decision. I think I need to invest in a*

blanket." At the sudden change of topic, everyone in the room dissolved into uncontrollable fits of laughter.

"Way to destroy the serious mood, Snarf." Conner threw a bundle of dark cloth at Snarf, leaving a trail of black smoke behind it as it flew. "Leish doesn't want it, but maybe you can use it."

Snarf backed away from the cloth with a look of exaggerated horror. Reaching out slowly, as if the cloak was going to attack him, he carefully picked it up with one claw. Holding it out from himself, much like a house wife who had just picked up a dead rat, he looked at it in confusion. "You can destroy that." Aleisha folded her arms and glared at the cursed cloth. "Conner only took it to make Tallen feel better after I rejected it." She wasn't sure why he'd kept it the whole way back to Might City; she would have dropped it on the way, leaving it for some unfortunate traveler to find.

Snarf opened his mouth and let out a narrow stream of flame, incinerating the black cloak in seconds. She didn't remember the morning well, as she had been mostly asleep when Tallen left, but she remembered him handing her the cloak. There had been another gift, too, she had thought. She remembered reading Tallen's note in the front of a book of some sort. Where had she put that book? Looking around the floor, she finally spotted the leather binding lying near Snarf's bed. Apparently, she had launched both objects to the other side of the room when she'd thought someone had hurt Snarf.

"I'm going to head to the library, would anyone care to join me?" Conner winked at her before walking toward the exit, followed closely by Byron and Grezald, "We'll be back before sundown. Enjoy your visit."

"It is good to have you back, Aleisha." Snarf moved to retrieve his bed, nudging her book out of the way so that he could push the cushion back to the middle of the wall. *"Come, tell me about your visit with Tallen."*

She stopped to retrieve the book before climbing up next to him, feeling the cold metallic texture of his bare wings as she prepared to tell him every detail that she could remember from the last week.

Chapter 41

"Are we intending to research anything in particular? Or are we just giving Aleisha and Snarf a chance to catch up?" Byron led the way through the long corridor leading to the main library, ambling slowly along to give them the time to discuss their destination.

"Well, I'm sure that Aleisha would appreciate the opportunity to read the scriptures, now that she has decided to follow the Creator, so I was thinking we could check out a copy, but I also wanted to look into a concern that she brought up a while back." Byron and Grezald paused at a fork in the corridor, waiting to hear him out before choosing a direction to continue. "She believes that Syris is smuggling dragonsilk for her former master, Cedrick. I promised her that I would look into it, but I have no idea where we could start with such research."

"I would think that we should look in the Library of Craft and Trade." Grezald moved to head down the left corridor.

"Dragonsilk is illegal in much of Elbot, so those who have worked with it will likely not admit the fact." Byron shook his head as he responded, *"What would that gain us?"*

"Only the most skilled of weavers would be able to produce it, so, rather than searching for those who boast a proficiency in dragonsilk, we search for those who have a reputation for other fine fabrics."

"That actually might work. We could build a list of craftsmen who might be able to create dragonsilk, and then eliminate those who could not be involved."

"You do realize, of course, that this exercise will do little to prove the validity of Aleisha's accusation." As they stepped into the Library of Craft and Trade, Byron immediately took flight, making his way to the top section of the library. *"I think that we can safely assume that Syris is not the one producing the dragonsilk, and finding potential craftsmen will require us questioning each one unless they have some obvious connection to either Syris or Cedrick."*

He was probably right, but Conner had to at least try to find some information. After all, they would need someone to help them weave Snarf's fur into a cloak, and what better person to do that than a craftsman already practiced with dragonsilk?

While Byron browsed the top shelf and Grezald spoke with the section's dragon librarian, Conner headed to the human librarian. "May I help you sir?" The elderly man smiled as Conner approached.

"I'm looking for a skilled weaver." The old man cocked his head, inviting him to continue. "I've come into quite a bit of money and would like to hire a craftsman who can make me a cloak worthy of my station."

"Well, sir" - he rubbed his chin with one wrinkled hand - "I could direct you to several different sources, but, in order to find the perfect craftsman, we'll need to narrow down the search. Just exactly how fine would you like you cloak?"

"Like I said, I've come into quite a bit of money; I want the best that money, or goods if necessary, can buy." The old man shrugged and reached for a thick book next to him. "I've heard tell of a man who can make silk from wool." That got his attention. The librarian placed the book back where it had been and leaned forward.

"You understand that I am but a keeper of knowledge? I cannot be involved in such illegal activities as that which you suggest."

"I only need to know where to look for such a man." The librarian looked about nervously, eyeing the dragons particularly carefully as he slid from his chair.

"Come with me, then, I'll show you where you might look for such specific services." He led him out of the library and down one of the many corridors snaking through the library interior. Conner had rarely gone through the particular section that they were in now, as it serves as a sort of an inn for visiting dragons. Since each of his brothers had a permanent room on the outer wall of the library, there was simply no need to venture this far in.

Several turns and staircases in, just about far enough that Conner was sure anyone else would have been thoroughly lost, the librarian stopped in front of a dragon room. "The Library of Secret Knowledge" - he turned and glared at Conner - "Even the library itself is secret to all but the librarians. You will find that for which you seek inside, though the dragon that presides over this library will not aid you in your search, so you may be searching for a very long time." He turned to the enchanted entrance. "We have a knowledge seeker here." He waited in silence a moment while the dragon responded. "I will wait for you for an hour, then you will have to find your own way back."

Conner nodded and entered the room. The most impressive thing about the huge room was not the size, though it stretched wider than he imagined possible unless this entire section of the building was made only to appear as dragon rooms to hide the secret library. The most impressive thing about this room was the dragon lying in the middle of the room, watching Conner closely.

Until this moment, Byron was the largest and oldest dragon Conner had ever had the privilege to meet. This dragon was easily twice the size of Byron and pure black. His golden eyes almost shone in contrast to his beautiful fur as he peered at Conner with a strange expression; he'd never seen a dragon gaze at a human in awe. What must this beautiful creature see in him that he would respond so curiously?

"You are the babe of Philimina," the ebony dragon did not ask; he somehow did not need to. *"What is your name?"*

"Conner." The dragon closed his eyes and sighed. *"How do you know me?"*

"I am Zwarte," he said it as if it should mean something to him, *"It has been many centuries since I last knew the wielder of my magic."*

"Your magic?"

"My magic" - he furrowed his brow - *"Has Philimina not told you the story of where your magic came from?"*

"The Creator gave Philimina the power of the dragons…"

"No, the Creator gave Philimina the power of one specific dragon: me" - he cocked his head at Conner - *"What did you think was the reason that you are so much more powerful than all other human magic users? Only Philimina was given the power of a dragon. All other Dictators were given an imitation magic. That is why you are the only one who can do dragon enchantments and breathe fire."*

"I have never used an enchantment of that level, and I'm rather sure that I cannot breathe fire." At his statement, Zwarte became visibly upset, shaking his head in anger as he growled in frustration.

"Have you ever tried? Has Philimina so shirked his responsibilities as your Dictator that he never taught you?" The black dragon lowered his head to Conner's, not usually a motion that would have intimidated him, but he'd never encountered such a large one as Zwarte. *"Let me see your wings, Conner. Every Dragonsoul from the line of Philimina bares my coloring; it is a sign of your lineage."*

Conner stood straight and let his magic flow freely through him, transforming his body into the large beast. As soon as the transformation was complete, he saw the dragon lower his head. *"You are as much my babe as you are Philimina's. It disgusts me that he has not taught you well."* He sat back and considered Conner for a moment, relaxing his angry expression after several seconds. *"So, Dragonsoul, how can I help you?"*

"I um." He was still reeling from the idea that he could breathe fire; he needed a moment to regather his thoughts and remember why he was here. *"I suspect a young man in the city of Fonishia to be smuggling dragonsilk, and I would like to seek out his supplier to collect evidence against him."*

Zwarte glared, *"Just give me the name and occupation of the smuggler. I can have him questioned and, if need be, stopped."*

Conner reached up to scratch his neck. That would fix one of their problems, though they would still have to search for someone who could weave Aleisha's cloak. *"I admit, I have another reason for my search."*

"Go on."

"I travel with a young girl and a family of dragon brothers. One of the brothers has decided to give of his own coat to provide a cloak for the young girl."

"He what?" Zwarte smashed his head into the ceiling as he reared back in surprise and horror. *"How old is this dragon? Does he have any idea what he is doing?"*

"Aleisha is very important to him; he completely understands what he is doing." Zwarte continued to gawk at Conner, his jaw slack as he stared in shock. *"He has already been shaved, but we need to find a weaver who is skilled in working with dragonsilk."*

Zwarte turned his head toward a set of shelves in the far corner of the room, *"You may find an adequate weaver among those volumes. As for the smuggler, I would still suggest that the best option is to give me his name and location, though you may find his supplier among those same weavers."*

"Thank you, Zwarte." He bowed to the great dragon and headed to the shelves, pulling out a book entitled *The Masters of the Craft of Dragonsilk*.

Opening to the front page, he saw that the book was a self-updating volume, enchanted by a powerful dragon to include the most current information. Turning to the chapter on Might City, he saw, as he had expected, nearly half a dozen names and locations of craftsmen who knew how to work with dragonsilk. Three names specified weavers, while the other two belonged to tailors. He had not considered, though he should have realized, that both would be necessary for the cloth to be of any use. Noting the names of the men he would need to speak to, he turned to the section on Fonishia; he theorized that, if Syris really was involved in smuggling dragonsilk, his producer would either reside in Fonishia or Jaboke.

Fonishia had only one weaver and no tailor. Jaboke was mentioned only once, *"A trader by the name of*

Darksoul

Cedrick sells the cloth but seems to neither know nor care about its origin, only the profit it can and does bring to his household." So Aleisha was right; Cedrick was selling the cloth and, most likely, Syris was his smuggler. Having found all that he needed, he left the information about Syris with Zwarte and moved to head back to Snarf's room.

Chapter 42

Aleisha flipped through the pages of her father's book. It appeared to be a journal describing his search for the Elixir of Life. "This entry is dated nearly thirty years before I was born." She scanned the page, looking for any mention of the elixir or her mother. "This seems to have been written before he met my mother. He says that he's tracking down his first plausible lead in his search for nearly a decade." She paused reading a few more paragraphs. "It looks like he wrote this entry the day he learned of my mother; he says that he's learned of a mortal who has lived in the same village for nearly sixty years, but who appears no older than the young adults in the village."

She continued skimming through several more pages while Snarf waited silently. "Oh, the young immortal was not my mother. *'I was sorely disappointed to discover that the young woman was no more than a weak magician who had been hiding her magic from the foolish villagers, who would rather have an immortal that a magic user in their presence. In my anger and frustration, I dispatched of the lying fool.'*" She closed the book, disgusted.

"You knew who wrote this book, Aleisha. Did you expect anything less?" Snarf's sympathetic words urged her to continue.

Finding her spot again, she turned a few more pages and began reading aloud, "*'At last! I have found a true immortal. She is short and round, but fair as was eighty years ago and completely without magic. It was not difficult for me to gain her friendship, fellow elder that I am, and I expect quick progress from here.'* Wow, the next entry is dated nearly a decade after that one. *'I have always known and been prepared for the patience that it would require to gain the trust of an immortal, and my perseverance has finally paid off. Dorcas and I are to be wed on the new moon, and I do not expect that she would keep her closest secret from her beloved husband.'"* She had to stop reading this. She had known that Tallen had manipulated her mother, had known that he'd only intended to use her to gain the Elixir of Life, but she'd never fully comprehended how entirely consumed he was. She had never realized how long her mother had been with Tallen, how patient he'd been, how obsessed, how dedicated.

"It must be difficult to see this from your father's perspective; you've only known your mother's side of the story for so long." Snarf nuzzled her as he spoke, "Perhaps you should take a break." His head shot up, "What good timing you have, Conner, but I thought that you would return at dinner time." As Aleisha tied the leather strap, she tried to ignore Snarf's side of the conversation. "Of course, I wasn't thinking. Welcome." At Snarf's welcome, Conner, Grezald, and Byron stepped through the doorway. "What is this 'important discovery' which brought you back so early?"

"I met a dragon." Conner had the determined expression of a man who would stop at nothing to- What exactly was he so determined to do?

"I would hardly call a dragon, especially a dragon in the Great Library, an important discovery." As customary, Snarf teased.

"Patience, Snarf; let him explain." Byron, too, held a strangely fierce expression; earning a shocked and mildly concerned response from Snarf.

"I met a dragon named Zwarte, who has black fur and golden eyes." By Snarf's expression, Aleisha could see that that was significant, though she had no idea why. "He knew me the moment I entered the room, said that he could feel his magic radiating through me. Apparently, the magic from Philimina's line came from this dragon, which is why I bare his coloring."

"How did you find this dragon?"

"I was looking for a weaver who could aid us in making Aleisha's cloak; the librarian brought me to a section called The Library of Secret Knowledge. This library doesn't have a human librarian, only Zwarte, and he does not help knowledge seekers navigate the enchanted room, though he made an exception for me since I am of his lineage." Conner paced before them, motioning wildly with his hands as he did so, he looked very much like a child who had just learned a new game. "He said that, since my magic came directly from a dragon, that I should be able to learn dragon enchantments; I've never even considered learning magic that powerful. When I tried to leave the library, he told me that he would like to teach me how if I am interested, though I'm not certain that it would be wise." Now finished, he sat down, staring blankly across the room.

"So, what of the weaver?" At Snarf's question, Conner jumped and turned back to him. *"Were you able to identify a weaver who could assist us?"*

"There are three weavers and two tailors in the area who have the necessary skills. I would like to visit each of them to try and deduce which one, if any of them, can be trusted,"

"How can you tell which one to trust?" She was surprised by his mischievous smile.

"We ask him not to charge us for his work." That didn't seem fair; she couldn't imagine that working with dragonsilk would be an easy process. Would they really expect a master weaver to work for free? "The sale of dragonsilk is illegal, Leish. Any law-abiding weaver would produce it for free and would be honored to make the cloth at a dragon's request, while anyone who refused to produce it without compensation is breaking the law and not worthy of our trust or our patronage." She supposed their reasoning made sense, but it did not seem right to ask anyone to give away such specialized work without pay.

"We would not take advantage of this weaver," Byron must have guessed what she was thinking. *"We would provide him with a gift after he was finished. He*

would not be allowed to know of the gift beforehand, lest he work for our pay, but we would not leave him uncompensated."

"So, where do we start then?" Conner grinned at her and motioned for her to take a seat next to him.

"As I said, there are three weavers in or around Might City; one is in the market district on the west side, one lives on a farm outside the gates to the east, and the third in the warden of the weavers guild located on the east. I believe that the one working in the guild is the most likely to be an honorable weaver, as he is the only one who has an obvious reason for knowing the craft."

"And while you are on the east side, you can visit the farmer as well. I would be very interested to know why a farmer knows anything about dragonsilk." It made sense that Snarf sounded more interested in business than normal; it was, after all, his fur that they were talking about handing over to a man who none of them had met.

"When can we go?" All four of them frowned at Aleisha when she spoke. "When can we go talk to these men?"

"I will go tomorrow, and I will go alone." Conner shook his head and chuckled, "There are potential criminals, Leish, I'm not taking you with me, magic user or not."

Chapter 43

Conner stood in the front room of the guild hall, wondering if he was being too optimistic to hope that he would find a trustworthy and willing weaver on his first try. He wondered if, perhaps, he was being too optimistic in hoping that he would find one at all.

"Warden Collins will see you know," a young apprentice entered the room, trying his best to look important as he delivered his message. "If you'll come with me, I'll show you to his office."

Warden Collins' office was exactly as Conner had expected; fabrics of all types were strewn over every available surface, as if he'd been showing the differences and similarities to a pupil or potential client. Books on the weaving craft were lined up carefully on a shelf in the corner with a small loom set up next to it. What he did not see, however, was any sign of dragonsilk, though he hadn't necessarily expected it to be on display.

The warden himself was a short thin man with almost no hair. He stood in the midst of the messy office, smiling welcomingly as he greeted Conner and ushered him to a seat. "What can I help you with?"

"I've heard tell of a skilled weaver," he took the seat and leaned forward to allow him to be heard in his hushed tone, "a weaver who is rumored to be able to make silk from wool."

Warden Collins' eyes flashed with greed. "Such a thing is possible, but requires a very specific type of wool."

"I have every confidence that I will be able to acquire any material you may need." The warden's overexcited grin was not encouraging. "If, that is, you will be able and willing to produce this fabric."

"Of course, of course" - Warden Collins claimed a seat on the opposite side of the desk - "Now, dragonsilk is a very delicate cloth, as I'm sure you are aware; the manufacturing of such a cloth will be rather costly. I trust that that won't be too much of a burden for you."

"Unfortunately, I cannot pay you for your work; I am well aware of the laws of Ephriat and Might City, and I will not venture outside of those borders. I was hoping that you would be able to help me without charge, as the manufacture and ownership of the cloth is not illegal."

"You would dare to ask me to work for free?" the short man exploded from his seat, "Do you even know the magnitude of this thing which you ask me to do?"

As Warden Collins continued shouting angrily at him, Conner slowly stood, bowed, and moved to leave. "I'm sorry to have wasted your time." Even as he passed the young apprentice in the front room, his eyes wide with terror, he could hear the warden continue to shout insults from his office door.

He had not realized how hopeful he had been of his trip until that moment. If the guild warden could not be trusted to use his skills honorably, how could he expect to find a weaver whom he could trust?

Darksoul

He supposed he should still check on the farm outside of the city; after all, if he didn't visit now, he would have to return later. Making his way through the residential district, he exited the east gate and surveyed the horizon. Most of the land to the east of Might City was farmland, so finding the particular farm he was looking for could prove rather time consuming, though he did remember from past experience that the various farming families knew most of the others in the area, so he headed in the direction of the closest farmhouse, planning to ask the first person who opened the door where he might find the young man named Lenard.

Four farms and nearly an hour later, Conner, shivering violently from the cold which anyone else could have borne easily, was finally headed in the direction of Lenard's farm. Lenard owned the smallest farm in the area, which, while it surprised him, was an encouraging sign; anyone selling dragonsilk would surely treat themselves to a nicer, larger home than this.

He knocked on the front door, hoping desperately that Lenard would be finished in the fields for the day, so his wife could invite him into sit by the fire. After waiting a few minutes, he knocked again, this time slightly harder so as to be sure he could be heard. An attractive young woman with blond hair and bright green eyes opened the door, quickly ushering him inside when she saw him shaking. "My goodness, sir, whatever are you doing out in the cold? Come sit by the fire while I make you a hot drink." He barely had time to thank her before she hurried out of his sight. "Lenard, dear, we have a guest."

A tall man with dark skin and a thick beard hurried into the room, smiling broadly. "Good evening," he thrust his hand at Conner, who shook it, nodding in greeting as he was still too cold to offer much better. "What brings you to our area?" The young woman came back in and handed him a steaming cup that smelled like honey.

"Thank you, ma'am." She smiled and returned to the kitchen. "I'm looking for Lenard, the son of Melvin."

"That's me." He took a seat on a wooden chair, pulling the afghan from the back of it to hand to Conner, who gratefully wrapped himself in its warmth.

"I would like to discuss some rather important matters with you if now is a convenient time, though I can certainly come back at a later date if that would be more-"

"Come back?" he laughed, "Sir, you don't look like you should have ventured through the cold even this time." Even as he tried to control his shivering, his whole body spasmed with the cold. "If you have important matters to discuss with me, you had better do it now. Though I'll tell you now, we aren't selling the farm."

"No, sir, it's certainly not about the farm." Conner sipped from his mug, sighing as the hot liquid warmed him from within, "My name is Conner; I am a magic user and a friend of dragons." He figured he ought not waste their time with small talk, as he could smell something delicious cooking and did not wish to intrude on their dinner. "I have heard that you are trained in the art of weaving dragonsilk."

"I have never made a single spindle of yarn from sheep's wool, much less from a dragon's." Much to his surprise, Lenard's response seemed more terrified than angry. "The only reason I know anything about the craft is because of my father."

"Did your father produce dragonsilk?"

"If he did, it was only when he was very young." His wife returned to the sitting area and claimed a seat next to him, silently passing him a steaming mug as she sipped from her own. "My family made dragonsilk for three generations before it was outlawed, but we haven't touched it since; we're no criminals." Lenard shook his head and pointed to the back of the house. "I can show you the books my father passed down to me, I'll show you the spinning wheel and the loom; you can see for yourself how dusty and unused they are. I swear I only know the theory behind the craft; I've never used my knowledge. Not once."

Conner brought the mug back to his lips to hide his smile; this man might actually be able to help him. "May I ask, Lenard, would you be willing to work for a dragon if they asked you to use their wool?"

"I'm not sure I understand what you are asking." He and his wife exchanged confused glances.

"My friends are looking for a man of honor and integrity to handle a delicate matter. I believe that you are the only man within a day's journey who will be able to help."

"I told you, I will not go against the law." He no longer appeared afraid of Conner, but he did not yet look confident either.

"Out of respect for the law, we would not be able to offer you payment."

"Out of respect for the law?" he scoffed and stood, his confidence finally returning. "Finding a loophole to keep your actions technically legal does not respect the law."

"The loophole was an intentional provision made for the sake of the dragons. Once every millennium or so, a dragon might want to gift his own fur for the sake of a friend of dragons." Lenard was not looking convinced, but his wife leaned forward, listening with great interest. "This is that one time in a millennium. A kind and selfless dragon has volunteered his own fur to provide a magical cloak to help a young girl in need of a very delicate enchantment.

"Please, think about it. If you decide you would like to help us, come to the Great Library. Ask any librarian where you might find Byron; he will point you in the right direction."

"We'll think about it, but that's all I can promise." Conner stood and thanked them both before making his way back out into the frigid weather, shivering as the wind began to pick up.

Conner was still nearly a mile away from the library when the snow started. The first snow of the winter

Darksoul

was always the hardest on him; the shock of the icy cold on his flesh always left him feeling weak and vulnerable. Shivering violently, he wrapped his arms around his middle and growled at the cold as if to scare it into leaving him alone.

Chapter 44

Aleisha sat next to Snarf as she waited Conner's return. He had told them to expect him back before dinner, but they had finished eating nearly an hour ago and she did not see him in the street below. *"We could wait inside, you know."* Snarf had been trying to hide his shivers from her since they'd moved outside, but she knew that he must be as cold as Conner always was now that winter had officially arrived.

"Yeah, waiting in the snow isn't going to speed him up any." She turned to reenter the enchanted room, shedding her cloak as she adjusted to the warmer temperature. "What do you suppose is keeping him? Is it the storm?"

"I would not worry too much, Aleisha. Conner is an intelligent fellow who probably realized that a storm was coming, so he chose to remain with whomever he was meeting when it started." Even as he said it, he turned slightly to grant welcome to whoever was in the hall outside his room.

The beautiful green dragon from the Library of Magic entered and directed a look at Snarf. *"Thank you. I will let her know."* Snarf paused before responding again, *"He will be returning at the end of the winter."* The green dragon nodded and turned to leave, sneaking a concerned look at his bare wings as she did so.

"Byron and Grezald have left to retrieve Conner. They sent Genevieve to tell us so that they would not be delayed any further." Aleisha tried not to worry about what that might mean. She tried not to think about how worried Byron and Grezald would have to be to go searching for Conner in this storm. She tried not to remember every story she'd ever heard about people getting lost in snow storms, but she found that she couldn't think of anything else.

Nearly an hour passed before they saw the great red blur appear on the other side of the enchanted doorway. Snarf nearly leapt from his position by her side to invite them in, Byron carrying what looked to be a large black cocoon with concern and inquiry.

"What is that? Where is Conner?" Byron placed the cocoon on the floor before her, revealing the partially frozen fur of tightly wrapped black wings. "Will he be ok?"

"Sure he will," Grezald chuckled. *"He's never handled the cold well, and has often retreated into his wings when it gets to be too much for him. He'll come out when he warms up a bit."* Aleisha hurried over to where she'd dropped her cloak and draped it over Conner's huddled form. Sitting back to wait for him to come back out, she pulled Tallen's journal out from under the side of Snarf's bed.

She hadn't even finished one entry when she heard Conner grunt as he stretched to his full height, spreading both wings and arms as his back cracked loudly. *"You couldn't wait for the storm to end before venturing out?"* Snarf leveled a bored look at him as he continued to stretch.

"The storm started after I exited the farmer's house." He folded his wings behind him as he began to shrink into his normal form.

"So, what did this farmer say? Is he willing to help us?" All three dragons turned to look at Conner, waiting with great expectation for his answer.

"I don't know, Leish. He says that he only knows the concept behind weaving, and he had never actually done anything with dragonsilk." She sighed and sat back down; she should have known not to get her hopes up. "I told him who needs his help and how to find us. Hopefully, we will see him in the next couple of days; otherwise, I'm going to visit the fellow in the western side of town."

"Until then, Aleisha has something she would like to share with the group." Snarf nudged her forward, pulling everyone's eyes away from Conner and onto her.

"Tallen gave me this journal that he was keeping while searching for the Elixir of Life." Conner frowned, but both Byron and Grezald appeared excited by her statement. "He details events leading up to finding my mother, seducing her, and trying to gain her trust. He took great pains to record her interests, values, and desires so that he could better manipulate her, but I think that we might be able to use the information to help us deduce what the key might be for my map."

"This is excellent news." Byron nodded slowly as he answered, *"We were sent to help you find what you*

sought, and that objective has been delayed long enough."

"If you would be comfortable sharing this journal with Griffin," Aleisha turned to Conner as she spoke, "I think that he has the best chance of any of us to extrapolate the key from Tallen's notes. Do you trust him more than you trust Elam?"

"I would trust Griffin to keep any secret." At Conner's declaration, all three dragons nodded their agreement.

"Then I'll bring it to him." She could not deny the relief she felt at not having to be the one to read Tallen's journal; his tactics with her mother were disturbing to say the least, and, if her understanding of the timeline was correct, she was quickly approaching the entry detailing her mother's imprisonment.

Nearly a week had passed since Aleisha had brought Tallen's journal to Griffin. Most of Aleisha's days were spent sitting with one of the dragons in Byron's room, waiting for Lenard to come, reading absolutely anything anyone brought for her, mostly the old texts of the scriptures, and listening to endless stories about past adventures.

While she enjoyed her time learning and listening, she longed to join Conner as he visited Parata, the seamstress who would be making her cloak once the dragonsilk was made. Even as she was grateful to be away from Tallen and his castle, she missed spending her days sitting with Conner next to the hearth.

"Welcome." Aleisha jumped at Byron's voice; they'd been sitting in silence for so long that she'd almost forgotten that she wasn't alone. *"Just step through the barrier."*

A tall, dark skinned man with a bald head and a thick beard stepped through the barrier, wringing his hands as he stared, wide-eyed, at Byron. "I apologize, sir, I've never- never spoken to a- a dragon before."

"Please, sit." Byron nodded toward his own bed, speaking with exaggerated gentleness; the poor man looked ready to pass out from fright even at Byron's calm demeanor.

"I was told by Conner, your friend, to seek you out to offer my, um, my services." His eyes darted around the room as he spoke, "He said that you were not offering pay, so my skills will not be used illegally." The poor man looked about ready to run as he fumbled through his words, "I would be honored to help, but I'm no criminal. I have to know that the, um, dragonsilk will not be sold."

"We would not ask such a great favor of you if it was not of the highest importance." The tall man seemed to relax at that and claimed the seat. *"My brother has freely given of his own fur to be used in a magical cloak to help a young girl in need of our aid. Any dragonsilk you make will be used for this cloak, which will be gifted to the young girl for the express purpose of being used for her need and for her alone. Any extra dragonsilk will be disposed of by me personally. As stated earlier, we cannot pay you, as*

the selling of dragonsilk is illegal, but we ask for your assistance nonetheless."

Lenard just sat and stared for a full minute before finally speaking, "I never dreamed that I would have an opportunity to work with dragonsilk; I would be honored to help you." He turned to Aleisha then, as if he just noticed her presence. "Are you who the cloak is for?" She nodded. "With the current snow storms, I cannot work in my fields, so I can begin weaving the cloth at any time that you provide the wool."

"Then we will provide it today." Aleisha grabbed one of the sacks of Snarf's wool which was sitting in the corner and climbed onto Byron's back. Setting the sack between his shoulder blades, she climbed down to get the second. As soon as all five sacks were securely wedged between Byron's shoulders, Aleisha reclaimed her seat at his side. *"I can either give you a ride back to your farm, or I can follow you; whichever you would prefer."*

Lenard's eyes grew wider, giving him an appearance similar to that of a startled cat. "Um, thank you, um, for your offer. I, um, I think I would prefer to ride my horse."

"I'll head back to the house, so you don't need to worry about me." Aleisha picked up the book she had been trying to read that day and headed to the door. "Conner will be able to find me there."

Chapter 45

Conner opened the door to the house, exhausted and eager to get out of the cold. "Good evening, Sir," Mathias appeared with his usual grin as he offered to take his cloak. "Aleisha arrived a few hours ago; I believe that she is in her room."

"Thank you, Mathias. You and your family can head home." Mathias grinned and moved to leave, having long since accepted Conner's early dismissal to be the new normal.

Wondering what had prompted Aleisha to return home before him, he headed upstairs. "Hey, Leish," he knocked on her door as he called to her, "Everything ok?" Much to his surprise, she was smiling when she opened the door.

"Lenard came today; he agreed to help us." She was practically hopping in place as she reached out to grab his hand, pulling him into her room. "Byron left with him to bring Snarf's wool to his house so he could work on the dragonsilk during the winter storms. He looked terrified of Byron. I've never seen anyone's eyes grow so large; the poor fellow.

"Now that he's agreed to help and Parata has already promised to make the cloak, all we need is Dagmar with the enchantment and I'll be free." She laughed, "Oh brother, now I sound like you do in the mornings; I need to shut up."

"Excuse me!" She laughed even harder. "What do you mean like I do in the morning? I don't talk that much." As she continued giggling at his expense, the room seemed to fill with an odd glow, as if bathed in the same magic that had lit the room when he and Aleisha first returned to Might City from Tallen's castle. "It will be strange, not always knowing exactly what you are feeling; I'll have to learn how to read your facial expressions."

"Well I'm not used to everyone around me being able to read me so easily, so it will be nice to regain a bit of anonymity." This was great; he'd never seen her so care-free, so lighthearted. If this cloak did not help her, he didn't know what they were going to do. "What is that face for?"

"I like you happy; I think I'll keep you this way." She laughed again; her laughter was quickly becoming one of his favorite sounds.

"The only problem is, if he gets completely finished before Dagmar and Grizwald get back and the fabric itself needs to be enchanted as it is woven, we'll have to start all over." Conner, Lenard, and Byron had been discussing how much dragonsilk Lenard would be making.

"Yes, but Snarf provided more than enough wool to make two cloaks, so if Lenard makes enough material for one cloak, then we will have enough wool left over if the wool needs enchanting, but we will also have the material ready to be sewn if the enchantment can be added later." Byron was sitting just outside of Lenard's house so that he could communicate with them without them all having to sit in the snow.

"It would save time to have it ready already, especially since I will have to return to my fields as soon as enough of the snow melts to continue my plowing." Lenard sat near the fire, working his spinning wheel, while Lauren sat next to him, occasionally checking a pot of stew she had cooking in the hearth. "I can't guarantee that I'll be able to work on the dragonsilk much at all once I can get back into my fields; feeding my family has to come first."

"Alright then" - Conner clapped and stood - "make enough for one cloak, and we'll discuss more after Dagmar returns. Whatever happens, and however much you are able to help us, we will forever be grateful, and you can call on us if ever you have a need we can assist you with."

Lenard stood and shook his hand. "Thank you. It's an honor to be of service to you." Conner stepped out the door and transformed into his true form before climbing onto Byron's back. He'd made the mistake of transforming before leaving Lenard's house a few weeks ago and had scared poor Lauren near hysterics, so he'd been careful since then to be sure that he was out of her sight before donning his warm fur in the horrid winter wind.

"How much longer do you think it will take for Dagmar and Grizwald to get back?" Though he knew that Byron had no way of knowing, he found himself asking the same question almost daily. Byron was blessedly patient with him and always answered him the same.

"Any day now; winter is nearly half over, so he's had quite a chance to study under the dragon in Sprino." Conner shivered and wrapped his wings around himself just a little more snuggly. *"What grand adventures do you expect wait for us with Aleisha and Snarf today?"*

"Who can know with those two?" He chuckled; Leish had been in such a good mood since Lenard and Parata had agreed to help them, that each of them had at some point in the last month commented on how different she was now. *"I'm sure we'll be greeted with raucous laughter and warm hugs. Maybe even something hot to drink, or a heated blanket."*

"Now that's just wishful thinking." Byron laughed at him as they landed on Snarf's balcony.

"Come in," Snarf practically sang their welcome from inside the room, prompting Conner and Byron to look at each other suspiciously. What did he have to be so cheery about?

As they entered Snarf's room, they surveyed their surroundings. Nothing seemed out of place, save Aleisha's ridiculous grin, though even that had become the norm of recent weeks. "What are you two up to?" Aleisha started giggling uncontrollably, but neither of them said anything. Conner took another step into the room, shifting his eyes about him so as to avoid any surprises. "Leish, what are you hiding from me?" She tried to shake her head, but the warm glow slowly building in the room told him everything he needed to know. "Do share the good news."

"Aleisha, Control yourself." Conner chuckled at Dagmar's response; it wasn't often that he got in on the teasing. Wait! Dagmar? That was Dagmar's voice. When had he gotten back?

"Dagmar? Grizwald? Where are you guys hiding?" Both dragons simultaneously jumped through the doorway on the opposite side of the room. Conner and Byron each let out a hoot and ran to the pair. Conner couldn't think of a time that he had seen this group so lively; Byron, Dagmar, and Grizwald were all talking over each other, Snarf, Grezald, and Aleisha were all laughing and tripping over each other trying to get out of the way of the stampede that was the other three, and Conner just stood back and stared at the scene in awe. His family was complete for the first time in what felt like a century.

"Snarf and Aleisha have been talking our ears off since we got back." After the majority of the commotion calmed down, Dagmar's voice was the first Conner managed to distinguish in the chaos. *"I never thought I would see a human who could outtalk Grezald and Grizwald."*

"Yeah, Leish has gotten pretty, um, enthusiastic of late." He grinned at her feigned offence.

"So, tell me how the dragonsilk is coming." The serious tone of his voice told him that only he and Aleisha could hear him.

"He has nearly enough to make Aleisha's cloak, and plenty of extra wool in case he needs to restart for some reason." Aleisha frowned at him; apparently she

had wanted to hear the answer too. "Come here, Leish, we won't leave you out." She smiled and claimed the space next to him. He wrapped one arm around her and repeated his answer for her.

"Do you have an estimate on when he'll be done?" Dagmar lowered his head to Conner so that he could speak out loud and still be heard. *"I am eager to see if this enchantment will work."*

"From what I've seen, he's making quick progress. He has several yards of material ready for use, and was spinning more thread today so that he can add to that. As long as the weather continues as it has, keeping him inside and working on the dragonsilk, I would guess that he will be done in a week's time."

"That is good. They said that you have also found a seamstress who knows how to work with dragonsilk."

"Yes, Parata, she is ready to begin whenever we have the fabric; she has graciously offered to make Aleisha's cloak her top priority when the time comes." He turned to smile at Aleisha, only to see her glaring at the ground.

"Then bring me the cloak as soon as it is finished, and I will put the enchantment on it." Dagmar tilted his head in Aleisha's direction a moment before she jerked her head up and forced a smile. *"Alright then,"* he raised his voice so everyone in the room could hear him, *"We have slightly more than a week before we have Aleisha's cloak. From my observation of the magician prisoner in Sprino, we can expect her to be a*

little weak for a few days as she adjusts to her non-magical state."

"Will that be a problem, though?" Grizwald interrupted, "The magician in Sprino has heavily relied on his magic for most of his life, while Aleisha has only known of hers for a few short months."

"While that is a good point, I would caution against expecting to skip the weakness. After all, Aleisha has always had her magic and, whether she has always used it or not, it has always strengthened her."

Chapter 46

The next week could not have moved more slowly. Aleisha continued to spend most of her time in Byron's room, listening to stories and reading books, but the jovial teasing that she, Snarf, and the twins indulged themselves with simply didn't seem to help the time go by any more quickly. "When did Conner say that he would be back?"

"Before nightfall, he said." Snarf answered in the dignified tone of a messenger before shifting into his regular teasing manner, *"His parting words have not changed since the last time you asked, an hour ago."*

She could not stand the waiting any longer; she felt like she'd been waiting for a lifetime to be free of her cursed magic. Placing her book on the floor, she stood and started walking around the perimeter of the room. She made it round the room twice, carefully stepping over Grizwald's tail with each pass, before Dagmar stood and exited to the balcony. *"You should join me."*

She stepped out onto the balcony and stood next to Dagmar, waiting in silence for him to speak. He appeared to be watching something in the distance as he stared, unmoving, across the city. *"Can you see Parata's shop from here?"*

"I don't know where her shop is, much less whether or not I could see it from here." She tried to keep the offence out of her voice, but Dagmar was better at reading her than most people, so she knew that she had not managed to fool him.

"I can see Conner" - he nodded in the direction of the buildings below - *"If you look for his magic, you may be able to see him too."*

"How do I look for his magic?"

"Exactly like you did while we were training. His is the brightest white in that district." He nodded again, directing her attention in front of her.

She closed her eyes and tried to picture the city below, slowly filling in the blank sections as she struggled to remember the exact layout of the city streets. After several minutes of forming her magical vision, she began to see distinct figures wandering about the street. Most of the people below were just that, people, but she spotted four glowing white dots among the crowd, as well as several huge glowing shapes that looked very much like dragons flying above the city.

One of the white dots on the ground was so dim that she nearly missed it, most likely a weak magician, two of the others were stronger, but they walked together toward the southern end of the town, heading to the magic guild, no doubt. The last white dot shone brightly, like a fire pit among torches, and stood stationary in the middle of a small building. "I can see him."

"Good, then you can watch him from here and know as soon as he's on his way." Dagmar jumped off of the balcony and flew towards Parata's shop. A small child on the street in front of the shop pointed up at

Dagmar a moment before being ushered on by a woman whom Aleisha assumed to be his mother.

Dagmar circled above the seamstress's shop, descending slowly as he did. At first, Conner's form seemed to stop moving entirely, before suddenly moving to the front door, pausing for a few moments before moving back to his former position.

Dagmar circled the shop one more time before returning to the balcony. *"I let him know that you are eager for his return, so I'm sure he will urge Parata to work as quickly as possible."*

"Thank you, Dagmar." Aleisha turned away from the balcony, opening her eyes to return her vision to normal. *"I had not realized that I would be able to see magic even through walls."*

"Such vision is not often as useful as you might think, as it is quite difficult to maintain an accurate view of the landscape." Dagmar headed back toward the doorway to rejoin the others. *"We have used it from time to time over the years when one of us has had to break from the group for one reason or another."* Aleisha followed him back indoors, glad to be out of the cold once more. *"I must admit, Aleisha, I am as nervous as you seem to be concerning this enchantment. The intricacies of the magic used are beyond many of the enchantments I have attempted in the past. The very importance of my task weighs on me as I fear the possibility of failure."* He reclaimed the seat he had occupied before his flight to Parata's shop. *"No matter the outcome, I want you to know that I will*

not cease my search for a release from your magic until you are free from its influence." She leaned into Dagmar's side, speechless at his kind words.

While they continued to wait on Conner, Snarf entertained the party with stories of his first winter storm without his wings' fur. *"I'd never felt something so cold; It was as if my very blood turned to icy mud in my veins."* As he spoke in the most dramatic voice he could muster, the twins leaned in to listen. *"All at once, I understood Conner's unceasing complaints about the snow. This beautiful, white blanket which had once softened the scenery and reflected the glory of the sun's rays suddenly became a harsh, villainous element with the purpose only to harm my delicate wings and freeze my warm spirit."*

"Welcome, Conner, we have some very eager folks awaiting your return." Conner stepped through the door, grinning as soon as he spotted Aleisha and holding up the most beautiful purple cloth she'd ever seen.

"Oh, Conner." She hurried over to him, reaching out to touch the perfect cloth. The dragonsilk was every bit as soft as Snarf's wings had been and the same impossibly deep purple; anyone who saw her wearing this cloak would immediately know that it had magical qualities. "Oh, Snarf" - she turned toward Snarf, who looked exceedingly pleased - "this is beautiful. Thank you." She turned back to Conner, "Thank you."

"It's not finished yet, Leish" - Conner smiled at her enthusiasm - "I need to hand it off to Dagmar before I can give it to you." Dagmar stepped forward and held out one foreleg to take the cloak.

"I will need a few hours, but then you may have your cloak." Dagmar disappeared through the doorway, leaving the rest of the party to wait impatiently for his return.

"I can't believe how close we are." Aleisha resumed her circuit around the room, stepping over tails and around bodies as she circled both Conner and the dragons. "I'm finally going to be free of both chains and magic. I can finally begin my normal life. I don't even know what that means."

Conner stood and joined her in her rounds. He said nothing; he simply took her hand and walked beside her as she waited nervously for Dagmar's return.

As the sun began to set, reflecting its final rays of light off of the wet snow and casting Byron's room in a red and orange glow, Byron finally spoke, *"Welcome."*

Dagmar entered the room and placed Aleisha's cloak on the floor before them, *"I have done all that I can. Aleisha, come and try your cloak."*

Aleisha stood frozen for a few moments; as excited as she was to finally have her cloak, she found herself terrified, much as she had been when preparing for the dragons to arrive to take her from Cedrick's mansion so long ago. Was she ready to venture into this unknown? Conner squeezed her hand and let go, placing his hand on her back to gently push her toward Dagmar.

As she bent to pick up her new cloak, the fabric seemed to vibrate ever so slightly in her hands. Holding the purple cloth in front of her, she took in the flawless beauty of it; she would never have imagined that a man who had never woven a single cloth could have made this in a matter of a few short weeks. Swinging the cloak around, she draped it over her shoulders, fastening the frog to secure it in place.

All at once she felt both a surge of strong magic pulse through her entire body and a strange weakness leave her lightheaded and dizzy. She closed her eyes as she tried to regain her balance, only to find herself wrapped in Conner's arms as he caught her swooning form. "I've got you, Leish."

Chapter 47

Conner had spent the last two days mostly staying in the house with Aleisha, making her meals and helping her up and down the stairs until she adjusted to her new frailty. She had tried to take herself to bed on the day she got her cloak and nearly fell down the stairs for her lightheadedness. When he'd come to help her, she had tried to shoo him away, saying that he shouldn't have to help her and complaining the whole way to her room as he carried her to her bed.

He suspected that she so despised being served because she had spent so long being the servant; he supposed it only made sense that she would feel uncomfortable allowing someone else to take that only role she'd ever known. Even so, he'd dutifully ignored her protests and never allowed her more than a few feet away from him so that he could be next to her in a moment any time she needed him, though those times became fewer with each day as she became more comfortable in her mortal state.

He watched from his seat next to the fire as she paced across the room, every pass more graceful than the last as she regained her balance and confidence. He had to admit that he would miss her dependence on him once she felt strong again, but he was glad that her spirits were lifting as she reclaimed her independence. "Snarf came by this morning before you got up; he said that he had exciting news that he planned to deliver after breakfast."

"Snarf came by" - she spun around, nearly falling into a table in the process - "Why didn't you get me up?"

"You were sleeping; I like you better fully rested and so does everybody else." He grinned at her annoyed expression. "Would you really have been ok with me waking you up? Wouldn't you have spent the whole morning complaining about stupid doors and walls that magically move into your way as you stagger through the house like a drunken wench?"

He ducked as she threw the closest object at him, which in this case happened to be a skein of yarn she'd been trying to learn to knit with. "I do not stagger." She tried to glare at him, but her eyes betrayed the smile she was attempting to hide.

"Sure, you do." He stood, preparing himself to flee on the chance that she was feeling strong enough to try to retaliate. "I have had the unfortunate experience of witnessing a drunken wench fleeing from the inn in which she worked; if not for your much more pleasant aroma, I might be fooled by your morning grace, or lack thereof." As he suspected, she tried to run at him, though he had no idea what she planned to do if she caught him, so he turned and darted through the foyer and into the kitchen, not stopping until he was safely positioned by the wood stove, a table and four chairs between him and Aleisha. "Now Leish, remember not to overexert yourself."

She reached up to undo the frog, letting her cloak drop to the floor, and lifted a hand in his direction.

Darksoul

"Good morning, Aleisha, Conner." At the sound of Snarf's voice, Aleisha seemed to forget about Conner and bent down to retrieve her shed covering.

"Good morning, Snarf. Conner tells me that you have exciting news."

"Yes, I came by earlier, but you were sleeping. Conner offered to get you up, but I thought that we would both be safer if we let you sleep." Conner laughed at the horrified expression on Aleisha's face, to which she turned and smirked at him.

"Am I really that bad?"

"Only in the morning, Leish, but we love you anyway." She grinned and turned away yanking her hood up in an attempt to hide the red flush crawling up her neck and cheeks.

"Griffin came by Byron's room this morning." As Snarf was flying above the house, he missed how embarrassed Aleisha was at the moment, so he kept talking as if nothing had happened, "He thinks that, even if he cannot pinpoint the exact key your mother used for your map, he should be able to figure out what kind of key she used if you let him examine the map."

"Really? He's gotten enough from Tallen's journal to deduce something like that?" She looked over at Conner, her eyes wide with the hope that she dared not indulge.

"That's what he said. Shall I tell him you will be coming over today?" Aleisha nodded wordlessly, either forgetting or not caring that Snarf could not see her.

"Tell him we'll be there soon." As the sound of Snarf's wings beating in the wind faded, Conner crossed the room and put a hand on each of Aleisha's shoulders. "Do you think we ought to get your map?" She nodded but didn't move. "If you tell me where to find it, I can go get it."

"No, I'll show you." She smiled and pulled away, grabbing one of his hands as she hurried out of the kitchen. She gave the stairs a valiant effort and made it nearly to the top before having to admit defeat and allowing Conner to help her the rest of the way up.

She took a moment to catch her breath at the top of the stairs before pulling him into her room and kneeling in front of her bed. "I keep everything I don't use regularly packed so that I'm already ready next time we have to leave." She pulled out a sack with a large package sticking out of it.

"What is that?" He nodded to the long package, which looked suspiciously like a sheathed sword wrapped in cloth.

"Oh yeah, I never did tell you about this." She had unfolded her mother's map and placed it on her bed to reach for the sword, unwrapping the cloth to reveal the simple sheath. "Elam gave this to me when I went to Tallen's castle the first time." She unsheathed it to show him the craftsmanship. "He thought that I might need to fight my way either in or out, but he was wrong." She smiled and turned to slide the blade back into the sheath, a seeming bout of lightheadedness causing her to miss the mouth and stab herself in the dorsum of her left hand, slicing a large cut between her thumb and forefinger.

As she yelped in pain, he leapt forward, taking both the sword and sheath from her. Quickly sliding the blade into its protective case, he thrust it back under the bed and turned to grab Aleisha's wounded hand, only to see her staring in horrified awe at the small pool of blood that had collected on her bed. "Leish, give me your hand." She obeyed, but she continued watching the red stain on her sheets as Conner attempted to stop the blood, which was spurting from the wound. Clasping the split with both hands, he heard her cry out ever so slightly as he directed his magic to reform the torn muscle and skin.

"Conner, the map."

"Don't worry about the map Aleisha, I need to take care of you first." He hadn't meant to snap at her, but seeing her hurt infuriated him, and the map, no matter how valuable, would just have to wait until he was done healing her.

"No, Conner, the map is changing." She tried to reach across his arms with her right hand to grab the map, but Conner grabbed her, determined to make her wait until he knew that she was ok. "My blood, it got onto the map."

Conner moved one of his hands to check his work, no longer listening to her continued comments about the map. The skin had healed nicely, leaving not so much as a scar where the blade had gone in. Using his shirt tail to wipe away most of the blood so that he could better inspect her hand, he sighed in relief and lifted her hand to kiss the now perfect skin.

"Conner, my blood was the key." Aleisha was still talking about the stupid map; she had no idea how troubled he was at the sight of her precious blood. "The keyspell needed my blood."

Darksoul

Coming Soon
Book 3 in The Soul Power Series
Lightsoul

Chapter 1

Clutching her mother's map in one hand and gripping Conner's hand with the other, she tried to hurry behind him as he pulled her toward the Great Library. Griffin had asked them to meet him at the library so that he could take a closer look at the map, confident that he could narrow down the possible keys to revealing the enchanted map's concealed directions. How exciting it would be to be able to tell him that they'd already discovered the key on their own, and quite by accident no less.

As they arrived at the library, Conner stepped to the side so as not to interrupt the man who was sweeping the newly fallen snow off of the front steps. Holding the door open for Aleisha to enter before him, he stepped inside and shivered. "I'll be glad when winter is over," Conner did not handle the cold well and often complained about the frigid weather. "How does your cloak handle the wind?"

"Very well, thank you." She smiled as she ran a hand across the impossibly soft fabric of her enchanted cloak. Snarf, the youngest of the five dragons that Conner and Aleisha traveled with, had had his wings shaved in order to have a magical cloak made for Aleisha. The cloak was designed to help her control her tainted magic, but it also served as the warmest covering she'd ever had the pleasure of wearing.

Conner led her through the winding tunnels of the Great Library, passing the Library of Ephriat History, the Library of Dragon Lore, and the Library of Magic before slowly climbing several flights of stairs and turning down the hallway that would eventually lead to Byron's room. They had barely stopped in front of Byron's enchanted doorway before the dragon spoke to their thoughts, *"Welcome."* They passed through the magical doorway, bringing the blurry image of Byron's room into focus. *"Griffin says he has made quite a bit of progress reading Tallen's journal."*

"Quite true." A young man with a wide smile stood next to the huge red dragon. "Your father kept detailed record of his interactions with your mother, reasoning that anything she said might help lead him to the Elixir of Life. I think that, if I may see your map, I might just be able to guess what kind of keyspell she had put on it."

"I would prefer if you did not call Tallen my father; he does not deserve such a title." Though Aleisha had recently reunited with the man who had sold her into slavery as a child, she still could not reconcile in her mind his position as her father.

"Of course" - the librarian's excited smile disappeared - "my deepest apologies, Aleisha."

"In any matter, the map?" Byron reminded her of the purpose of this meeting.

"Oh yeah, the map." Aleisha held the map in front of her, smiling at the jagged line between the two sections of the map: the section which was enchanted and still hidden from sight, and the section of the map which had absorbed her blood and now revealed a beautiful chart of Elbot. "While I was getting things ready to bring over here, I sort of happened upon the keyspell by accident."

"You 'happened upon the keyspell?'" Griffin stared at her with one brow raised. "How do you 'happen upon the keyspell?'"

"I, um." She was slightly embarrassed by the circumstances of the happy discovery, as her current, weakened state, had made her clumsy. "I cut my hand on the sword Elam gave me, and my blood got all over the map."

"You what?" Byron sounded as angry as Conner had looked when she hurt herself. *"Why would you try to handle a sword in your condition? Why would you let her even touch a sword, Conner?"* Conner dropped his head, unwilling to defend himself at Byron's frustrated growl.

"It wasn't Conner's fault; I should have been more careful." Everyone in the room stood in uncomfortable silence until Byron nodded. "As I said, my blood got on the map and seemed to burn away the gibberish which had so confused me" - she held the map a bit higher, showing it to Byron - "I can read it clearly now, though I'm not familiar with the region shown."

"I see no more than a clean parchment" - he tilted his head to look at it from another angle - *"even the revealed map must be hidden from all but you."*

"But I don't know anything about reading maps." She brought the parchment back to her own line of sight. "After all of this, we still won't be able to continue our search?"

"Leish," Conner chuckled beside her, "we can teach you how to read a map. I'll bring you to the Library of Ephriat History and we'll see if we can find a map that depicts the same area shown on your mother's map."

"Then we can leave?" Again, Conner chuckled; laughter was his standard response to her excitement. "I can't believe this is finally happening." She clasped her hands over her mouth, her eyes welling with tears of joy. "My mother would be so-" she gasped. Something was wrong. As quickly as her disappointment had turned to joy, her energy turned to exhaustion. "Conner," she reached for his arm to steady her as she was suddenly overwhelmed with dizziness.

"Leish!" As her vision darkened and she felt a sharp pain in her right side upon collapsing to the floor, the last thing in her vision was Conner's terrified expression.

Made in the USA
Middletown, DE
03 April 2019